If she says Ben
on her, then he doesn't.

The acid in Duncan's stomach called him a liar. Suddenly he'd had enough pretending. His voice came out harsh. "I'm a mess, Gwen."

"So am I." She sounded surprised.

"As messes go, we aren't even on the same scale. You'd be better off with Ben."

"You're probably right."

Startled, he stole another quick glance. She was smiling at him rather shyly. In spite of everything, an answering smile tugged up one corner of his mouth. "Not going to argue with me, huh?"

"If you're going to say stupid things, I can, too."

His smile lingered until he pulled into the driveway. It died before the car came to a complete stop. The lights were off. All of them.

Ben wasn't back yet. No one was. He and Gwen would be alone in the big old house.

Dear Reader,

"In like a lion, out like a lamb." That's what they say about March, right? Well, there are no meek and mild lambs among this month's Intimate Moments heroines, that's for sure! In *Saving Dr. Ryan*, Karen Templeton begins a new miniseries, THE MEN OF MAYES COUNTY, while telling the story of a roadside delivery—yes, the baby kind—that leads to an improbable romance. Maddie Kincaid starts out looking like the one who needs saving, but it's really Dr. Ryan Logan who's in need of rescue.

We continue our trio of FAMILY SECRETS prequels with *The Phoenix Encounter* by Linda Castillo. Follow the secret-agent hero deep under cover—and watch as he rediscovers a love he'd thought was dead. But where do they go from there? Nina Bruhns tells a story of repentance, forgiveness and passion in *Sins of the Father*, while Eileen Wilks offers up tangled family ties and a seemingly insoluble dilemma in *Midnight Choices*. For Wendy Rosnau's heroine, there's only *One Way Out* as she chooses between being her lover's mistress—or his wife. Finally, Jenna Mills' heroine becomes *The Perfect Target*. She meets the seemingly perfect man, then has to decide whether he represents safety—or danger.

The excitement never flags—and there will be more next month, too. So don't miss a single Silhouette Intimate Moments title, because this is the line where you'll find the best and most exciting romance reading around.

Enjoy!

Leslie J. Wainger
Executive Senior Editor

Please address questions and book requests to:
Silhouette Reader Service
U.S.: 3010 Walden Ave., P.O. Box 1325, Buffalo, NY 14269
Canadian: P.O. Box 609, Fort Erie, Ont. L2A 5X3

Midnight Choices

EILEEN WILKS

INTIMATE MOMENTS™

Published by Silhouette Books

America's Publisher of Contemporary Romance

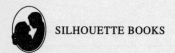 SILHOUETTE BOOKS

ISBN 0-373-27280-4

MIDNIGHT CHOICES

This edition published by arrangement with Harlequin Books S.A.

® and TM are trademarks of Harlequin Books S.A., used under license. Trademarks indicated with ® are registered in the United States Patent and Trademark Office, the Canadian Trade Marks Office and in other countries.

Visit Silhouette at www.eHarlequin.com

Printed in U.S.A.

EILEEN WILKS

is a fifth-generation Texan. Her great-great-grandmother came to Texas in a covered wagon shortly after the end of the Civil War—excuse us, the War Between the States. But she's not a full-blooded Texan. Right after another war, her Texan father fell for a Yankee woman. This obviously mismatched pair proceeded to travel to nine cities in three countries in the first twenty years of their marriage, raising two kids and innumerable dogs and cats along the way. For the next twenty years they stayed put, back home in Texas again—and still together.

Eileen figures her professional career matches her nomadic upbringing, since she's tried everything from drafting to a brief stint as a ranch hand—raising two children and any number of cats and dogs along the way. Not until she started writing did she "stay put," because that's when she knew she'd come home. Readers can write to her at P.O. Box 4612, Midland, TX 79704-4612.

This story is for those who have fought and won
against breast cancer...and for those whose fight is over.
It's for those of us who love them.
And it's for my own beloved warriors:
Doris Elizabeth Hembree. Kia Cochrane.
Rosalie Whiteman.
Edie Duke. Day LeClaire.
Courage, like life, happens one step at a time.

Chapter 1

Highpoint, Colorado

Humidity fogged the kitchen window where Duncan stood, gathering in tiny droplets at the bottom of one pane. Spaghetti sauce simmered on the stove, layering the air with scent—oregano, basil, the sweetish bite of onion and the meaty aroma of the Italian sausage he liked to use instead of hamburger. The phone was ringing.

Probably his brother. If not, the caller would either give up soon or leave a message.

He wiped a circle clear of fog and left his hand on the glass. It was cold. According to the calendar, spring had arrived, but winter died slowly in the mountains. It was likely to hang on, snarling and snapping, for another few weeks.

He looked out at the line of cedars his father had

planted along the back fence when he was three. They were nearly thirty feet tall now. He tilted his head and saw a gray sky sliced and diced by the bare black limbs of the oak that sheltered the rear of the house.

Three rings...

Duncan counted heartbeats in the silence between rings. His pulse was still elevated from his workout. A drop of sweat meandered down his neck. His arm throbbed like a mother, but that was to be expected. He'd learned to stop before throbbing turned to solid pain. Pushing for more than his body could give just slowed his recovery, and he couldn't afford any setbacks. He'd maxed out his personal leave; added to medical leave, that gave him just over a month to get himself in shape.

In more ways than the obvious.

Four rings. Idly he rubbed the raised tissue of the new scar on his forearm. It was cold outside, but free of ice or snow. He could run.

With a click, the answering machine picked up. After a pause he heard his brother's gravelly voice: ''You'd better be in the shower or something, not out running in this weather. I'm in no mood to nurse you through pneumonia.'' Another pause. ''I'll be a little late—a problem with a supplier.'' Then the click as he disconnected.

Duncan shook his head. Habits died hard—especially with someone as thickheaded as his big brother. Did Ben think the army only let them go out to play when the weather was nice?

Still, he should pull on a dry sweatshirt. He headed for the stairs at the front of the old house.

The doorbell rang. He paused with one foot on the step, tempted to ignore it as he had the phone. But this intrusion had arrived in person and would have seen his

Jeep out front. He or she would probably keep ringing for a while, and it was cold outside.

Reluctantly he moved to the front door, turned the dead bolt and pulled the door open.

The woman on his doorstep looked cold. Her hands were pushed into the pockets of a pale pink cardigan that zipped up the front; it was the exact shade of her creased trousers. Her sneakers were pink, too, with shiny silver shoelaces. The flat white purse slung over her shoulder had the soft look of expensive leather. Her hair was icy blond and very short, revealing complicated little knots of wire and gems that dangled from her ears, which were small and pink with cold. So was the tip of her slightly crooked nose. Otherwise she was pale. And tiny. If she were to step straight forward into his arms, the top of her head would fit easily under his chin.

His heartbeat picked up. His mind skittered for purchase.

She was too young, too skinny. Her hips were no wider than a boy's, and the hand she pulled out of one pocket was long and narrow. He wasn't attracted to tiny, fragile-looking women a decade younger than he was.

What color were her eyes? In the fading light he couldn't tell.

Then those uncertain-colored eyes met his. And his thoughts spilled out, leaving his mind blank.

"Is Ben here?" she asked. "Benjamin McClain?" When he stared dumbly at her, her eyebrows pulled together.

Dear God.

"I have come to the right house, haven't I?"

What is this? What just happened? He licked dry lips. "Ben will be home soon. I'm his brother, Duncan. Dun-

can McClain.'' After a long moment it occurred to him
to step aside. ''Come in.''

Gwen stepped across the threshold. It was, thankfully,
a good deal warmer inside. Somewhere spices were sim-
mering in tomato sauce. It was a homey smell…a homey
place, she thought, glancing around. The entry hall was
large, with a door opening off it to the right—probably
a coat closet—and a staircase diagonally across from the
front door. An open arch on the left led to the living
room. The wooden floor was clean enough, but dull, as
if it had been a very long time since it had received more
than perfunctory care.

There was a coatrack next to the door. It held a black
ski cap and two jackets—a dark green parka with a hood
and a denim jacket. Both obviously belonged to large
men—to Ben and this man, she supposed. Duncan
McClain, Ben's brother.

Her hands were balled into fists in her pockets. She'd
known Ben wasn't married or living with a woman. If
he had been, she would have approached him differently.
But she hadn't asked the detective to find out if he was
living with anyone else—like a brother. This was a com-
plication she hadn't allowed for.

When in doubt, fall back on manners. That was one
lesson her mother had taught her that Gwen often found
useful. ''I'm Gwendolyn Van Allen.''

He nodded without speaking. Obviously the name
meant nothing to him. What odd eyes he had—very pale
gray, rather striking with the dark hair and those straight,
slashing eyebrows. Something about his eyes made her
uneasy and she looked away.

A pair of muddy boots sat next to the coatrack—work
boots, the brown leather much scuffed and discolored.

They were huge. She glanced from them to the running shoes on Duncan McClain's feet. The boots were bigger. They must belong to Ben.

"May I take your sweater?" Ben's brother asked.

"No, thanks. I'm a little chilly." Training enabled her to find a social smile and a topic, but her cheeks felt stiff. "I thought I was prepared for the weather here, but I'm a Florida girl. Your version of spring isn't what I'm used to."

He didn't say anything. He didn't look much like Ben—at least, not like the photograph the detective had enclosed with his report. For a long time Gwen hadn't wanted to remember Zach's other parent, and she'd succeeded all too well at forgetting. Now she couldn't summon a clear image of Ben's face. Other things, yes, but not his face.

A flash of shame slid the smile from her face. "You did say you expected Ben soon?"

"Yes."

That was it—just yes, no elaboration. And he was looking at her so intently... Nervously she sought for a topic that might drag more than a monosyllable from him. "I hadn't thought he'd be working late at this time of year. Construction work is seasonal, surely?"

"Some of it is. You don't want to pour concrete when it's below freezing, for example, but if we waited for good weather to put up a building, Highpoint would be a very small town."

"Do you work with your brother, then?"

"No. Your eyes are green, aren't they?" He turned and started for the arched opening to the left. "You can wait for Ben in the living room."

What an odd, abrupt man, she thought. Perhaps he was shy. He moved smoothly, though, like a man who was at home in his body and knew he could depend on it. He was taller than she was—well, almost everyone was taller than she was—but not as tall as his brother. Or as brawny. She did remember that much. Ben was an outdoors type. He'd seemed to bring a breath of mountains and open spaces into the trendy little club in Florida where they'd met.

The living room was large and old-fashioned, with moldings framing the ceiling and a carved wooden mantel that looked older than the house itself. The floor was wooden here, too, but mostly covered by a large gold area rug with brown borders. Two armchairs upholstered in a nubby beige fabric flanked a chocolate brown couch. Throw pillows in flame colors littered the long couch and one of the chairs; an orange pillow sat on the floor next to the other chair. The coffee table and end tables were cluttered and didn't match, but the effect was comfortable rather than careless.

He turned on a lamp beside the couch. Though it was only five o'clock, it was dreary outside, dim inside. "Have a seat. Can I get you something to drink?"

She shook her head and sat, though she would rather have paced. Her insides felt jittery, as if she'd had too much caffeine. He sat in the chair at right angles to the couch, his long body loose and apparently at ease. Then he just looked at her, those curious eyes intent, as if she posed a puzzle he meant to solve before he spoke again. She curled her toes up inside her sneakers, resenting him. "Do I have a piece of broccoli between my teeth or something?"

He smiled slightly. "Am I staring? Sorry. You must be used to it, though."

"No," she said, startled, then she flushed. "That

didn't come out right. I wasn't angling for compliments.''

''Of course not. Why would you?'' He crossed his legs, resting an ankle on the opposite knee. He was wearing baggy carpenter pants and a black sweatshirt. ''How old are you?''

''I beg your pardon?''

He shook his head. ''Never mind. I take it your business with Ben is personal.''

''Yes.'' She rubbed her hands together, trying to warm them and hoping to distract herself from the urge to jump up and pace. ''I can't explain. I'm sorry.'' *This man is Zach's uncle.* She was talking to her son's uncle and he didn't know it, and she couldn't tell him. Not until she'd told Ben.

He studied her face a moment. ''I'm not clever with small talk, but there's always weather. Folks around here never get tired of talking about that, so I can probably hold up my end. Of course, we're not as good at it as the English. They've elevated the discussion of weather to a fine art.''

''Have you been to England, then?''

''Briefly, a few years ago. Beastly weather,'' he said, shifting flawlessly into upper-crust English. ''Rained the whole bloody time.''

Surprise curled in the pit of her stomach. *Why, he's good-looking,* she thought. His face was thin, but the strong cheekbones and eyebrows gave it character. As she saw him for the first time as a person instead of a hitch in her plans, her face relaxed into a more genuine smile. ''I'm not sure how long I can talk about the weather, not being as well trained as you are. In Florida we don't take much note of rain unless it's horizontal and tree limbs are whipping by at seventy miles an hour.''

''I'd take note of that, too. Have you ever been through a hurricane?''

He'd claimed to lack skill at small talk, but he was very good at asking questions. And listening, truly listening, to her answers. As they talked, the nerves in her belly eased until at one point, when his eyes met her eyes in that direct way he had, she felt a sharp tug of pleasure.

Her eyes widened in surprise. It had been so long...not that attraction was appropriate. For heaven's sake, this was Ben's brother. But she couldn't help being pleased. She was truly healing. Surely that meant she'd been right to take the steps she had.

Then she heard the front door open and all her nerves came rushing back. Before she'd thought about it, she was on her feet again. Facing the doorway.

''Smells good,'' a deep male voice rumbled as the door closed. ''We have company for supper?''

She knew his voice. It gave her a jolt. She hadn't expected the quick hit of familiarity.

Then he was standing in the doorway, a big, solid man in a flannel shirt and worn jeans. He looked at his brother first, she noticed—a quick, assessing glance. Then he turned to her, a slight smile on his hard face, a question in his eyes. ''You going to introduce me, Duncan?''

He didn't recognize her. Humiliation burned like acid. ''We've met. Though I see you've forgotten, so I'll reintroduce myself. I'm Gwen. Gwendolyn Van Allen.''

Shock slapped the smile from his face. Good. At least he remembered her name. This would have been even worse if she'd had to remind him of what had happened between them five years ago. She pulled a photograph out of her purse and crossed to him, holding it out. "And this is your son, Zachary."

Chapter 2

Cold air cut into Duncan's chest with each breath he took. His feet thudded steadily on the hard ground beside the road. Overhead the sky was a dingy black, with a few shy stars peeking out where the cloud cover thinned. His sweatshirt clung damply to his chest and back beneath the denim jacket he'd grabbed when he'd escaped the house. His heart was slamming hard against the wall of his chest. His arm ached.

He needed to cool down. He'd been running about an hour—not long enough. He couldn't go home. Not yet. She'd still be there.

So he'd walk awhile. He eased to a jog, then a walk as he crossed Elm.

Dammit, she wasn't even his type. Too pale, too thin. Her hair was too damned short. He liked long hair on a woman.

But her image kept intruding on his run in fragments, vivid and raw like the jagged memories of an accident victim. He saw her hands, the thin fingers nervously rubbing together for warmth. The ring she'd worn where a wedding band would go—silver and simple, with a single pearl. The small mole on her neck, right where a man would taste her pulse. He saw the quick bloom of anger in her cheeks when Ben didn't recognize her, and those silly silver shoelaces, a single note of whimsy in a polished package. He remembered the way she'd risen from the couch, drawn upward by the sound of Ben's voice. Forgetting Duncan was even there.

He worked hard at not moving from remembered images to imagined ones. Like the way that delicate body must have looked locked in his brother's arms.

It didn't matter. It couldn't. Whatever had hit him when he'd opened the door to her would fade.

A car slowed as it passed him, turned into the parking lot and pulled up at the gas pumps at the convenience store on the corner. Maybe he should fuel up, too. He could get a cup of coffee, drink it in the store where it was warm and let the sweat dry. Then run some more.

She'd had his brother's child.

Or so she claimed. Maybe he shouldn't take her words at face value. People did lie. And Ben was the owner of a successful construction firm—not a bad target for a paternity suit.

But he remembered the way she'd looked. The clothes, the makeup, the cropped hair—she'd had a shine to her, the kind of gloss that means money. Hard to believe a woman like that would need to trick money out of a man.

He wished he'd seen the photograph of the boy. The second he'd realized just how personal her business with his brother was, though, he'd taken off. But he'd seen her face when Ben had made it clear he didn't have a clue who she was.

He'd seen Ben's face a moment later, too.

Ben believed her. Duncan's lips thinned. Damn Ben's righteous hide! How could he have fathered a child he didn't even know about? Ben, of all people. His big brother was no saint, but on some subjects he was about as yielding as the mountains they'd grown up in. A man took responsibility for his actions. A man used protection *every* time, and if he was ever fool enough to forget that, he'd better head straight to the courthouse for a marriage license, because he couldn't call himself a man if he allowed his child to grow up without a father.

Yet Ben had had a son by a woman he hadn't even recognized. A son who'd done some of his growing up without a father. Duncan felt cold and wild inside. He wanted to smash his fist into his brother's face.

There was a cop car in front of the 7-11. Duncan hesitated. But the wind was picking up, pushing a cold front ahead of it. He shivered, grimaced and told himself not to be an idiot. It would be a helluva note if he caught some stupid bug because he was so determined to avoid Jeff that he ducked out of sight every time he saw a police car. Ben would make his life hell if he got sick.

It was with a certain grim amusement that he saw his suspicions had been right. Jeff pushed the door open just as Duncan reached it. He was holding a steaming plastic-foam cup. He grinned. "Hey, there, GI Joe. You aren't out running at this hour, are you?"

"Hey, copper. No, I flew in. Left my wings in the bike rack."

Jefferson Parker chuckled. Jeff was a head shorter than Duncan, a lot chattier, several shades darker in skin tone and every ounce as stubborn. They'd been friends in high school, where Jeff had been one of very few black faces in the crowd—and the student-body president two years in a row. Which said a lot about his ability to get along with others and his determination to excel. "Better leave 'em parked or I might have to run you in for impersonating an angel. Not that anyone would believe it, between that ugly face of yours and those goose bumps you're sprouting instead of a halo. You going to let me buy you a cup of coffee?"

Duncan eyed him. Jeff's dark eyes were friendly and incurious. What a crock. The man was nosier than a hound on a scent and just as hard to sidetrack. It had been a huge mistake to take Jeff up on his offer of using the police firing range to keep in practice.

Still, he supposed he might as well see how long it took Jeff to get to the point this time. He didn't have anywhere else he needed to be. "Sure."

Jeff introduced him to the young clerk, Lorna, claiming she made the best coffee in Highpoint—an exaggeration bordering on outright falsehood, Duncan thought as he sipped the industrial-strength brew. His old friend kept up a steady stream of chatter that included the shy young woman. He was good at that sort of thing, never at a loss for words. People relaxed with him.

Probably a good trait in a cop, Duncan thought, watching.

"Well, how about that," Jeff said as they left the store, stopping to stare in mock surprise at the bike rack by the curb. "Someone must have run off with those wings of yours." He shook his head. "Criminals are sure getting bold these days."

Duncan smiled slightly. *Here it comes. The Highpoint police are looking for a few good men...*

"That Lorna...." Jeff nodded at the clerk on the other

side of the brightly lit window. "She's nineteen, lives with her mom. Got a little girl her mother watches while she's at work. Can't afford day care, you know? She has to work nights because her mother works days down at Jenkin's Drug."

Duncan's eyebrows lifted. Where was Jeff going with this? "No support from the father?"

"Bastard skipped town a couple years back when Lorna turned up pregnant."

"That's rough. She's in school?" Jeff had asked her how her classes were going.

"She goes to community college two nights a week, works here the other five. Got her GED last year." Jeff pulled a package of gum out of his pocket and offered Duncan a stick. Duncan shook his head. "We don't have a lot of crime here, compared to L.A. or Houston. But Highpoint isn't Mayberry, either. We've had two convenience stores hit in the past three weeks."

Duncan glanced into the 7-11. Lorna was stuffing bills into a narrow white envelope. She had a pimple on her chin and pretty brown eyes bare of makeup. When she bent to slide the envelope through the slot into the safe, her hair fell forward. It was long, brown and shiny clean. She brushed it impatiently behind her ear, revealing a tiny gold earring in the shape of a cross.

The girl—little more than a child herself—had a baby girl waiting at home for her. Duncan looked back at Jeff. "Looks like she follows the rules, doesn't keep much cash in the register."

"She doesn't. But that's no guarantee." Jeff peeled the foil from a stick of gum. "I stop by every night and the black-and-whites keep an eye on her when they can. That's no guarantee, either, but this perp picks his times. He hit the other stores when they were empty except for the clerk. First thing he does is shoot out the security camera. Hits the lens square on, single shot with a .22 handgun.''

Duncan frowned. A .22 pistol was a couple of notches above a water pistol for accuracy. Maybe. ''Where's the camera?''

''Far left corner.''

He glanced back into the store, automatically calculating the angle. ''Does he come in with his weapon drawn?''

Jeff shook his head, popped the gum in his mouth. ''Draws from inside his jacket as he pushes the door open.''

''Then he's a helluva shot.'' Duncan could have made the shot himself. Not many others could.

''Yeah. He's good, but jumpy. Killed a dog.''

''A *dog?*''

''When he was headed out of the last place he hit. A stray came around the corner of the store, startled him. He shot it and ran.'' Jeff stuffed the empty gum wrapper in the trash can next to the door. ''So we've got bullets, but not much more. We know he's male, around five-seven, average build. He wore jeans, a dark jacket, gloves and a ski mask both times. No skin showed. We don't know if he's white, brown, black or yellow with blue polka dots.''

''No one made the vehicle?''

''One of the clerks thinks it was a dark compact, not new. She didn't get much of a look at it. He makes 'em lie on the floor once they empty the register.''

''Did he...'' Duncan stopped, shook his head. Damned if Jeff hadn't gotten sneakier with his pitch. He'd nearly reeled Duncan in this time, gotten him involved enough to ask questions. ''You'll catch him sooner or later. If this guy was really bright, he wouldn't be hitting convenience stores. They don't have much cash.''

''Sooner's better than later. A jumpy, not-so-bright gunman makes mistakes. People get hurt then.'' Jeff started for his car. ''You going to let me give you a ride?''

''I need to finish my run.''

Jeff nodded, reached for the handle, then gave Duncan a steady look. ''What you've been doing—that's important. No doubt about that. A cop doesn't get much chance to save the world the way you army types do. Sometimes all we can do is drop in on a nineteen-year-old mother who works nights when she isn't trying to learn bookkeeping. Maybe that will keep this perp from hitting this store, maybe not. We don't get a lot of sure things in our line of work.''

Duncan's mouth quirked up. ''I remember when you used to try to get me to volunteer for some damned committee or other. Roped me in a few times, too. If you'd had the good sense to go into the army instead of the police force, you'd be their ace recruiter by now.''

A grin lit Jeff's face. ''I'm getting to you. Duncan, we need you. I know it wouldn't be fun to be a rookie, not when you're used to being a big-deal sergeant, but if you take some courses, you can move up quick. The chief's keen on getting a sharpshooter.''

Duncan's smile slid away. He gave a single shake of his head that combined refusal and warning.

''Okay, okay.'' Jeff held up his hand as if to stop a flow of protests. ''But you'll think about it.''

Duncan watched his friend pull out of the parking lot and didn't think about anything except whether he needed to stretch again. No, he decided. His muscles were still loose and warm.

He'd just started running again when a shot rang out.

He dropped and rolled, reaching for a weapon that wasn't there. Then lay on his stomach on the cold concrete, his arm throbbing fiercely. Little by little, understanding seeped in. Along with humiliation.

Not a gunshot. A backfire. From a '92 Chevy packed front and back with teenage boys, some of whom were staring and laughing. Yeah, pretty funny, all right, he thought as he pushed to his feet and slowly resumed his run. Watching a grown man nearly mess himself because your car backfired would be one hell of a good joke to kids that age.

He concentrated on keeping his shoulders loose as he ran. They had a tendency to tense up when his arm was hurting, which made the jarring worse. The Chevy turned west at the light.

It was a shame Jeff had already driven off. If he'd seen how Duncan reacted under fire these days—or anything that passed, to his screwed-up senses, for being under fire—he sure as hell would drop the subject of Duncan trading one uniform for another when his enlistment was up. Which would happen in two and a half months.

He very carefully didn't think about that, either.

Ben was sitting in his favorite chair next to the fireplace, which still held the ashes of its last fire. His shoes were on the floor beside the couch, his feet propped on the coffee table. One of his socks had a hole started in the heel. A glass half-filled with bourbon sat on the table beside his feet. He'd poured it after Gwen left, then forgotten it.

He was holding the photograph. It was all he could see, all he could think about, the grinning boy in that picture.

Zachary. His son.

Zachary *Van Allen*. Not McClain.

The front door opened, then shut. He lifted his head, scowling, and saw Duncan standing in the doorway, staring at him with no expression on his face.

Ben didn't try to read his brother's expression. Even as a boy Duncan had been good at tucking everything away out of sight, and the older he'd gotten, the better his poker face became. But he saw the tense way Duncan stood and the stiff way he held his left arm. And he saw his bare head.

"Damnation," he growled, rising to his feet. "I thought they operated on your arm, not your thick skull, but only an idiot would go running for hours with a half-healed wound. And in this weather, without a hat! I don't know what they taught you in Special Forces, but a jacket isn't enough. Half your body heat—"

"Not tonight." Duncan's voice was hard. He advanced into the room, voice and body taut, like a big cat ready to strike. "I'm in no mood for your bloody nursemaid act tonight."

Ben took a deep breath, fighting back a surge of temper. Nagging Duncan to take better care of himself was the wrong way to go about things. He knew that. But in the past Duncan would have greeted Ben's bossiness with a raised eyebrow, maybe a polite "yes, ma'am" or some other nonsense.

He'd changed. Ben didn't know what had happened on this last mission, but it had damaged more than Duncan's arm. "It must be close to freezing out there," he said in the most reasonable tone he could muster.

"Believe it or not, the army doesn't make us stay in at night when the weather's bad. But we aren't going to talk about my sins tonight. We're going to talk about yours." His pause was brief. "Her car is gone."

Ben's empty hand closed and opened again. This was going to be hard. "I offered Gwen a room here, if it's any of your business. She preferred to stay at a hotel."

Duncan just looked at him. He'd never been one to fill the air with words, and seldom used two when one would do, or one word when a nod or a glance was enough. Right now, though, his silence felt crammed with accusation.

Ben's scowl returned. Damned if he was going to put up with any lectures—silent or otherwise—from his younger brother. "She didn't tell me. I didn't know the boy existed."

"I know that," Duncan snapped. "There's no doubt in your mind that he's yours?"

Duncan's irritation reassured Ben. At least he hadn't needed to be told that his older brother would never have ignored his son if he'd known the boy existed. He answered Duncan's question by crossing to him and handing him the photograph.

Duncan's eyes widened, then clouded with some emotion Ben couldn't read. After a long moment he handed the photo back. "Poor kid. He looks so much like you it's scary."

"Yeah." Ben couldn't say anything else right away. He didn't know what to do, what to think—his emotions were so full, so contradictory, he was afraid he'd start cursing. Or maybe bawl like a baby. He cleared his throat. "Not that I would have thought she was lying, even if he hadn't turned out to look like me."

"You knew her well, then?"

There was a subtle insult in the tone. Or maybe the insult lay only in Ben's mind. "No. Not exactly. Hell." He ran a hand over his hair. "It was pretty much a one-night stand, all right? We met, we hit it off, and... You remember that vacation Annie nagged me into taking a few years ago? Gwen and I met then. We spent a couple days together." And one night.

"Then you walked away without realizing you'd fathered a child."

"She could have told me." Ben began to pace. "She should have told me. I've missed so much... He's four. Four and a half years old." His voice held wonder and loss and anger.

"So why didn't she tell you?"

Ben felt all the weight of his own guilt in those softly spoken words. "That's between her and me."

"When I think of all those Friday-night lectures you used to hand me and Charlie about responsibility and safe sex..." Duncan's mouth tightened. "Dammit, Ben. What the hell happened? How could you not know there was a chance you'd started a child in her?"

The disillusion in Duncan's eyes was harder to face than his anger. Ben stopped by the big picture window. He'd forgotten to pull the drapes, and his own reflection stared back at him from the night-darkened glass—a big, dark man in worn jeans and an old flannel shirt. "I knew," he admitted gruffly. "We used protection, but..." He couldn't bring himself to go into detail, but the fact was, she'd put the condom on him. Only she hadn't gotten it on right, and he hadn't noticed until afterward, too intent on what he felt, what he wanted.

Just the sort of thing he used to warn Duncan and Charlie against.

He grimaced. "The odds of her getting pregnant were

pretty small. When I didn't hear from her, I assumed everything was okay.'' He'd convinced himself of that. He hadn't wanted to think about her. Or the way he'd ended things between them almost as soon as they began.

Duncan didn't say anything. It was Ben's own reflection that stared back at him accusingly from the dark glass. The image wasn't clear enough to show the touch of gray that had appeared in his hair lately, but his mind supplied that. He was pushing forty, and he was alone. It wasn't how he'd ever thought his life would work out.

But he had a son. He straightened his shoulders and turned to face Duncan. ''She's coming here with Zach in a couple weeks. They'll stay here to give me a chance to get to know him, let him get to know me.''

''I can go back to the base.''

''Hell if you will! This is your house, too. Your home. And—'' he grimaced ''—maybe it will be easier if we have someone else in the house. She and I have a lot to work through.''

''A single night together doesn't exactly constitute a relationship. There can't be that much to work out.''

''I'm going to marry her.''

Duncan's eyes went blank. After a moment he turned away, shrugging out of his jacket as he spoke. ''She came here because she wants you to marry her? It seems…belated.''

''Don't be an idiot.'' Irritation at his brother's denseness eased some of the other feelings. ''That isn't why she came here, and I haven't asked her yet.''

''But you think she'll agree?''

''She's the mother of my child.''

For the first time that night, there was a hint of humor

in Duncan's voice. "She might not see the two as being equivalent."

"That's why we'll have a lot to work out."

Duncan looked as if he might say something more, then shook his head and headed for the hall to hang up his jacket.

Ben was starting to feel better. They'd gotten through some of the worst of it. He remembered the drink he'd poured earlier and went to get it. The liquor tasted warm and mellow, but there was a bite beneath the smoothness. Tonight he needed that bite. When Duncan came back into the room, Ben swirled the amber liquid in his glass without looking up. "So, are you going back to the base, or are you going to stay here where you belong?"

"Do you need me to stay?"

Ben almost snapped out something about wanting and needing being different, but stopped himself in time. Duncan was the one who needed help, not him. But he was too stubborn for his own good. He'd hang around if he thought Ben needed him, though. "Yeah," he said, though it wasn't easy.

"All right. Ben..." Duncan seemed to struggle for words. "For God's sake, think about this. You spent a couple days with her five years ago. You didn't even recognize her."

"She looks different now. Her hair was long then."

"You didn't know her," Duncan repeated. "And now you want to marry her."

"She's got my son."

Duncan turned away. "How old is she?"

"What does that have to do with anything?"

"Do you even know?"

Ben searched his memory. "I think…probably close to thirty now. Maybe."

"At least you didn't rob the cradle," Duncan muttered. He still wouldn't look at Ben. "You have feelings for her, or do you just plan on using her to get custody of your son?"

It was strain Ben heard in his brother's voice, not anger. He reined in his own temper as firmly as he could. "I don't use women."

Duncan turned slowly to face him. His eyes were winter-gray and unreadable. "If you didn't want her enough to hang around five years ago, what kind of marriage can you have?"

"Things have changed. She didn't need me then. She does now."

"Because of the boy."

"That's part of it." Ben took a deep breath, let it out and got the rest of it said. "Twenty months ago she was diagnosed with breast cancer."

Chapter 3

Andrews, Florida, three days later

Gwen tucked the letter neatly back in its envelope. She took a deep breath, striving for calm.

The moist air carried the taste of home into her lungs—Florida air, flavored with hibiscus and jasmine. Outside a mockingbird welcomed the evening. The orange-gold rays of sunset streamed at a familiar slant through the windows of the porch. An easy profusion of light filtered through the leaves of the big bay tree to dapple the wooden floor, the glass table where she sat and the long white envelope with the Colorado return address.

Ben had booked and paid for the flight for her and Zach. He'd sent a terse little note to let her know, sent it overnight mail. Dammit. She pushed to her feet and started pacing.

She'd agreed to come to Highpoint with Zach. She'd agreed to stay in Ben's house so he and Zach could spend normal, everyday time together. But she *hadn't* agreed to letting him pay for their airfare.

He'd done it anyway.

Well, he was a proud man. A proud, stubborn jackass of a man. She rubbed her temple. This probably wouldn't be the only time they butted heads over money. Benjamin McClain had a real problem with the fact that she had more of it than he did. She'd known that.

She hadn't known she was still so angry with him about it, though.

At the other end of the house, the front door slammed. "Mom! Mom! Guess what! Where are you, Mom?"

She stopped moving, a smile easing the tight muscles of her face. "In the Florida room, honey."

Feet pattered, light and swift, down the uncarpeted hall toward the sun porch where Gwen waited. "We went to see the seals, Mom, and I fed one!" Three feet, one inch of towheaded tornado whirled into the room, legs pumping.

"You did?" She hunkered down and held out her arms. Her son hurled himself into them. "All by yourself?"

"Mostly." Zachary was ever judicious in his assessment of truth. "I got to hold the fish myself, and the man held me. I told him he didn't have to 'cause I'm four now, but he did, anyway. And their teeth are really big, Mom. Did you know that?"

"Big teeth, huh? Bigger than mine?" She made chomping noises and pretended to bite him. He giggled, and her arms tightened.

Oh, God. She wanted so much for him, so much....

"You're squishing me, Mom." He wriggled.

"Sorry, light-of-my-life. Tell me about the seals."

"The man said they're called seal-ions, not just seals. And they bark like dogs. Like this." He demonstrated.

Her mother spoke from the French doors, her voice dry. "He did that all the way home."

The muscles across Gwen's shoulders tightened. "The condition of his clothes tells me he had a good time."

"We both did." Her mother gave Zach the soft, faintly surprised smile that only her grandson seemed able to elicit.

All her life, Gwen had heard how much she resembled her mother. It was true. Her nose lacked the symmetry of her mother's, due to the time she'd fallen out of a tree when she was seven. Otherwise, looking at Deirdre Van Allen's face was too much like peering into her own physical future—the same eyes, mouth, chin, even the same small ears tucked flat to their heads. The same wheat-pale hair and easily burned skin. Aside from age, there was only one obvious difference between the two women: their height. The fine bones and flat chest that made Gwen look like an undernourished child were transformed on Deirdre Van Allen's taller frame into a model's willowy elegance.

Sometimes Gwen had rebelled against the resemblance, sometimes she'd taken comfort from it. These days she mostly just hoped she'd be around to find out how accurate that genetic mirror turned out to be.

Two sticky hands seized her face and turned it toward a small, square face with dark eyes and a determined chin. "I want a dog."

Her mind snapped back to the moment. "You do, huh?"

"I been telling you and telling you that."

"Mmm-hmm. And what have I been telling you?"

His mouth drooped. "That I can't have one till I'm older."

"That's right." He looked so sad, with that pouty lip. And so stubborn, with those frowning eyebrows. And not like her at all. Her heart hitched in her chest. For a long time she'd managed to forget that Zach had come from two sets of genes, not one. She couldn't do that anymore.

"But you never say how much older. I'm getting older all the *time*."

"So you are. What did your grandma stuff you with, anyway?" She poked his T-shirt-clad tummy. "I see a purple spot, a red spot…"

He giggled. "That's grape drink and ketchup."

"And was that ketchup on something or did you take it straight?" She scooped him up and stood—and God, but it was good to be able to do that again, to rise easily with the warm weight of her son in her arms. The radiation had left her so weak, tired all the time.

All that was in the past. "I also see a bath in your very near future."

He frowned, considering that. "With bubbles," he informed her. "An' my army guys."

"Sure thing." She glanced over her shoulder at her mother as she started for the French doors that led to the rest of the house. "There's a pot of decaf in the kitchen, if you'd like a cup."

"Wine sounds better right now."

"You know where it is."

Several minutes later she left Zach in a tub that was more bubbles than water, surrounded by battalions of "army guys."

She would tell him about his father tonight. Oh, she'd had reason enough to wait until she'd seen Ben, spoken with him, but she'd returned from Highpoint two days ago. There was no excuse to delay any longer. Ben had made it clear he wanted a relationship with his son.

How would Zach feel about suddenly acquiring a father?

Her stomach clenched with nerves. She saw that her mother had poured her a glass of merlot and left it on the counter. She picked it up and took a sip, letting the rich taste of the wine linger on her tongue.

It was so important to handle this right. She'd tried to prepare herself for the questions Zach would ask, including the big one: why hadn't she told him about his father before?

Unfortunately she still didn't have a good answer for that one.

Sighing, she looked at the open doors to the Florida room. Might as well get this over with. Her mother wouldn't leave without making one last push to change Gwen's mind.

"Battles are being waged," Gwen announced as she stepped into the sun porch. "Campaigns plotted, and bloody war declared. I think the green guys are going to win again, though."

Dusk had replaced the warm colors of sunset. Her mother stood in silence and dimness, her back to the house, looking out at the shapes and shadows of the garden. Her back was as straight as ever, but the way she hugged her arms to her made her look oddly vulnerable.

"Mom? Is something wrong?"

Deirdre turned, her face pale in the dying light. "I saw the letter from *him*. You're going through with this, aren't you."

Gwen grimaced and flipped the light on. "It wasn't addressed to you."

"I didn't read it," her mother snapped. "But I couldn't help seeing the return address." She waved at the glass table, where a glass of wine sat next to the envelope with McClain Construction in the upper left corner.

Gwen took a deep breath. Arguing with her mother wouldn't help. It was probably inevitable, but it wouldn't help. Her throat ached as she crossed to her mother. "Yes, I'm going through with it. Everything is arranged—we leave on the tenth and will stay with his father for two weeks. I'll tell Zach tonight."

"Oh, Gwen." Deirdre closed her eyes tightly for a second. "I don't understand this obsession of yours. For heaven's sake, you had to hire a detective to track the man down!" She shuddered delicately. To Deirdre Van Allen, anything connected with a detective was implicitly sordid.

"That was partly my fault. I've told you that."

"The way you make excuses for this man worries me."

Was she doing that—making excuses? Wearily Gwen rubbed her temples, where a headache was starting. "This is about Zach, not me."

"Is it? I don't think so. With all that Zach's been through in the past eighteen months, the last thing he needs is another major change to deal with."

Gwen turned and headed for the kitchen. Deirdre followed. "We've been over this and over this. You know how I feel."

"And this is about *your* feelings, isn't it? Not mine. Not your son's. You're cherishing some sort of romantic pipe dreams about this man, a man who walked out on you without a backward glance.''

Gwen wanted to scream. She wanted to just stand there and yell as loud as she could, but that would be as cruel as it was childish. It would frighten her mother and Zach.

Her mother was already scared. Gwen understood that; fear lay behind the protests and opposition. So she carried both their glasses to the sink, emptied them and rinsed them and opened the dishwasher. ''This man has a name, you know. And a son. He deserves to know his son.''

''And what does Zach deserve? To have his life turned upside down for the sake of some man you picked up in a bar?''

Gwen's breath sucked in. The jolt of pain came as a surprise. It shouldn't have, she thought, yanking a paper towel loose from the roll, then bending to grab the spray cleaner from under the sink. Her mother had never put it quite so bluntly before, but then, she wasn't one to give up without using any and all weapons within her grasp.

There were always fingerprints to be cleaned from the refrigerator. She moved there quickly, sprayed and wiped.

''I'm sorry. I shouldn't have said that.'' Deirdre came up behind Gwen. ''For heaven's sake, Gwen, sit down. It's difficult to hold a conversation when you're bouncing all over the place.''

''I can't think when I'm sitting still. You know that.''

''You're not thinking now. What happened five years ago was an aberration on your part. But this man—''

''Ben,'' Gwen said, angry. She turned to face her

mother. "His name is Benjamin McClain. And it was an aberration for him, too."

"No doubt that's what he told you." Deirdre's lips thinned. "Be realistic. He's a construction worker. Picking up women in bars is no doubt quite normal for him."

She drew a deep breath, struggling to find a measure of calm. "No, Mother, he isn't a construction worker. Not that there's anything wrong with that, but he owns a construction company. Though he likes swinging a hammer when he gets a chance."

"I suppose he told you that, too."

"Yes, he did. And guess what? The detective confirmed it. And the letterhead you peeked at should be a clue, too."

Most of the details of that long-ago night were smudged, like a charcoal drawing left out in the rain. But Gwen had been forced to salvage what she could of those neglected memories when she'd gone to the detective two months ago. She'd remembered Ben saying he preferred working on a site to shuffling papers. He'd looked like a man who enjoyed working with his hands, too—a big man with broad, callused hands, the kind of man a woman could depend on.

Appearances could be deceiving.

Deirdre's gaze didn't waver. "Is he married?"

"No. And he wasn't married *then,* either."

Her mother looked down, rubbing her forehead with a pianist's long, slim fingers. When she spoke, her voice was unusually quiet. "I'm worried about you."

Why did her mother always do this—pull back just before things went too far, say the one soft, right thing that crumpled Gwen's defenses? Gwen hugged her arms around her middle and wished she knew whether the skill was intentional. "You raised me to do the right thing, even when it hurts. I know this is right."

"Mo-om!" came a singsong cry from inside the house. "Come get me! I'm ready to get out!"

"Coming, sweetie," she answered, relieved to have a reason to end the conversation.

"Let me get him ready for bed," Deirdre said.

Gwen hesitated, wondering…but that was unfair. Her mother had never let their own difficult relationship spill over onto the little boy they both loved. "All right."

"Gwen—" Deirdre surprised Gwen by laying a tentative hand on her arm "—you're searching for something, I can tell. Ever since…well, you've had reason to question your life, your choices. But please don't act hastily. Promise me you're not going to sign away any of your rights to this man."

Gwen met the green eyes so like her own and saw all the feelings Deirdre Van Allen would never put into words—fear, anger, frustration…and love. She didn't doubt that her mother loved her.

"Mom." She laid her hand over her mother's. "I don't know how things will work out. I'm trying not to make plans, not to expect things to go a certain way. But whatever happens, you can't lose Zach, not really. You'll always be his grandmother—his only grandmother, as it turns out. Ben's parents are both dead."

Though he had brothers. She'd met one of them—a dark, watchful man whose pale gray eyes seemed to be stuck in her memory like a burr.

Deirdre's breath sighed out. She stepped away. "You mean well, I know. I'd better go get Zach out of the tub." She left the room, moving with the angular grace Gwen had always envied—like an egret, Gwen thought, striding long-legged and slow through murky currents.

The currents had been murky enough tonight. Gwen rubbed her temple. They often were, between her mother and herself. It was amazing how two people who loved each other could misunderstand each other so thoroughly and so often. Though her mother had surprised her tonight, showing an insight Gwen hadn't expected. She'd said she knew Gwen was searching...and it was true.

What woman raising a child alone wasn't searching? Of course she wanted more. The comfort of a man's body next to hers at night—yes, she wanted that. The passion, too, she admitted. But she wasn't indulging in romantic pipe dreams. Maybe the thought had crossed her mind once or twice that something might develop between her and her son's father. There had been a connection between them once—surely she hadn't imagined that. And Ben had asked her if she was seeing anyone.

But she wasn't pinning her hopes on a fairy-tale ending. Childhood dreams of happy-ever-after might be hard to give up, but she was too much of a pragmatist to mistake wishing for reality. And the reality was that Zach needed to know his father...just in case.

The surgeon had removed the lump along with part of her breast. It had been very small, very close to the surface of her skin. Radiation should have killed any lingering cancer cells. Statistically, her chances were good. But no one could say for sure. Cancer cells might be lurking somewhere in her body right now, malignant fugitives hiding in some organ, waiting for some unknown trigger to start them growing again.

Her mother was sixty-one. She loved Zach and would do her best for him if Gwen died, but when Zach was fifteen his grandmother would be over seventy. Gwen had no other close relatives. Oh, she had friends—one in particular whom she'd trust with her son. But the courts gave preference to close relatives. If Deirdre fought for custody of Zach, she might well win.

She wouldn't win against Zach's father.

Gwen glanced around the spotless kitchen. It was much too soon to make any decisions, but she'd put things in motion. Her mother knew that and hated it, and Gwen couldn't blame her. But she had to think of Zach first.

There wasn't a blasted thing left to clean, so she headed for her study, where work of another sort waited.

The law was a tidy goddess, and it suited Gwen. Not criminal law. There, the stakes were too high, and she knew herself too well. She could be seduced by the clarity of order and lose sight of the greater good the law was intended to serve—justice. Nor, in spite of her father's pressure, had she been drawn to corporate law. He'd been bitterly disappointed when she told him she wouldn't be working for Van Allen Produce, Inc.

Surprisingly her mother had supported her choice. Perhaps Deirdre understood how well real-estate law suited Gwen. It called for patience, thoroughness and attention to detail. Gwen loved the historical sweep of performing a title search, the feel of the law stretching backward in time, the digging through old records. She liked bringing her findings to the present by checking statutes on environmental protection, wildlife habitats, zoning requirements, native lands—all the written code, the regulations both federal and state, that a developer had to observe.

Since becoming a mother, she'd especially appreciated being able to do a large part of her work from home, plugged into various databases.

Gwen's chair was already occupied by what looked like a shabby fur pillow. The pillow opened its eyes and blinked balefully at her. "You know what I'm going to do now, don't you, Natasha?" Gwen said. Careful of old bones, she scooped the cat up and deposited her on the floor.

Natasha glared and stalked to the window, where she levitated onto the broad sill and began licking her ruffled fur back into place. Gwen smiled a little sadly. Natasha was old, cranky and set in her ways, no pet for a lively four-year-old boy. But the cat had been with Gwen for almost sixteen years, ever since she finished high school. She was one of the reasons Gwen hadn't given in and gotten her son the puppy he craved.

Natasha wouldn't appreciate being deserted for two weeks, but she'd be all right. Gwen's mother might be deeply unhappy with her decision to go to Highpoint, but she'd never refuse to take care of the cat. She'd done it before. The two of them had an understanding. Natasha let Deirdre know what she wanted, and Deirdre gave it to her.

Gwen smiled as she settled in front of her monitor. The old cat was the one being other than Zach who pretty much always got what she wanted from Deirdre Van Allen.

Gwen turned on her computer. Distantly she could hear water splashing and Zach giggling. Natasha had turned herself into a purring lump again. The computer hummed.

But what she saw as she brought her fingers to the keyboard was the careful sterility of a doctor's examining room. She remembered the chart opposite the examination table—why did doctors always put up those colorful drawings of people's insides for their patients to brood over? The paper covering the exam table had crinkled every time she moved.

She'd shifted a lot.

Sitting at her desk with the cursor blinking imperatively at her, Gwen's heart raced as it had that day. Her palms felt clammy.

Until the diagnosis, she hadn't known fear. Not really. Now the two of them were intimate. Gwen inhaled slowly: *I breathe in and my body is calmed; breathe out, and I smile.*

According to the therapist who led her cancer support group, meditation kept you anchored in the moment, and anxiety was reduced or eliminated when you dealt only with the present moment. So far Gwen hadn't had much success with it. Meditation required stillness, and that didn't come naturally to her. She was working at it, though. Even the stodgiest western medical practitioners these days agreed that the mind affected the body.

After a moment, her heartbeat slowed.

Maybe I am getting better at it, she thought, pleased, and called up the land plat she was researching.

Oddly enough, it wasn't the day she'd been diagnosed with cancer that had come back to her so vividly just now, but the day of her last checkup. When Dr. Webster had told her everything looked good. That was the day she'd broken down and bawled like a baby, her nose running and sobs choking her.

It was also the day she'd known she had to make some changes in her life. The day she'd decided to find her son's father.

Maybe it wasn't so odd, after all, that she would remember that day.

Gwen took another slow breath and started to work.

Chapter 4

"Are we there yet?"

Gwen rumpled the silky hair on her son's head. "Has the plane landed yet?"

"No, but we're almost there, aren't we?"

"About thirty minutes still to go, champ." Assuming the flight was on time. She prayed that it was. If Zach got wound up any tighter, he'd be bouncing off the walls.

"An' my dad will be waiting for us when we get there, right?"

"He sure will. At the baggage claim." That question had been asked at least as often as the traditional "How much longer?" Gwen bent and pulled a book from the tote that held a few small toys, some dried fruit and her laptop. "How about a round of *Green Eggs and Ham* to fill in the time?"

Gwen had read the Seuss story too many times for it to provide any distraction from her own thoughts, but she hoped it would work some of its usual magic on Zach. She began reading, with Zach chiming in loudly on the parts he knew.

A father, it turned out, was at least as exciting as a puppy.

Gwen had spoken with Ben briefly two days ago. He'd asked to speak to Zach—and Zach had been hanging by eagerly, waiting for his chance. Of course, as soon as the phone was in his hands, her ball-of-fire, never-met-a-stranger son had turned shy, barely able to breathe a yes or no to whatever Ben had asked him. He was always like that on the phone, she'd assured Ben. The rest of the time, his mouth worked just fine.

"'Would you like them in a house?'" she read, thinking about last Christmas and wondering if the next one would be different. If she would have to share her son for part of the holidays. "'Would you like them—'"

Zach tugged on her arm. "What does his house look like?"

"Well…like the picture here, I guess."

"My *dad's* house," he said impatiently.

Of course. What other "he" was there these days? "It's painted white and has a staircase and a big front porch. I think all the bedrooms are upstairs, so we'll probably have a room on the second floor."

"Will we be next to my dad's room? Or my uncle's?"

"You have three uncles now, remember? Your dad's two brothers are your uncles, and his sister is your aunt, so his sister's husband is your uncle, too. That makes three." Ben's sister and her husband were someplace in Africa at the moment, and the youngest brother was a long-haul truck driver who lived with Ben when he wasn't on the road. And the other brother, the one she'd met, would be there at the house, though he didn't usually live there. "Which uncle did you mean?"

"The army uncle," Zach said. "I forgot his name."

"Duncan," she said, her mouth oddly dry. "He's your uncle Duncan. I don't know where our room will be, sweetie. We'll just have to wait and find out." She began reading again, hoping to stem the flood.

Zach had been brimming over with questions ever since she told him about his father—but they weren't the ones she'd expected. And dreaded. He'd wanted to know what his dad looked like and if he liked little boys. How long would they stay there? Were there other kids to play with? Could he take his army guys with him? How big were the mountains? Could he climb one? Did his dad have a dog?

Puppies hadn't been entirely eclipsed by the advent of a father.

Gwen didn't fool herself that the other questions wouldn't come up at some point. When she'd told him about his father, she'd tried to scale her explanations to a four-year-old's understanding, saying simply that she hadn't known how to get in touch with Ben when Zach was born, so his dad hadn't known about him. "You didn't have his phone number?" Zach had asked.

"No, I didn't. I didn't have his address, either, so I couldn't write him."

"So how come you found him now?"

"I hired a private investigator."

Zach had been desperately impressed. A real private eye? Wow. He'd wanted to meet the man and maybe see his gun. Gwen had been glad the investigator and his gun, if any, were safely distant in Denver...and selfishly relieved she hadn't had to face the other questions. Yet.

When they finished the book, Gwen judged it time to make a trip to the rest room or else Zach would undoubtedly need to go the moment they were instructed to stay in their seats. "C'mon, short stuff, time to take a walk down the aisle."

Since Zach was fascinated by airplane washrooms, he didn't object. No doubt he was tired of sitting still. So was she. Her mother often said she was as fidgety at thirty as she'd been at three. She wasn't far wrong.

An older woman who reminded Gwen vaguely of Aunt Bee from *The Andy Griffith Show* was already waiting her turn. She fussed over Zach, insisting he go ahead of her—"it's difficult for them to wait at this age, isn't it, dear?"—and asked him if this was his first time on a plane.

"I been on lots of airplanes," he informed her. "My mama an' me like to fly. We don't like airports very much 'cause they won't let you run, even if there is lots and lots of room. But we like airplanes."

She smiled at him indulgently. "Are you going on vacation, or is this a family trip?"

"We're going to see my dad. He lives in the mountains in a big house with a porch, an' he likes little boys. My mama said so."

"Oh, ah…how nice." She gave Gwen a quick glance, her eyebrows raised. "I assume he's talking about a new stepfather?"

Zach answered before she could. "No, he's my dad. A private eye found him for us."

The woman's rather protrudent eyes bulged further. Fortunately the rest-room door opened just then. Gwen breathed a sigh of relief and chivvied her talkative son inside. Zach was blithely unaware there was anything odd about meeting his father for the first time at the age of four. She didn't want some stranger's attitude casting clouds over this visit, making him worry about things he couldn't understand.

Not that Gwen herself didn't worry. How could she not? Between her mother's furious disapproval and the expectations Zach had built up in the past eleven days, she had plenty to worry about.

Her nervous stomach clenched tighter as she helped Zach refasten the snap on his jeans. Heaven knows her own expectations had been knocked sideways when she'd seen her son's father again—expectations she hadn't known she'd had.

The plane was descending when they emerged, and she had the dickens of a time keeping Zach halfway still through the landing process. Finally, though, they were off the plane and headed for the lower level, where they could claim their four suitcases. And one father.

Over Zach's protests, she scooped him up onto her hip before stepping on the escalator. She'd read a horrible story about children whose clothing got caught in the treads....

"Do you see him, Mama? Is he here? Do you see him yet?"

"Zach, you have to be still or I'm going to drop you." The tote was trying to slip off her shoulder. She didn't have a hand free to anchor it, and her heart was pounding, pounding.... "Ugh," she said, shifting him slightly. "I must be feeding you too much. You weigh two tons."

He giggled.

Gwen looked over the top of his head. Waiting at the bottom of the escalator were two men. Two, not one.

Her face felt hot. Ben had brought his brother to welcome his son to the family—and that was good, that was wonderful. She was here because Zach needed his family—all of it. But it wasn't what she'd expected. *Why do I keep expecting things?* she thought fretfully. *It doesn't do any good. I just trip over those stupid expectations every time.*

Ben's gaze was fixed on the boy in her arms. As the moving stairway carried them to him, a smile spread over his hard, square face. The man who waited with him neither moved nor smiled. His expression was every bit as intent as Ben's. But his gaze was on her, not her son.

Gwen's mouth went dry. "Zach," she whispered. "Zach, that's your dad waiting for us at the bottom. The man in the blue windbreaker."

He twisted around to stare. The little arm around her neck tightened. "There? The big one?"

"Yes." She swallowed. "The big one."

The escalator deposited them on level ground. She stepped aside to let those behind her get off, then cleared her throat. "Zach, this is your dad. And this is your uncle Duncan."

"The army uncle."

"That's right."

Zach's choke hold on her tightened. The boy's blue eyes met the man's brown eyes—met and held in the same straight-on way. Two male faces focused completely on each other, one of them large and hard, the skin weathered and shadowed by beard; the other small, soft and rounded, but with the same stubborn jaw and short, blunt nose.

"You're my dad," Zach whispered.

"Yes." Ben's throat worked. "Yes, I am. I'm so glad to see you, Zach. So damned glad."

Zach nodded solemnly. "I'm dam' glad, too."

Duncan made a choked noise. "Ah…been a while since you were around kids, hasn't it, Ben?"

"Yeah." Ben's eyes never left his son's face. "Your uncle Duncan means I wasn't supposed to say 'damn.' You shouldn't, either."

"Okay." Zach squirmed around so he could capture Gwen's face in his two small hands. "Mom, put me down. Put me down now. I'll show my dad our suitcases. I bet he can carry all of 'em. He's really big."

Slowly she lowered Zach to his feet, stricken by a pang of separation so acute it was a physical ache. She wanted to scoop him up and run away, but it was already too late. "Keep hold of your father's hand, Zach. Don't be running off."

He held up a hand, his face turned up to Ben's in sunny confidence. "C'mon. Mom packed hunnerds of things. I brought all my army guys. We're gonna stay with you for two weeks!"

"So I hear." A large hand reached down and swallowed the little one. Ben glanced at her. "I won't let him get lost."

She nodded. "I'm not sure which carousel is ours."

"I'll find it. I know your flight number." He looked down at Zach, his expression soft and grave. "I don't know if I can carry hundreds of things. I might need some help."

Zach giggled as they set off. "It's all in *suitcases*. Do you have a dog?"

Gwen smiled. And swallowed hard. Dammit, she was *not* going to cry.

"Ben's good with kids," the man still beside her said quietly. "And he's already gone on this one."

"Zach's good with everyone." She gave Duncan a smile—and looked quickly away. Damn, damn, damn…

"I take it your flight was uneventful?"

"Aside from reading *Green Eggs and Ham* twenty times, yes." What was wrong with her? Couldn't she get anything right? She tried to pull her thoughts together, watching as Ben and Zach stopped at the first of the baggage carousels.

Ben hunkered down, putting himself at Zach's level. Zach was chattering away. His clear voice carried enough for her to catch a few words—something about his army guys. Then he pointed at a blue suitcase. Ben stood and heaved it off the conveyor belt.

They were so delighted with each other. She couldn't do anything to mess that up.

The man beside her spoke quietly. "The two of them look right together, don't they?"

"Yes. Yes, they do." Her body was humming to itself, making her feel so alive. Making her feel, for the first time in so long, very much a woman.

Stupid, treacherous damned body—this wasn't the first time it had betrayed her. "We'd better catch up with them," she said. "My luggage isn't blue."

Chapter 5

"Hey, buddy, you paying attention? Gotta bid if you wanna stay in the game." Pat grinned at Duncan. *"You chickening out on me?"*

Pat looked just as he always did, the red hair a few weeks past a trim, his fatigue shirt unbuttoned. His stubby little excuse for a nose was peeling as usual— Pat always said he could get a sunburn from standing under a hundred-watt lightbulb. He was sitting in the notch of the old oak out back, leaning against the trunk, holding a hand of cards.

Duncan was straddling the same wide limb, his legs dangling down on either side. He used to sit out here like this with his brother Charlie.

Part of Duncan knew this wasn't right; Sgt. Patrick McConaughsey didn't belong to the time of his life when he'd sat in this old oak. But it seemed rude to ask Pat why he was here in Highpoint when Duncan was so glad to see him. "Hey, Pat, it's good to see you."

"You gonna play cards or not? It's jacks or better to open."

Duncan glanced down. Sure enough, he was holding a hand of cards. All jacks. All red Jacks, in fact. Alarm trickled in. "Pat, there's something wrong here. Something wrong with my hand."

"Is it your hand or your eyes? Look again."

There was *something wrong with his eyes. He couldn't seem to focus. No, maybe it was getting darker. He looked around, his alarm deepening. Everything was dark, murky. "There's some weather moving in. We'd better get inside."*

"Duncan, we need you on the force." That was Jeff, standing on the ground beneath the branch Duncan straddled. "We need you to kill for us. You're good at it. Here's your rifle." He tossed it up.

"No!" But he caught the rifle one-handed—he couldn't let it fall to the ground. It was loaded. He knew it was, and even as he protested, his hands were checking it out, making sure everything worked. "You don't understand. I can't do this anymore."

"Duncan, you playing cards or not?" Pat demanded.

Horror bit, clear and sharp through the darkening air. He remembered. "Pat, you're—"

Gunfire. They were under attack. They—

"It's a backfire," Jeff said. "Just a bunch of kids. Nothing to worry about."

"Duncan," Pat said again, but his voice was wrong. All wrong, breathy and liquid. Duncan knew what he'd see when he turned his head, but he couldn't stop himself. He couldn't stop any of it.

Pat leaned against the trunk of the tree, his legs straddling it as before. But he wasn't grinning. He didn't have enough face left to grin. In the middle of the drip-

*ping, meaty mess that used to be his face, the blood
bubbled.*

He was still breathing.

*"No!" Duncan screamed and he grabbed Pat's shirt
and shook him. "No, no, no—damn you, don't keep doing this, coming back and dying on me. Damn you!" he
said again and shook him over and over, and his friend's
blood spattered everywhere, on his face, his chest, his
hands—*

Knocking. Someone was knocking on…on his door?

Duncan sat bolt upright in bed. Daylight slanted
through the blinds to fall in bright bars on the blue bed-
spread covering him. He shoved his hair out of his face.
His hand shook, but it wasn't bloody.

God, he was sick of that dream.

Rap. Rap. Rap. Out in the hall, but not on his door,
someone was knocking. A little boy said impatiently,
"Aren't you ready yet?"

Zach. Duncan recognized the voice, but hung still between horror and waking. What did Zach want him to
be ready for?

"Mo-om!" the boy's voice rang out.

The bathroom door opened. "Shh," Gwen said in a
low voice. "Keep it quiet, okay? I think your uncle Duncan is still asleep."

Oh. Right. The boy wanted his mother, not his uncle.
Of course. Duncan had a sharp sense of dislocation as
he swung between the horror of his dream and the cheerful, everyday sounds outside his door.

He threw back the covers, climbed out of bed and
crossed to the window, lifting one of the slats of the
blinds so he could look out. Mrs. Bradshaw, the neigh-
bor who used to baby-sit for his mother back in another
world, was digging in her flower bed.

His unconscious mind wasn't exactly subtle. Over and over it hammered home the same points. The script changed slightly—this had been Jeff's first time to make an appearance, for example—but the essence was the same every time. At the start of the dream, Pat was alive and well and wanted to play poker. At the end he was a bloody wreck…and still horribly alive.

Zach's whisper was every bit as audible as his normal voice. "I'm *hungry,* Mom."

He heard Gwen say something, her voice still low. A giggle from Zach. Then the thud of little feet, fading as they headed down the stairs.

This was supposed to be reality, wasn't it? Crisp, sunny spring mornings. Neighbors weeding their flower beds. Little boys who were hungry for breakfast, mothers who tried to keep them quiet. It was all so blasted normal.

It was a reality he didn't fit into anymore.

Get a clue, he told his unconscious. Pat was dead. One hundred percent dead, not breathing in bubbles through his ruined face.

The ruined face had been all too real, though. Duncan scrubbed his hand over his own face. So had the blood.

He turned away from the sunshine and grabbed his sweatpants. She'd headed downstairs with her kid, which meant the bathroom was empty. He wanted a shower, hot as he could stand it and as soon as he could get it.

The bathroom smelled of woman stuff. There was a tidy little makeup case by the sink and a plastic cup holding a yellow, adult sized toothbrush and a smaller red one. The yellow one was damp. The shower stall was wet and smelled like flowers.

One good thing, he thought as he scrubbed skin that didn't show the bloodstains from his dreams. At least he'd gotten over his weird initial reaction to her. He'd discovered that when he'd gone with Ben to pick up her and her son at the airport. Not that he'd stopped reacting, but that spooky whatever it was he'd experienced the first time he'd seen her had faded to normal lust. He could handle that.

He lathered his face, then reached for the razor he kept on the small shelf. There was another razor beside it. A pink one.

Had she noticed his razor when she showered earlier? *Oh, no,* he told himself. Don't go there. But it was too late. The instant mental picture of her, wet and naked, annoyed him as much as it aroused him. He held the skin of his cheek taut with one hand and started shaving. She needed to be sharing a bathroom with Ben, not him. But Ben's bathroom opened off the master bedroom. Chances were, she'd start using it once Ben talked her into his bed again.

Ouch. Damn. He'd cut himself.

Ben had better start paying more attention to her than he had last night. First he'd insisted Duncan go to the airport with him. Then he'd barely spoken to her, either on the ride back to Highpoint or once they arrived. That was no way to impress the woman. Duncan had suggested that he go out for a while, leave the three of them alone, but Ben had been unusually nervous— about seeing Gwen again? Duncan wondered, frowning. No. Nervous about getting to know his son.

Well, what of it? He snapped off the water. Of course Ben was focused on Zach. That was the way it should be.

It did seem that if he'd been half as interested in Zach's mother five years ago, he would have known about his son all along.

But that didn't make any difference. Gwen wasn't free, not in any way that counted. Maybe he didn't see her as a sister-in-law yet. That, he thought grimly as he dried off, was going to take time. But once she was sleeping with his brother again, his body would get used to the idea that she wasn't available.

Right now, all he had to do was go downstairs and act normal. He grimaced as he opened the bathroom door. That shouldn't be too hard. He'd been acting normal for a month now.

The mingled smells of coffee and bacon drew him to the kitchen. He paused in the doorway.

Ben stood at the stove, pouring batter into neat circles onto the griddle. Zach sat at the table, elevated on one of the couch pillows. He had a milk mustache, a piece of bacon in his hand and a plate empty of everything but syrup. His mother sat beside him with her back to Duncan. She wore a sweater the color of raspberries. In the bright sunshine, her pale hair was almost incandescent.

They looked like a family.

"Hi, Unca Duncan! My dad made us fatjacks for breakfast!"

A smile eased onto his face. "Fatjacks huh? Is that sort of like flapjacks and do I get any?"

Ben spoke from the stove. "I'm putting yours on now. You'll have to flip them yourself—I've got to get out to the site."

Gwen pushed her chair back. "Come on, Zach, let's wash a few layers of syrup off your hands and get you dressed."

"No need for you to rush just because my day starts early," Ben said.

"I need to rent a car, remember?" She flashed Ben a

quick, polite smile on her way to the sink, where she yanked off a paper towel and dampened it. "I was hoping you could drop me at a rental place on your way in. Hold out your hands, Zach."

Ben's jaw set in a way Duncan knew all too well. "You don't need to rent a car. I told you that. I've got my work truck, so you can use the Chevy. It's old, but I keep it in good shape."

"Thank you, but I'd rather rent a car. I explained that when I agreed to come here."

"If an old Chevy isn't good enough for you, you can use Duncan's Mustang."

Her eyebrows lifted. "How kind of you to offer me the use of your brother's car. As I said, however, I prefer to make my own arrangements."

Oh, but she did that well, Duncan thought, a grin tugging at his mouth. Princess to peon, with more than a whiff of mad for flavor.

"Why spend the money on a rental when you don't have to?" Ben demanded.

She finished wiping her son's hands and gave him a pat on the bottom. "Upstairs, short stuff. I laid your clothes out on the bed."

Zach protested, glancing uncertainly between his mother and Ben. Kids always picked up on it when there was anger in the air, Duncan thought. And these two fairly simmered with old anger.

People didn't carry anger around this long unless other strong feelings were involved. He made himself face that. While Gwen was busy with Zach, he crossed the room, took the spatula from Ben and said under his breath, "Try to remember you're not her big brother."

Ben shot him an annoyed glance. "I'm real aware of that."

"Then stop grabbing the reins. She's an adult. She doesn't need you to steer for her." Gwen didn't really know either of them, yet she was living in their house. Of course she wanted to have her own car, rather than depend on them.

Zach ran out of excuses and left to get dressed. She carried his plate to the sink, every stiff inch of her announcing her displeasure. "I would rather we didn't argue in front of him."

"Okay, you're right about that," Ben admitted. "Look, can we settle this later? I need to get out to the site if I'm going to have any chance of finishing up early enough to take Zach to the movies the way we planned."

"If you're in a hurry," Duncan said mildly, "I can drop Gwen off at the rental place on my way to the shooting range."

Ben scowled. "All right, all right. Do it your way. I should be back by noon."

The door didn't quite slam behind him, but it came close.

"Well." Gwen slid the plate into the dishwasher. "Thanks for offering me a ride. We'll be ready whenever you are."

"His bark is worse than his bite, you know." Duncan flipped his pancakes. They were a little singed.

"No doubt. I'm not crazy about being barked at, though." She grabbed another paper towel and began wiping off the table.

He sliced a chunk of butter into a small bowl and stuck it in the microwave. "Ben can be bossy, but he's not a tyrant. Just stubborn."

"Maybe so. But I'm not one of his employees."

There it was again—that princess lilt to her voice. He shook his head, wondering why that cool, snooty tone appealed to him so much. "Oh, Ben picked up the habit of being in charge long before he had any employees to boss around. He's been running the family—or trying to—ever since our folks died. God knows what would have happened if he hadn't taken charge of the lot of us then."

She paused, a little V between her eyebrows, the crumpled paper towel in her suddenly motionless hand. "I didn't know. I mean, I knew his parents were dead. That was in the PI's report."

He stared. "You had Ben investigated by a PI?"

"I needed a PI to find him." She jerked one shoulder in a quick shrug. "I thought I might as well find out if he'd gotten married or something in the past five years. Since I was planning to introduce him to his son."

"I see." He took the melted butter out of the microwave and drizzled it over his pancakes.

"You're either remarkably tactful or lacking in curiosity."

The amusement in her voice made him look at her, really look at her. *Mistake,* he thought as his groin tightened. *Down, boy.* But there was such self-deprecating humor in her eyes that he couldn't help smiling back. "Oh, I'm curious, but devious about it. I was the middle child until my little sister was born. Middle children learn to be tricky."

"Do they?" When she relaxed into her smile like that, she reminded him of her son—no trace of the princess now, just warm, sunny woman. "I wouldn't know, being an only child. We don't bother to be devious since the world revolves around us."

He chuckled and carried his pancakes to the table. "I can't remember the last time Ben made pancakes for breakfast. Thanks for inspiring him."

"Zach's the inspiration." She threw herself back into motion, heading across the kitchen. "Which is wonderful, just what I'd hoped for. Being Zach's father is obviously important to Ben." She opened the door. "Where's the trash?"

"Under the sink. You don't stand still much, do you?"

"Not willingly." She hurried back across the room to toss the paper towel in the trash. "I guess that's all the damage I can do here without snatching your plate away. Most people get testy if I do that before they finish eating."

"Something of a neatnik, are you?"

"It's one of my more annoying flaws. I'd better see what's keeping Zach."

"He's okay. We haven't heard any loud crashes." Duncan took a sip of coffee. "I was fifteen when my folks were killed. Ben was twenty-one. He dropped out of college, talked the construction company where he'd been working in the summers to take him on full-time and persuaded the court he was a fit guardian for the lot of us." Duncan put down his mug. "You didn't ask, but I thought you ought to know. He comes by his managing ways honestly."

She tipped her head to one side. "I always wanted a brother or sister—someone who could do for me what you just did for Ben. Someone with all that shared history. I never intended for Zach to be an only child, too."

"Does he have to be?"

"I don't know." She had a look on her face that made him think she wanted to clean something, and quick. Her glance fell on his mug, which was half-empty. She grabbed it and carried it to the coffeepot, which put her back to him. "I'm not sure what you know. What has Ben told you about my health?"

Ah. Easier to talk about some things when you weren't eye to eye. "He said you were diagnosed with breast cancer a year and a half ago. The lump was small and they think they got it all. You had radiation before the surgery, and you're on some kind of hormonal treatment."

"Tamoxifen. I'll take it for another three years. It suppresses estrogen production. They think high estrogen levels are linked to the type of cancer I had."

Duncan's grasp of female biology tended to be more hands-on than scientific, but he thought he saw where she was headed. "Would pregnancy affect your hormone levels?"

"Yes. They don't know how much of a danger that is, though." She turned around, his mug steaming gently in one hand. "You have no idea what a relief it is to talk to someone who can say 'cancer' right out loud without stammering."

"Ben's not usually one to tiptoe around a subject."

"A lot of people are uncomfortable talking about it, though. My mother avoids the word as if it referred to a social disease." The quick flash of her grin suggested this was a harmless oddity, nothing that troubled her.

"She's afraid for you."

"Yes. Yes, she is. And now I really need to check on Zach. If you think the only kinds of trouble he can get into are noisy—well, obviously it's been a while since you were four."

"Okay. But I'll appreciate that coffee a lot more than he would."

She frowned at the mug she was about to carry out

of the room, gave a little shake of her head and crossed
to hand it to him.

Their fingers brushed. He allowed for the quick jab of
pleasure and congratulated himself for pulling his hand
back smoothly without spilling the hot coffee—in spite
of the slight jerk of her hand.

She blinked, stepped back and gave him one of those
polite smiles before leaving the room.

Duncan sat at the table without moving, looking at the
bright blue square of sky framed by the window over
the sink and trying not to enjoy the slow burn of arousal.
Or the knowledge that she'd felt it, too.

It seemed they were both going to have to be careful.

On Gwen's third morning in Highpoint, she stood
with her eyes closed, letting water stream over her back
and shoulders, and blessed the unknown genius who'd
invented showers. Sometimes she thought the only thing
keeping her sane were these few minutes at the start of
every day when she could stand beneath lots of lovely
hot water.

Sanity, of course, was relative. Her mother thought
she was nuts to have contacted Ben in the first place,
but Gwen was more certain than ever that she'd done
the right thing. Zach and Ben had bonded so fast it had
been like watching some kind of cosmic superglue in
action.

There were other aspects of her journey she wasn't so
sure about.

She'd wanted answers, she admitted as she poured a
dollop of baby shampoo into her palm. Closure. Oh,
she'd hoped for more—hoped there might still be a spark
between her and Ben. Something to build on.

Well, she had gotten one answer, hadn't she? Smiling

ruefully, she lathered and rinsed. There was no doubt at all that Ben had fallen, and fallen hard, for their son. He barely seemed to know she was in the same room when Zach was around. And frankly she'd seen more of Ben's brother than she had Ben.

And that was okay. The whole purpose of this trip was to give Zach a chance to develop a relationship with his father, one that didn't depend on having her around. So she'd encouraged Ben to take Zach to the movies, the park, wherever.

The fact was, the spark wasn't there for her, either. Not anymore.

Maybe the connection she'd felt five years ago had been the product of wishful thinking. Or maybe it had gotten buried under their mutual anger or had simply withered over the years. Heaven knew she wasn't the same person she'd been five years ago. She'd been so angry after her father's death, flying off in all directions.

Gwen squirted lavender-scented bath gel into her hand and smiled. The scent made her think of the friend who had given it to her. Kelly laughed loudly, cried easily and took life in bigger bites than anyone Gwen knew. She never let fear dictate her choices. Gwen wanted to be like Kelly when she grew up.

Of course, Kelly would probably say Gwen was looking for labels, not answers—tidy little pigeonholes where she could file memories and feelings.

She'd probably be right.

Gwen reached for her razor. Her fingers brushed the other razor sitting on the shelf, nearly knocking it off.

Duncan's razor.

A little thrill shot through her. How absurd. But it had been a very long time since she'd shared a bathroom with a man. A long time since she'd shared anything remotely intimate with a man.

It was inappropriate to think of sharing the bathroom with Duncan as some sort of intimacy, she told herself as she drew the razor along her leg. No, it was just plain dumb. She frowned and started on her other leg. It would be worse than dumb to think about intimacy and Duncan. More like courting disaster.

Quite aside from the sexual buzz she got around him, though, she liked him. She liked the way he moved and the way he smiled—slowly, as if a smile was something to be savored, not rushed into. Most of all she liked the way he listened. When she talked to him, she felt as if he gave her his complete attention. Rather the way most men focused on the Super Bowl or sex, she thought, and sniffed. As if nothing else mattered.

The buzz wasn't going to be a problem. She wasn't about to act on it, so it would fade in time. For now...well, he wasn't around all that much.

Gwen shut off the water, grabbed a towel and stepped out of the shower stall, automatically facing away from the big mirror over the vanity. Whatever Duncan did with himself during the day, mostly he did it away from the house. Something was eating at him....

And why did she think that? Gwen shook her head and rubbed herself briskly with the towel. It wasn't as if she was good at reading people. The law was so much easier to understand.

"Mom! Mom!" Zach called from the other side of the door. "I'm gonna go eat breakfast now!"

"Okay, sweetie." Gwen wrapped the towel around her hair and reached for her lotion. "Save me some toast."

"'Kay!"

She heard his feet thudding down the stairs. How could such a small boy sound so much like an elephant in a hurry? She smiled and smoothed lotion up her arm to her shoulder, and down over her breast. Then the left side—arm, shoulder and breast. The little ridge of the scar. The dip on the side of her breast where there used to be a plump curve.

Gwen's hand hesitated. Then, impulsively, she faced the mirror.

The surface was still fogged over. She pulled the towel off her head and swiped it across the mirror, then stood still and looked.

Narrow shoulders, on the bony side, but okay. A flat stomach with thin white stretch marks around an "innie" belly button. Skinny thighs, but a nice butt, she thought. Pubic hair more white than blond—she'd wondered sometimes if her mother's hair was this pale down there. Then felt guilty, as if she were intruding on her mother's privacy. Deirdre was a very modest woman.

Then there were her breasts. Modest little things *they* were, to be sure. She'd always wished they were a teensy bit bigger, but had been secretly pleased with their shape. At least she wouldn't have to worry about sagging when she was older, and she'd always been able to go braless. Even now, though she never wore snug-fitting tops anymore.

Pretty little peaches high on her chest…wall-eyed, lopsided breasts.

The surgeon hadn't told her that her nipples might not match after the surgery. Her left nipple pointed out slightly, pulled toward the scar. And here…she found the spot with her fingers, as well as her eyes. Here was that dip, the funny-looking dent in the side of her breast where the surgeon had removed breast tissue along with the lump.

She was extremely lucky. Gwen stroked the dent lightly and assured herself of that. Maybe her breasts weren't as pretty as they once were, but ten years ago they would have taken her whole breast, not just scooped out a bit of it. Twenty years ago they would have taken the breast, all the lymph nodes and the chest muscle.

Twenty-two years ago her aunt had died...*after* they cut away her breast, lymph nodes and chest muscle.

Gwen looked away, reaching for her sweater. Then made herself stop and look back at the mirror. What would a man think, how would he feel, about her lopsided breasts?

She used to think she was pretty good at sex, however lacking she might be at relationships. There were rules for sex. Some were obvious: be considerate. Don't lie. Both partners should be free. Always use protection. Don't have too many partners—well, that one was a bit ambiguous. Gwen interpreted it to mean, "Be very, very picky." Kelly claimed that was just another way of playing it safe, but Gwen thought playing it safe was sound policy for the relationship-impaired.

People didn't come with rules. She wasn't good at people, and she wasn't sure she'd still be good at sex, either. It had been so long....

Gwen ran her fingertips over the side of her breast again. The dent was very noticeable to her eyes, her touch. Maybe it wouldn't be so obvious to a man, though. Men were usually focused on the main event, weren't they? Football was all about scoring, and sex meant intercourse. Although Duncan wasn't as—

Horrified, she dropped her hand and snatched her panties from the neat pile of clothes on the closed lid of the toilet. No way was she going to think about sex and Duncan. He was an interesting man. She liked him. Nothing wrong with that. But add a jolt of sexual sizzle to liking, and you ended up with a recipe for trouble. He was her son's uncle, for heaven's sake!

Gwen pulled on her panties and slacks, yanked her sweater over her head and grabbed her hairbrush. The plain fact was, her hormones did a happy dance whenever Duncan was in the room. The good news was that he didn't have a clue. Neither did Ben, thank goodness.

She wasn't responsible for her hormones, just her actions. As long as she made sure everyone else remained in the dark about that blasted sizzle, they didn't have a problem.

Chapter 6

Colorado air was different from Florida air, crisp and dry and spiced with pine instead of hibiscus or jasmine. It was also too damned chilly.

Gwen sat on a wooden lawn chair and tried to ignore cold fingers and toes, the distractingly different air and a sky so huge and blue she felt as if she'd fall up into it if she stared too long. She *had* to make some progress with this title search. She'd been online most of the morning trying to conduct a search of the Bureau of Land Management's database, but her little jumping bean had different priorities.

Finally she'd taken Zach outside to run off some of that energy. Her laptop could run off the battery for a while, and she had a decent connection speed with her cell phone.

"Look at me! Look at me, Mom!"

She glanced up—and swallowed. "Wow." She stood and the thirty-five-hundred-dollar laptop nearly fell to the ground before she caught it and closed it. "That's super, honey," she said as she walked really fast to the tree where he was dangling upside down.

She got her hands on him just as he started to slip. Her heart was playing handball off the wall of her chest. "You're a great acrobat, but gymnasts use a spotter, you know."

"They do?" he said as she guided him to the ground. "What's a spotter?"

"Someone who stands by to help them do their tricks right. So they don't fall on their pointy little heads." She wanted to get on her knees and hold him tight. She ruffled his hair.

He giggled.

"He keeps you busy, doesn't he?" a feminine voice said.

Startled, Gwen glanced to her left. An older woman stood at the fence beside a newly budded bush. Her hair was a tight cap of grizzled gray curls. She wore glasses with lavender frames, a plain white shirt and jeans. Everyone in Highpoint seemed to wear jeans. But, Gwen thought, this woman surely bought hers in the boys' department. She was tiny, no hips.

Even tinier than Gwen was herself. "That he does," she said, delighted. Her father used to say she was no bigger than a minute. On that scale, this woman was forty seconds, max. "I'm Gwen Van Allen."

"Naomi Bradshaw. I couldn't help noticing that you're trying to get some work done."

"'Trying' is the operative word. Yes, honey, what is it?" she said in response to Zach's urgent tugs on her sweater.

"I gotta go."

"Do you want me to go with you?" At his vehement

denial, she bent to undo the top button on his jeans. He could usually manage it when he had time. From the way he was hopping around now, though, time was of the essence. Good thing there was a half-bath just off the kitchen. He'd never make it upstairs.

The second she undid the snap he took off like a bullet for the back door. Gwen glanced at her new acquaintance, slightly wary. She had no idea what, if anything, Ben had told people about her and Zach.

The woman's eyes were bright with curiosity, but she didn't ask any questions. "Maybe you'd like to send your boy over here sometime. Heaven knows I'm set up for kids." She waved at an elaborate jungle gym behind her.

There was a sandbox, too, Gwen saw as she walked up to the chain-link fence. And a swing hanging from the broad limb of one tree. "You sure are. Grandkids?"

"Oh, I've got plenty of them, Lord knows, though only two are here in town. But the equipment's been around longer than they have. Over the years, I've probably baby-sat for half the families in this town." Her eyes twinkled behind the glasses. "I charge for it, I'm afraid. I wasn't offering just because I love kids, though I do."

"Do you keep any other children Zach's age? He's used to spending his mornings at a day care, where he has lots of kids to play with."

"The Murray twins will be here in less than an hour. They're five."

"We may have a deal, then. At the rate I'm going I'll never finish the first title search, much less the rest of the work I'd planned to finish while I'm here."

"Title search? Are you in real estate?"

"A real-estate attorney, for my sins. I hope you don't mind if I ask for references?"

"Not a bit. Simplest would probably be to ask Duncan. I used to watch him and Charlie and little Annie sometimes. Though it's been a while." She grinned. "Scamps, every one of them, but good kids."

Gwen couldn't resist probing for more. "Scamps, huh? What about Ben?"

"He was a handful, too, but I never baby-sat him, which is why I didn't suggest him as a reference. He was too old to need a sitter by the time Johnny and me moved here."

"Is Johnny your husband?"

"He was. He's gone now."

"Oh, I...I'm sorry."

Mrs. Bradshaw chuckled. "Gone, honey, not dead. That man always did have itchy feet. Couldn't see a road without wanting to travel it. That's why I started baby-sitting—had to do something when he took off. Johnny sent money when he could, but he wasn't what you could call reliable."

"That must have been hard."

"Water under the bridge now. Some folks do seem to be born to wander. Take Ben's and Duncan's father. You couldn't have kept that man in one spot if you'd tied him down. Just like my Johnny, though he did take his wife with him when he could." She chuckled. "That part wasn't like my Johnny."

Gwen hunted for a sensitive response, but all she came up with was a nod and a smile.

Naomi Bradshaw didn't seem to need much encouragement. "I don't want to drag up that whole nature-versus-nurture argument, but I swear wandering is born in some people."

"Well, if there is such a gene, it must have missed me. Except for college, I've lived in the same city all my life."

"A homebody, are you? That would suit Ben."

"Ah—" Gwen felt her cheeks warm "—I don't know that I'm a homebody, exactly. I suppose you're curious about why I'm here. About Zach."

"About to burst with it, but that isn't your problem. Though I'd be much obliged if you'd tell me which of 'em you're here for—Ben or Duncan."

"I'm here for Zach. He's Ben's son."

Her eyebrows shot up. "Is he? Well, now I am surprised, though I suppose I shouldn't be. Ben's as human as any of us, even if he did get a double helping when the good Lord was handing out 'responsible.'"

That he had. Ben was the sort of man she'd always dreamed of finding one day—stable, strong, dependable. It was no wonder it had taken her so long to forgive him for dumping her—something he never had apologized for, had he?

And maybe she hadn't truly forgiven him, either.

"I'd been wondering if the boy was Duncan's," Mrs. Bradshaw confided. "He's in the army, after all."

Amusement eased the frown from Gwen's face. "Those army men are a wild bunch," she agreed.

"It comes of hanging out with no one but other men. They get their priorities mixed up. Not that I mean to say anything against Duncan. He's a good boy, always has been, and a genuine hero, too."

"What do you mean?"

"Haven't they told you anything about it? Well, if that isn't just like a couple of men, keeping all the good stories to themselves! He'll be getting a Purple Heart, I'm sure." Mrs. Bradshaw nodded firmly. "The poor boy was shot all up on his last mission. Very hush-hush stuff, I hear.''

"Good God. That's how he was hurt? I knew he was on medical leave, but no one said anything about him having been *shot.*"

"Oh, yes. Not that he or Ben have said one word about it to me, in spite of us being neighbors. Trisha Rayburn told me about it. I watch her son sometimes now that she and Harold have split up. She's been taking night courses, but she'll have to go to Denver soon to finish up.''

"Mm,'' Gwen said, unsure how to respond. She'd wondered what Duncan did all day, other than work out and go to target practice—he was very fond of that big rifle of his. She'd seen him cleaning it in the kitchen. How annoying that the obvious answer hadn't crossed her mind. If he was seeing someone who worked nights, of course he'd be gone a lot during the day. "I guess Trisha and Duncan are good friends.''

"I don't know about that. Her daughter, Layla—Layla keeps her little brother most of the time when her mother's in school—she's been seeing Jeff Parker, and Jeff's an old friend of Duncan's. Trisha said Duncan had to have a lot of surgery on his arm. The bone and muscles were all chewed up. They have to give him a Purple Heart for that, don't they? Being wounded in the line of duty.''

"I'm not sure how it works. You know, I really think I'd better check on Zach. He's taking a long time.''

"Sure thing, honey. Just let me know if you want to bring him over.''

Gwen hurried for the house, alarmed by her reaction to learning about Duncan's injury. She felt shaky. It was absurd. She knew Duncan was okay—he went running all the time, didn't he? So he must be recovering just fine. Yet it made her sick to think of him having been shot, his bones and muscles "all chewed up" by bullets.

What kind of action had he been in? Was Mrs. Bradshaw right about it being some sort of hush-hush work, or was that embellishment? "Zach?' she said, letting the back door close behind her.

The bathroom door was closed. Automatically she went there first, turned the knob and opened it.

Duncan stood at the toilet. Not, thank God, using it— he had one foot on the closed lid and was rubbing something smelly into his thigh.

His bare, muscular, hairy thigh. He was wearing boxers. And nothing else.

She gaped at him. There was no other word for it. Sweat gleamed on the muscles of his neck and shoulders and chest, and she stood there and gaped at him as if he'd stripped on stage and invited her to stare at his body.

Lord help her, what a body he had. The long, red welt of a scar on his biceps didn't lessen the impact one bit.

"I'm sorry," she gasped much too late. "I didn't think. I was looking for Zach. You might try vitamin E for the scar," she added as her face went hot. Then she fled, leaving the door standing open behind her.

"I'm not sure this was a good idea," Duncan said from the doorway two hours later. "Zach's having a great time, but I think he and the twins are planning a military coup in Mrs. Bradshaw's kitchen."

Gwen glanced up from her laptop, her eyes wide and wary as a startled doe's. Her smile didn't enter those worried eyes one bit. "Thanks for taking him over there."

"I figured I'd better. I hadn't been to visit Mrs. Bradshaw since the nurses persuaded the doctors I should make my brother's life miserable while I'm recovering, instead of theirs. She had a lot of probing to do."

Humor broke through her guard in a chuckle. "I take it you're a lousy patient. Zach seemed to be enjoying himself when you left?"

"Judging by the decibel level, he and the twins were having a blast. If it was anyone but Mrs. Bradshaw keeping tabs on those three, I'd be worried."

"She seems like a very nice woman. If you'll excuse me," she said, closing her laptop, "I need to go get—"

"Uh-uh." Duncan shook his head. "I warn you. If you leap up from that couch and run out of the room on yet another made-up errand, I'm coming after you."

She froze halfway to her feet, then eased back down. "Not going to let me wallow in embarrassment, are you."

"Nope." Duncan sauntered into the living room, showing her with every relaxed inch of his body that they were going to treat this lightly. "Look, it was more my fault than yours. I should have locked the door. I'm out of the habit, but that's no excuse. I had a muscle cramp after my run and went straight for the medicine cabinet without stopping to think."

"I really was expecting to find Zach."

"So you've mentioned." Three times now—just before she bolted, obliquely when he and she and Zach sat down to lunch and again just now. "I believe you. Otherwise I'd suspect you desperately wanted a peek at my body. In which case, I'd have to assume you were disappointed, judging by the way you raced off. And my ego refuses to buy that."

"Well." Her smile flickered and her cheeks turned

pink. "To think I'd be grateful for the male ego. I didn't want you to think the scar upset me. I've been worrying about that," she admitted, "after the way I blurted out advice about vitamin E."

He knew why she was upset, but neither of them was going to mention that. He could only be grateful for the way his leg had hidden his reaction to having her gaze travel over him so intently. "Did you use vitamin E after your surgery?" he asked, coming over to sit casually beside her. *See, we can both handle this.*

"Yes, I did." She looked faintly surprised. "I think it helped, too. Of course the scar from a surgical incision is likely to be a lot neater than one from a...a bullet wound."

"I've got both—a scar from the original damage done by the bullet, and the one the surgeon made when she went in to fix things."

She ducked her head. "I don't like to think about you being shot."

"Neither do I." That was the understatement of the decade. He didn't like thinking about the reason for her scar, either. But he had a feeling she needed to talk about it, and people were usually comfortable giving advice. "So how much vitamin E should I take?"

"Oh, you don't take it. Not for this. You apply it topically, right on the incision."

She told him about vitamin E and how you shouldn't worry about how the scars looked now—they would fade in time. She talked about keeping his skin supple, and the possibility of keloid scars, the tendency to which was an inherited trait.

He listened. And he watched her.

Looking was all he could do, but there was pleasure in it. She darkened her eyebrows and lashes—not obviously, but they must be as pale as her hair naturally. He wondered what she looked like when she awoke in the morning with her eyes all naked and sleepy.

And yanked his thoughts back before his imagination could seize that image.

Her mouth was untinted and generous. The smooth, dense cream of her skin curved over cheeks soft and round as a child's—one reason it was easy to misjudge her age. Not that he knew what that was, exactly. Ben hadn't been sure. But the fine lines around her eyes made him think she must be in her late twenties.

Smile lines. She smiled easily and often, but her smiles weren't all equal. The one she flashed him now was self-conscious. "I'm blithering on, aren't I? I'm sure your doctor told you how to take care of the incision."

"She told me to keep it clean and dry. I suspect army doctors aren't that concerned about scarring."

"Probably because you rough, tough soldiers don't worry about scars. Yours is a sort of badge of honor, isn't it?"

God, no. He couldn't keep from stiffening. "A scar speaks of survival. If that makes it a badge of honor, yours certainly qualifies."

"That's how I ought to look at it, I guess. But let's face it—people consider a scar on a man interesting, not disfiguring. You can still take your shirt off at the beach and women will flock around."

If she took her shirt off anytime, anywhere, men would definitely flock around. He didn't dare point that out when he was trying so hard not to think about her with her shirt off. "Is it 'people' who consider your scar disfiguring, or is it you?"

She sighed. "Me, I suppose, since no one else has

seen it, except for my doctor. Uh-oh.'' She rolled her eyes. ''*That's* more information than you needed.''

His laugh surprised him, rolling right up from his belly before he knew it was coming. Gwen turned beet-red, then giggled.

Chapter 7

The first thing Ben heard when he walked in the door was Duncan's laugh. He stopped. It had been way too long since he'd heard his brother laugh out loud that way.

He heard Gwen giggle and he smiled, pleased. Ben was pretty sure Duncan had been avoiding her, and he knew why. Duncan was hung up on the fact that his big brother had had a one-night stand, and he wasn't giving Gwen a fair shake. It wasn't like him to be judgmental, but a lot of things about Ben's little brother weren't normal right now.

Sounded as if they were moving in the right direction now, though. Ben shifted the shopping bag to his other hand and headed for the living room.

Gwen's face was a bright, embarrassed red, and her eyes were lit with mirth. Duncan sat beside her on the couch, half-turned so that he faced her, not the doorway.

"Is this reprobate giving you a hard time?" Ben demanded, delighted.

Duncan turned. His face was strangely blank, as if he hadn't decided what to put there. Gwen smiled, her color fading to a pretty glow. "I managed to put my foot in my mouth all by myself. And no, I'm not going to tell you what I said. I've embarrassed myself sufficiently for one day."

"I wasn't expecting you for a couple hours," Duncan said. "You were heading out to the Morrow site, weren't you?"

"The siding hadn't been delivered, so I spent some time in the office instead, tracking down the problem. Where's Zach?" he asked, glancing around. In only five days he'd gotten spoiled. The boy usually made straight for him the moment he came home. "Don't tell me he ran out of energy and is taking a nap."

"No, he's playing next door. Is that for him?" She nodded at the bag in his hand.

Since the bag had the logo of a popular toy store on it, he knew what she was really asking. She'd warned him not to spend the entire two weeks buying things for Zach. "It's just a puzzle. You said he liked puzzles."

"He'll be tickled." Gwen closed her laptop, which was sitting on the arm of the couch, and stood. "I'll go get him, although I warn you—you're in for some stiff competition. Mrs. Bradshaw has five-year-old twin boys at her place."

Ben lost his smile. "What's he doing at Mrs. Bradshaw's?"

"Having a blast, from what Duncan tells me."

"I don't see why you took him over there."

Duncan raised his eyebrows. "So he could play with

the twins and Gwen could get some work done. What's bugging you, Ben?''

Ben scowled at his brother, who ought to know enough to stay out of this. ''Maybe she has to use sitters when she's in Florida, but not here. If you *had* to work,'' he said, switching back to Gwen, ''Duncan could have kept an eye on Zach until I got here.''

''Duncan isn't at your disposal. More to the point, he isn't four or five years old. Zach needs time with kids his age.''

''I don't want him staying with a sitter while he's here.''

''*You* don't want?'' She tossed her hands in the air. ''Sure. Okay. I don't know how we limped along without you making these decisions for us until now. If that's how you want things, be home by noon every day to take over so I can get some work done, too. And be sure to explain to Zach why he can't play with the twins anymore.''

''I've cleared as much time as I can. I can't just dump everything and take off.''

''You think I can? You think practicing law is a hobby for me?''

''I don't know why you're practicing law at all! You don't need to work. With your money—''

''Is that the only reason you work? For the money you can make?'' She stepped closer, her face tight with anger. ''If you think Zach needs a stay-at-home parent full-time, sell your business and move to Florida. I'll give you my money—the money I inherited, at least, which is the part that sticks in your craw, isn't it? Then you can afford to take care of Zach while I play at being an attorney.''

He was so mad he could barely pull words together. "It will be a cold day in hell before I live off a woman!"

"Ben." Duncan stood. "You might want to shut up now."

He rounded on his brother. "And *you* might want to butt out."

"You aren't angry because Gwen left Zach with a sitter. You're angry because he's with Mrs. Bradshaw—who is going to tell everyone about the son you didn't know you had."

"That's bullshit. I'm proud of Zach."

"That's right. It isn't Zach you're ashamed of."

Ben opened his mouth to rip apart his brother's stupid ideas—and shut it again as a sick feeling welled up inside him. He took a few steps away, running his hand over his hair. Was it getting thinner on top? "I've never cared what people think."

And that was true, dammit. So why did he feel so rotten?

Duncan nodded. "True. You've always known what was right and lived your life accordingly, and to hell with what anyone else thought. I don't know what went wrong with you and Gwen, but I know you. I'll bet that when you decided not to see her again, you were sure it was the right thing to do." He paused, letting a brief silence weight his next words. "You're not sure anymore. That's what's eating you."

Ben paced restlessly, coming to a stop by the window. The grass out front was starting to turn green. It wouldn't be long before he had to drag a mower across it. He had a good lawn, thick and healthy. He ought to—he'd been tending it for years. Alone.

He could have watched a chubby, diaper-clad Zach toddle across that lawn a couple of years ago…if he hadn't ended things with Gwen the way he had. If he hadn't been so blamed sure he was right.

Ben sighed. Ever since Gwen turned up in his life again, he'd been mad—at her, at fate, at everything that had kept him from knowing his son for four years. But Duncan was right, damn him. Most of all, he was furious with himself.

Had there been times he'd questioned his decision? He couldn't remember now. He'd put Gwen firmly out of his mind, as finished business. A mistake. He did remember that it hadn't been all about sex with them. She'd been so pretty and lively and feminine, and he'd felt good with her. Hopeful. When he'd realized how wealthy she was, he'd been hugely disappointed. It had seemed best to cut things off cleanly, since there was no chance of a future for them.

He'd barely given a thought to the possibility of a child. Having made up his mind she was wrong for him, he'd decided there wouldn't *be* a child—as if God would agree she was wrong for him and withhold any sticky consequences.

How could he have been so stupid?

"I'll go get Zach," Gwen said quietly.

"Hold on a minute." Ben rubbed the back of his neck. It was forever too late for him to see Zach as a newborn, as a toddler. But he might still be able to watch his son turning crooked somersaults on that grass this summer. If he didn't screw up again. He turned.

There were probably things he hated worse than apologizing, but offhand he couldn't think of what they were. "I dumped on you for all the wrong reasons. I didn't mean most of what I said. I'm sorry."

Her eyebrows lifted. "I'm tempted to ask which parts you *did* mean, but never mind. We've argued enough."

Ben grimaced. "Do you suppose this will get easier?"

"I don't think being a parent ever gets easy."

"No, I mean…sharing the parenting. You're not used to it, and I'm too used to being in charge."

"Well—" her smile flickered "—I guess as long as we can both talk things out when we disagree, there's hope. It's harder for people who don't know each other well, isn't it? A married couple grows used to negotiating their differences, hopefully before they have to do it as parents. Not to mention the fact that when things get rough, they can smooth out the edges in bed."

He felt his body respond to the idea. It was past time he did something about his goal. "That can be arranged."

Silence fell—brief, taut, complicated.

Duncan broke it. "I'll get Zach."

Gwen watched Duncan leave. She wanted to grab him and make him stay—or run away herself. But that would be childish.

"I wasn't offering you a quickie," Ben said. "That wasn't what I meant."

Reluctantly she faced him. She wasn't sure what he had in mind. Or if she was ready to find out. "You have a real talent for saying things you don't mean."

He grimaced. "Yeah. Lately that's been true. I guess I haven't known what I mean myself half the time." He started pacing, the random motion of a man unable to be still when his thoughts were unquiet.

She knew the feeling.

"I've been pretty shook up ever since I found out about Zach."

She smiled tentatively. "I'm used to thinking I'm right most of the time, too. It took me a while to adjust to the idea I could be really, really wrong. I was wrong not to find you before now.''

"The fact is," he said heavily, "I blamed you. When you showed me Zach's picture, I blamed you for everything. For cheating me out of the first four years of his life.''

It was guilt she saw in his eyes now, not anger. "And you don't anymore?''

"I can see how it seemed to you. I broke things off between us. I didn't contact you, which left you with the responsibility for everything—not just for having the baby, but for making sure I knew about your pregnancy, too. That wasn't right.''

Gwen's chest ached and she rubbed it absently. She admired Ben. He was so forthright, so responsible. She was beginning to like him again, too. But she didn't *want* him. What was wrong with her? "I should have let you know. I see that now. At the time…" She gave a short, pained laugh. "Maybe if I'd had your address, I would have listened to my conscience instead of my temper.''

His face darkened. "I gave it to you. You didn't have to pay a damned detective to find me.''

"I was furious when you gave me that little speech about our lifestyles not meshing. As soon as you left, I tore up your card. I trashed the flowers, too.''

"You're kidding. You were so cool and collected—I didn't think it mattered much to you.''

"I didn't know how to fight. I'm still not very good at it." She sighed and let her hand drop. "We do need to talk, Ben, but Duncan will be back any minute with Zach. Maybe we should save this for later.''

He waved dismissively. "He won't be back right away. He knows better. We don't have much time to talk when Zach isn't around—let's make use of what we've got.''

Nerves tightened her stomach. ''What do you want to talk about?''

''You've had a chance to check me out. I figure that's one reason you came here—you wanted to see how I'd work out as a father in an everyday way.''

Wary, she nodded.

''So what do you think?''

Was that all he needed to talk about? Relieved, she smiled warmly. ''You're a wonderful father. You're patient and tolerant and you give him time and attention instead of presents.''

''If you hadn't given me a hint ahead of time,'' he admitted, ''I probably would have bought out the toy store.''

That amused her, since her hint had consisted of an outright ban on expensive gifts. ''But you've resisted the urge, and I'm sure that wasn't easy. If I'd set out to design a dad for Zach, I couldn't have come up with a model half as good as the real thing.''

''Good.'' His voice turned gruff with pleasure. He shoved his hands in his back pockets. ''That's great. I'd do anything for him.''

''It shows.''

''I don't want to be a part-time father.''

There was a look in his eyes she didn't understand, except that it made her uneasy. ''I sympathize with your feelings, truly. And I respect you for wanting to be a father all the time. But I've only been here five days. Let's not rush into any decisions so quickly.''

''I don't want to rush you, but dammit, you're only giving me two weeks. Gwen.'' He moved closer, stopping within arm's reach.

All of a sudden she knew what the look in his eyes meant. Man-woman stuff. Sex, in a word.

For some reason it panicked her. She changed the subject hastily. "When I found out I was pregnant, I was still mad—at you, at the whole blasted world. It seemed so unfair. But isn't that what adolescents always whine when life doesn't fall in with their plans? I had a lot of growing up to do."

"You strike me as very much a grown-up." The look in his eyes agreed with his words.

She smiled brightly. "Becoming a mom made a difference. Being diagnosed with cancer was another major kick in the maturity department."

"You've had it rough. I wish I'd known."

Was she supposed to feel guilty for not telling him about that, too? A spurt of annoyance almost made her ask what he thought he could have done if he *had* known. She bit it back. He meant well.

"The thing is," he added sheepishly, "I'm great in a crisis, but I can be a little overbearing the rest of the time."

That surprised a laugh out of her. Without thinking, she put a hand on his arm. "I'm glad we talked. We've been avoiding that, haven't we? Maybe it will be easier now to share the parenting."

His eyes darkened. "There's still your other idea for working off the rough edges, too."

She jerked her hand away. "Tell me you aren't suggesting we go to bed together in order to be better parents."

"No. Well, yes. I mean... Hell, I'm doing it again, aren't I."

"You'd better find a way to say what you mean this time."

"Okay." He took a deep breath, as if steeling himself for something. "Marry me."

How many years had it been, Duncan wondered, since anyone had needed a pillow to sit at this dining-room table?

He hadn't noticed anything lacking in his life before Zach showed up, but it had been a long time since he'd been around kids. It came as a surprise to realize he'd missed that.

Just now, the kid was wired. Exhausted, but too wound up to know it yet. Zach had been chattering away nonstop ever since they'd sat down. Which was just as well, since no one else seemed to have much to say. Whatever had happened while Duncan lingered at Mrs. Bradshaw's, it didn't look as if the other two had settled anything.

To be specific, Duncan thought—*and I may as well be specific since I can't stop thinking about it*—*obviously Ben didn't take advantage of having Gwen to himself to take her to bed. He'd be looking pleased and relaxed then, not tense and determined.*

He chewed and swallowed and wished he weren't so damned relieved. It would be better if Gwen and his brother did have sex. Better for him, at least. Then he could start putting this...this whatever-it-was behind him.

Zach had been rattling on about the fun he'd had with the twins. "So your new friends like to play army, too?" Duncan said to him.

"Uh-huh." He stuck a heavily loaded fork into his mouth. "Carson an' James's mom—"

"Swallow first, then talk," Gwen interrupted gently.

Zach chewed industriously. It would take him a while, given the size of the mouthful he'd just shoveled in.

"I need seconds," Ben said heartily. "I don't know how long it's been since I had stir-fry. This is great."

Duncan hid a smile as he handed the bowl to his brother. The last time Ben had eaten stir-fry had probably been while their sister was living here, and Duncan would lay odds he'd complained about it. Ben liked his vegetables to know their place, not take over the whole plate.

But Gwen wasn't a mere sister. And Ben had good reason to want to please her. Duncan's amusement faded.

"Thank you," Gwen said, smiling one of her polite smiles. "Stir-fry is one of Zach's favorites. Of course, we're big on vegetables in my family, being in the produce business."

An awkward silence fell. The Van Allens weren't in the produce business in any small way.

"Zach especially likes the water chestnuts," Gwen added.

Zach nodded and, at last, swallowed. "They crunch. I pertend they're bugs. Mom, I've been trying and trying to tell you. Carson an' James are gonna have a baby sister. That's why their mom is so fat. The baby is in her stomach. Is that weird or what?"

Duncan grinned.

"That's the way it works." Gwen's face took on something of her princess look, which meant she was uncomfortable. "Moms make babies in a special place in their stomachs."

"But how did the baby get in there? I asked Carson an' James, but they didn't know. So I told 'em I'd ask you." He looked up at his mother in utter confidence.

"Um…" She cleared her throat. "This really isn't a subject for the supper table."

"Why not?"

"Well, you remember what I told you about the difference between boys and girls?"

"Sure. I got a penis an' girls got a 'gina." He thought about that. "You said not to talk about my penis when there's company."

"Right." Her cheeks might have grown pinker, but she didn't fumble the ball. "It takes two people to make a baby, a man and a woman. The man starts the baby growing in the woman with his penis."

Zach's eyes rounded. He looked down at his lap, amazement writ large on his small features.

Duncan nearly choked, turning a laugh into a cough.

Ben put his fork down. "It takes a grown man to start babies. Your body won't be able to do that until it goes through some changes, and that won't happen for years and years."

"It *changes?*" Zach was still staring at his lap.

Duncan grinned. What kind of bizarre transformations was Zach picturing that part of his body undergoing?

"Tell you what," Gwen said. "Why don't you help your father with the dishes after supper, and you can ask him whatever you like then. Right now I think we should decide what we're going to do tomorrow."

"I thought Zach might like to go into work with me," Ben said. "See the office, maybe visit a construction site. We've got earth-moving equipment at one site that's pretty neat to watch."

Zach's face lit up.

Gwen looked dubious. "Putting 'Zach' and 'heavy equipment' in the same sentence scares me."

"I'll keep him with me every second."

"You won't get much work done."

"Mom, please?" Zach pleaded. "I'll be real, real good."

Gwen and Ben exchanged a long glance, then Gwen nodded slowly.

Duncan felt superfluous. They were the parents—he was just an uncle. "Why don't I do the dishes?" he asked, pushing back from the table. "You cooked and Ben worked most of the day. My turn to be useful."

"You went to the store for me," Gwen protested. "Believe me, I considered that useful."

Ben turned a frown on him. "I'll do the dishes. You've been favoring your arm."

He tried to suppress the snap of temper. "I promise not to bench-press the dishwasher. Would it reassure you if I carried the plates in my left hand?"

"I have to carry plates with *both* hands," Zach said. "Just in case."

"You've got a point," Duncan said.

Duncan did the dishes. And, dammit, his arm did ache. But no worse than his leg, which was still sore from the cramp that morning.

The cramp that had led to her walking in on him in his skivvies. And staring as if she'd never seen anything so delicious in her life.

Rain washed the window over the sink, a quiet, liquid sound that irritated him. He wouldn't be able to run tonight. Not that he'd planned to. It just bugged him that he couldn't.

Fact was, he was in a real pisser of a mood. He wouldn't hang around the others tonight, he decided as he closed the dishwasher and turned it on. Maybe he'd play pool, have a couple beers. He didn't need to expose the other two to his mood—or expose himself to whatever version of the mating dance they settled on.

When he went to the living room to let them know he was going out, Ben was sitting on the floor with Zach. They were working on the new jigsaw puzzle. Duncan wanted to shake him. Gwen might as well have been in Florida still for all the attention Ben was paying her. Was that any way to beguile a woman?

Then he looked at Gwen. Maybe Ben was going about things just right, after all. Her face was soft with happiness as she watched father and son playing together on the floor.

Duncan took a deep breath. He couldn't compete with the man who was the father of her child. Since that man was his brother, he shouldn't *want* to compete. "I'm going to head over to Binton's, play some pool."

Ben grinned crookedly. "I guess you'll take my head off if I tell you to drive carefully."

"I might," Duncan said, but the corners of his mouth tugged up.

"Say hello to Ella for me," Ben said, referring to Binton's owner. "Are she and Jeff still dating?"

Gwen grinned. "According to Mrs. Bradshaw, Jeff is dating someone named Layla. If we're talking about the same Jeff, that is. An old friend of Duncan's?"

"Mrs. B would know," Ben said dryly. He turned back to Duncan. "Speaking of Jeff, did I tell you he stopped by the office today?"

"No." Duncan felt the muscles along his spine tense, resisting what was coming. He didn't think Jeff was interested in Ben's professional services. McClain Construction handled mostly commercial jobs these days. "Did he want you to recommend a residential contractor?"

"He mentioned that," Ben said oh, so casually. "He also said he's been trying to talk you into joining the police force when your enlistment's up.

"Yes. He has." Duncan turned away, his shoulders bunching with the effort to hold back his anger. He started for the door.

"Hold on a minute." Ben's voice signaled that he'd stood and was following. "I hope you're considering it."

"I haven't decided anything." He didn't turn or stop.

"Don't you think it's time you did?" Ben demanded as he laid a heavy hand on Duncan's shoulder.

"Back off, Ben." He shrugged off his brother's hand and grabbed his jacket from the coatrack.

"I know you talked about being career army at one time, but that was before—"

"Before I got shot up?" Duncan spun on the balls of his feet, his hands opening and closing. "Am I supposed to change my mind now that it looks like I can get hurt?"

Ben leaned in closer, scowling. "You're supposed to show some sense."

"Why bother? I've got you to tell me what to do."

"Someone has to pound some sense into your thick skull! You've given the army ten years of your life. You don't have to prove anything, for God's sake. It's time to consider doing something else while you've still got enough working pieces left to do it with!"

"What the hell makes you think I've got enough working pieces *now?*"

Duncan saw the way his brother's face changed, fury chased out by alarm, followed fast by what looked damnably close to pity. Cursing, he flung open the front door, then slammed it shut behind him.

Faint but clear, he heard Zach pipe up with, "Mom, my dad and my uncle Duncan yelled real loud."

Duncan hesitated, caught between curiosity and a furious need to be somewhere else. Anywhere else.

Gwen's voice was muffled by the door. "I noticed that."

"Why?"

Her next words came through crisp and clear. "Because they're mad at each other. Sometimes when grown men are mad, they yell and stomp their feet just like little boys do."

A second ago he would have sworn he didn't have a smile in him, but his mouth crooked up as he took the steps down from the porch in a single leap and headed for the driveway.

Chapter 8

Sometime after midnight Gwen gave up. Sleep just wasn't happening. She slid out of bed, careful not to wake Zach.

Though that was a faint worry. He slept as if he'd been knocked out, always had. She remembered a few terrified "new mother" moments when she'd actually woken him up just to make sure she could.

The house was dark and quiet as she descended the stairs, the air chilly even with her quilted robe. It would be colder outside. She grabbed an afghan from the couch and carried it with her.

The McClain house had a fabulous front porch. It ran almost the whole length of the house and was covered by the roof, so the porch swing was dry when she ran a hand over it, testing. The air was still.

There were stars. She didn't see the moon—maybe it wasn't up, or maybe it was hiding behind one of the peaks that cradled the little town. But the earlier drizzle had dried up, the clouds had moved on, and the dome of the night was thickly salted with stars. Gwen sat on the swing, tucked her feet up and wrapped herself in the crocheted warmth of the afghan. And let her thoughts spin.

She wasn't sure how long she'd been sitting there when headlights swung around the corner, splashing light across the damp pavement. The streetlight gave her a glimpse of the car headed in her direction—a dark, late-model Mustang purring quietly down the street. In the still air the shush of tires on wet pavement was louder than the engine as the car slowed. Its headlights angled as it turned into the driveway.

Silence returned as the engine died.

Duncan was home. And here she sat in her nightgown and robe and freezing toes, bundled up in an old afghan. As if she was waiting for him.

Was she?

The muscles in her stomach went tight and anxious. It was very dark. If she sat absolutely still, he might not even know she was here. Especially if he'd been drinking.

She knew it the second he spotted her. He froze with his foot on the first step. His head turned toward her. "It's late."

"I couldn't sleep. Did you demolish someone at pool?"

"Won one game, lost the others. Temper doesn't mix well with games of skill."

He surprised her then. He sat right there on the porch next to one of the posts that held up the roof, stretched one leg out along the steps and cocked the other up.

It's safe enough, she thought, without naming what,

exactly, she was safe from. He was sitting some distance away.

"I'd rather have picked a fight," he said. "Didn't care for the chance I might be arrested by my old buddy Jeff, though."

"I think Jeff was the one you wanted to pick the fight with."

In the darkness she could just make out the shrug of his shoulders. He was wearing the denim jacket she'd seen on the coatrack the day she'd told Ben about Zach. "Since it didn't seem like a good idea to jump Ben with his son watching, yes."

"Good grief. Do you *do* that at your age? Get into fistfights with your brother?"

His grin flashed in the darkness. "That's right—you don't have any brothers, do you? No, I don't, not anymore. But I used to enjoy a scrap with Charlie now and then."

Gwen tried to get her mind around the idea of brothers fighting each other for the fun of it. "Men are weird."

"Probably."

"I guess you could get in trouble for picking a fight in a bar. Being in the service and all, I mean. I saw a movie once where a Green Beret fought to protect his wife in the parking lot of a bar. He accidentally killed one of the attackers, and the jury ruled it was murder because he'd had all that special training." She shook her head. "I always meant to check out the code on that. It didn't seem reasonable."

He looked away. "I'm a sharpshooter, not a martial-arts expert. But you're right. The U.S. Army doesn't encourage Special Forces personnel to pick fights in bars."

"A sharpshooter?" She brought her knees to her chest

and hugged them, wondering what, exactly, that meant. What kind of assignments did a sharpshooter receive? "I don't know much about the army," she admitted, "except that most of the soldiers I've seen looked terribly young."

"Seen a lot, have you?"

"We don't get as many as places like Panama City do, being on the west coast of the state. Fewer beaches mean fewer tourists. But soldiers come from Georgia and Alabama, and air force and naval personnel from bases in Florida. They all look like kids to me, but they cruise the bars and crowd what beaches we do have."

"I'll bet your mother warned you to stay away from them when you were younger."

"She did." Gwen grinned. "Zach's passion for everything military drives her nuts." She hesitated, sure she shouldn't say anything about his argument with his brother. But maybe it was the darkness, or the way the sky glowed down on them both, or the late hour. For some reason she couldn't seem to stop herself. "Are you still angry with Ben?"

"You aren't going to give me advice, too, are you?"

"I'm supremely unqualified for that. And I'm sure I don't have to say this, but…you do know that he's just worried about you, don't you? Because he cares?"

His sigh barely reached her it was so soft. "I know."

Of course, Ben was an idiot. He showed his concern by trying to boss his thoroughly adult little brother around. It was distressingly familiar. Though her mother had never offered to pound some sense into Gwen's thick skull, she remained convinced she could manage Gwen's life better than Gwen did.

One thing was different, though. The brothers fought hotly, not with the chilly courtesy she and her mother used.

"I hope we didn't upset Zach," Duncan said.

She hesitated. Not because she thought Zach had been upset. Because she had been. For a second, when Duncan had spun so quickly to face his brother, he'd looked poised, ready…dangerous. For that second she'd actually thought he was going to attack Ben. "He's not used to raised voices," she said at last. "But I don't think he was frightened."

"I heard what you said to him."

"Um, well, I'm afraid I was sarcastic."

"But accurate. Though it's little girls who stomp their feet, isn't it? Boys are more likely to swing at each other."

A sudden image of Duncan stamping his foot like a prissy little girl made her grin. "I guess so. We pout, too, though I prefer to call it maintaining a dignified silence."

"But you don't yell?"

"Well, I don't. At least, I suppose I must have when I was small, but I don't remember. I'd like to yell," she added wistfully.

"I'd offer to give you shouting lessons, but I'm not much of a yeller myself. Until recently."

She rubbed her thumb absently back and forth over a small hole in the afghan. Chances were excellent that if she said anything more, it would be the wrong thing. Women were supposed to instinctively pick up on all sorts of subtle clues that gave them insights into people. Gwen was convinced she'd been shorted in the instinct department. She always guessed wrong.

But saying nothing could be a mistake, too. "Do you want to talk about it?"

"There's not much to say." He turned, leaning against the post. "I don't know what I want to do, so naturally it infuriates me when other people think they know what's best."

"You aren't sure if you want to stay in the army?"

"If I were, Ben's fussing wouldn't get to me."

That made sense. Her lips twitched. "After you left, Ben muttered about how some people are too pigheaded to take advice, so I offered him some. I don't think he's going to take it."

His chuckle warmed her. Apparently she hadn't messed up yet. She lowered one foot long enough to push against the wooden floor of the porch and set the swing to swaying.

He sat in comfortable silence with her awhile, broken only by the faint squeak of the swing's chains. Then he asked, "So what's keeping you from sleeping tonight?"

The answer slipped out before she'd even decided to tell him. "Ben asked me to marry him."

Duncan didn't say anything. For much too long, he didn't say a word, just sat there, utterly still. Why had she blurted it out that way?

Her foot was freezing. She brought it back up and tucked the afghan around it. "I shouldn't have said anything. I haven't given him an answer yet."

There was another, shorter pause before he said. "I knew he was going to ask you."

"Actually, he didn't. Make it a question, I mean." *Marry me,* he'd said. Once she'd regained the power of speech, she'd told him it was much too soon for her to make a decision like that. He'd given her a level, determined look and asked her to go out with him.

She'd put him off about that, too. Gwen shook her head. "I don't remember him being this way before."

"Bossy, you mean?" Duncan asked dryly. "No, don't answer that. I shouldn't…he was on vacation when you met him, wasn't he?"

"Yes. So maybe I only saw part of him, the part that comes out to play when he's away from home and responsibilities. It didn't seem that way, but the fact is, I barely knew him." She sighed, melancholic over her young, hasty self. The swing had drifted to a stop. She contemplated unwrapping her foot long enough to give it another push, but didn't move. "The thing is, he still doesn't know me. I was a different person back then." Yet he'd asked her to marry him. However he'd phrased it, that was what he'd meant.

For Zach. That was why Ben wanted to marry her. She wanted…oh, she didn't know what she wanted, except that she didn't want to be married for her son. Did that make her foolish, selfish? A dreamer? Her mother would say it did, but her mother would also say she was a fool to consider marrying Ben.

Of course, Deirdre didn't want to share Zach with his father.

"Different how?"

"I was a mess." She gave a short laugh. "Maybe I seem like one now, too, but I was really a mess back then. Needy, immature…my father had died about two months before I met Ben. I was so *angry*."

"That's not an uncommon response to death."

"I suppose not."

"What was he like? Your father, I mean."

There was no simple answer for that. Gwen took her time putting words to a man and a relationship she hadn't understood until long after he died. "Stern, almost Calvinistic. He had tremendous personal integrity—George Washington had nothing on him in the 'cannot tell a lie' department. He was religious about the value of hard work. Everything had to be earned with him.'' She heard the bitter edge in her voice and added quickly, ''Not that that's a bad thing. He and Mother were very conscious of the way so many children with wealthy parents are given too much, too easily. It ruins some of them.''

Duncan's quiet voice soothed her. ''Was he hard to please?''

''If I brought home all A's and one B, he lectured me about how to bring the B up. He wasn't harsh,'' she said quickly. ''Or unreasonable, not really. He loved me. I knew that. But...I only knew it in pieces, a glimpse now and then. I didn't have it in here.'' She pressed her fist to her chest. ''So I was always trying to earn another piece of his love.''

He was looking straight at her now. Starlight reflected off the liquid surface of his eyes, making them gleam faintly in the darkness. ''When he died, you couldn't collect any more pieces. Of course you were angry.''

''Yes.'' She was so surprised she forgot about keeping her foot warm and stretched out her leg to give the swing a push. ''That's it exactly. It was a long time before I realized I didn't need pieces. His love had been there all the time. I just hadn't known how to see it.''

Duncan turned his head slightly and his eyes lost that stolen bit of starlight, falling back into shadow. ''So you met Ben while you were furious with your father for dying and leaving you. Then Ben left you.''

Her mouth gaped. ''Oh,'' she said. ''Oh, I never thought of that. Why didn't I? It's so obvious.'' That was why she'd been so furious at his rejection, why she'd clung to her anger for so long. Had she confused Ben with her father in other ways?

It was not a comfortable thought.

Duncan propped his foot on the top step, letting his arms hang over his thighs. "Can I ask you something?"

Anything, she thought, and was alarmed at herself. She wrapped her arms around her knees again. "What?"

"I can't figure out why Ben did leave you. He isn't one for flings, and you... I don't get it. Can you maybe enlighten me?"

She wasn't sure what she'd expected him to ask, but that wasn't it. "A lot of men react one of two ways when they realize my family has money. Some like the idea too much. Some run the other way." She shrugged. "Ben didn't like it."

In his silence this time she read all sorts of things. Mostly, though, she knew them for her own thoughts. She still had more money than Ben. And he was still uncomfortable with it.

"At the risk of sounding like Mrs. Bradshaw, one more nosy question. Just how rich are you?"

"My mother's rich. I'm not."

He spoke dryly. "We may have different notions of what 'rich' means."

"Mother inherited the family business and most of the other investments. I do have a trust from my father, though." She hesitated, then told him how much that trust amounted to. She wasn't sure why. Maybe just because he'd asked. Ben never had. He was probably hoping her money would go away if he ignored it.

He whistled softly. "That's not pocket change."

"It's less than lots of people win in lotteries every month. The income from it means I don't have to work if I don't want to, true, but it hardly makes me a jet-setter."

"I doubt that's much comfort to Ben. And you stand to inherit a good deal more one day."

Yes. She wasn't looking forward to that, and not just because she wanted her mother to live forever. Money on that scale came with strings, responsibilities. "My mother may leave a lot of it to Zach."

Duncan didn't say anything, and this time she knew he was thinking the same thing she was. Ben would have a hard time with that.

"Well," she said at last, speaking lightly, "now you know why my mind was too snarled for sleep. I notice you're too clever to offer advice."

"Easy enough to restrain myself. I have no idea what's best for you."

"Still, you helped. I'm not good with problems unless they involve contracts, deeds or case law. I'm afraid I wasn't as helpful to you as you've been to me."

"I'm a lot more screwed up than you are." Abruptly he stood. "You must be getting chilly."

"Just my feet." Reluctantly she put them on the wooden floor and gathered the afghan around her.

"You're barefoot?" He shook his head. "Better not let Ben see you wandering around without slippers."

"I don't own slippers. At home I go barefoot all the time."

"You're not in Oz anymore, Dorothy."

She chuckled. "I think California is nicknamed Oz. Not Florida."

But she wasn't thinking about what she said. She was thinking that if she married Ben, she would be the one to relocate. A law degree was more transportable than a construction firm. There was a test she'd have to take to be accepted into the Colorado State Bar, but after all those years of proving herself to her father, she was good at tests. Her speciality would transfer to Colorado easily—like Florida, most of Colorado's land-ownership records went back only to the late nineteenth century, which made it simpler to research titles.

It was cold here most of the year. Too cold to go barefoot.

And that would be a pathetic reason to turn a man down. Wouldn't it?

He waved a hand in front of her face. "You still in there?"

"Sorry." She grimaced. "I'm getting spacey. Must be time for me to go to bed." She stood.

The swing creaked as her weight left it. Somewhere in the distance a dog barked. Duncan was standing so close, right in front of her. This close to him, she could smell the malty, brash scent of beer.

He didn't move.

Her heart began to pound, heavy and slow. She searched his face in the darkness and found only the suggestion of eyes meeting hers. Her fingertips tingled. A little shiver shook every drop of sleep from her cells. He was going to kiss her...

He spoke, quiet and dispassionate. "We'd better not indulge in any more late-night tête-à-têtes."

Gwen thudded back into reality, landing hard, with a vague stir of nausea. "I don't know what you're talking about." When she moved forward on icy feet, he fell back. She had the front door open when he spoke again.

"Yes, you do."

She hesitated for a second in the doorway, then hurried inside without turning around, her heart pounding and pounding in her chest.

The swing was still warm from Gwen's body when Duncan sat in it. He shoved it into motion with his foot, then sat and rocked.

Hard to believe he'd actually played Dear Abby to his brother's woman. She thought he'd showed restraint by not offering advice. His mouth twisted bitterly. Oh, yeah, he'd restrained himself. But not that way.

Gwen was rich and vulnerable and the mother of Ben's child. She was everything he had no business wanting. But dammit, she was also smart and funny, so determined to do the right thing, and so wryly unsure what that might be.

She stirred him.

Duncan knew it was time to leave Highpoint. He had an apartment near the base; he could bunk there while he figured out what he was going to do with his life. He needed to get out of here before he did something unforgivable.

Chapter 9

For the next three days, Gwen was courted. On Thursday Ben brought her flowers, a cheerful bouquet of daisies and freesia. On Friday he took her and Zach out for pizza and a movie. He was paying attention now.

And he touched her. Not constantly, and not in an implicitly sexual way. In a *claiming* way. He was announcing his intentions, and he wanted them made public. He ruffled her hair at the pizza parlor and introduced her and Zach to the owner, whom he'd gone to school with. He helped her in and out of his truck as if she'd turned feeble. Standing in line at the movies, he chatted with several people—with his hand resting at the small of her back.

But an announcement was as far as he went. Arm, shoulder, back—he touched her, but he didn't kiss her, didn't do anything Zach couldn't see. Even when Zach wasn't there.

No, once they were alone, with their son tucked up in

bed, she and Ben talked. And that was all. They discussed the construction business and the law, and of
course they talked about Zach.

They didn't talk about cancer. She'd deliberately introduced the subject once, mentioning the way she'd cut
back on her work hours while undergoing radiation. Ben
had looked determined and said she'd gone through hell,
and thank God it was over.

Radiation was over, yes. She didn't know how to tell
him that she still lived with cancer every day, that the
changes it had made in her life, in her body and in her
sense of self hadn't ended when the treatments did.

After that, she stopped bringing it up.

Duncan went out every night. Once he went to the
bar; other nights he went running. Ben looked worried
when Duncan ran at night, but he didn't nag.

She didn't think he knew Duncan sometimes ran in
the middle of the night, too. She'd heard him leave a
couple of times after everyone was in bed and should
have been asleep.

Duncan. Oh, God, what was wrong with her? She kept
thinking about another late-night conversation that had
been more intimate than any she'd had with Ben. On the
front porch, with Ben's brother.

That Saturday Gwen sat at the kitchen table, frowning
irritably at the blinking cursor on her laptop's screen.
Out back, Ben and Duncan were playing touch football
with Zach and the twins, men against the boys. The boys
had been winning the last time she checked. That might
have had something to do with the handicap the men
had assigned themselves. Dashing for the end zone while
hopping on one foot with one arm held behind the back
didn't lead to many touchdowns—though Gwen thought

she'd have been laughing too hard to score against the two men, herself.

An excited squeal, the pounding of feet and a distinct crash sounded through the screen door. No one screamed, cried or cursed, though, so Gwen tuned that out easily enough. Yet still the cursor blinked at her, forgotten.

Her thoughts were harder to ignore.

Was Ben trying to show respect by not asking for intimacy? Did he want to keep her guessing? Or was he responding to the signals she couldn't help putting out? The ones that said "this far and no further."

Gwen was vastly confused, all right. But most of the confusion welling up from the tangles inside was about her, not Ben.

For so long she'd held on to her anger toward him like a child clutching a tattered scrap of blanket for comfort. But it was gone now. It had evaporated the night she talked with Duncan, just dried up and blown away. Her inability to forgive Ben had been wrapped around threads of rage and loss spun by her father's sudden death. Twice abandoned, she'd confused the source of one hurt with the other.

Without the security blanket of her anger, Gwen had no defenses left against Ben.

She sighed. Apparently she didn't need them.

How could she like the man so much and find it impossible to stop thinking about his brother? Gwen was thoroughly put out with herself. She scowled at the screen, placed her fingers on the keyboard and typed directions in the search box.

A jaw-cracking yawn caught her before she could add the latitude.

Dammit. This coming back to life, sexually speaking,

had its drawbacks. She hadn't been sleeping well, and it wasn't just her mind keeping her awake nights.

She had a date with Ben tonight. A real, dress-up-and-go-somewhere date. Without Zach.

She sighed, her hands dropping away from the keyboard. When he'd asked her out last night, she'd said yes. It was right and reasonable to give him a chance, wasn't it? And, she admitted, to give herself a chance. Ben was everything she'd always wanted in a man—steady, honest, a rock to depend on in good times and bad. And she'd wanted him once. Surely, given the unruly state of her hormones lately, she could get past this little problem she had with seeing him as a lover. If she just gave both of them a chance.

If she could just stop dreading the evening.

A wounded dinosaur howled out front. She jumped. *Good grief,* she thought, putting a hand over her thudding heart. A truck's horn. That was what it had been. She called herself an idiot and forced her attention back to her work.

While she'd been brooding, the database had dutifully followed her instructions. She was copying the results of the search into the appropriate file when the screen door slammed open and a herd of wild beasts thudded into the kitchen.

One of them called out in Zach's voice on the way to the front of the house, "It's my *other* uncle! The one I don't know! An' he's driving a humongous truck!"

Charlie McClain was a tall, rangy man with a narrow face that nature had crowded with features not designed to fit it or each other—until he smiled. Then somehow those mismatched features sorted themselves into something altogether charming.

He smiled a lot.

He'd driven up in just the cab part of his rig, having left the trailer at the lot. Gwen didn't see much of him that afternoon. He thrilled all three boys by taking them for a spin in the humongous truck, then left on some business after dropping the boys back at the house.

Duncan left with him. No surprise there.

But it bothered Ben. He and Gwen were in the kitchen, belatedly washing up from lunch. Zach and the twins had migrated back to Mrs. Bradshaw's, and Ben was loading the dishwasher while Gwen put things away.

"Something's not right," he muttered. "Charlie's up to something."

"What do you mean?" Charlie had seemed perfectly cheerful to her, but then, she wasn't good at picking up subtle clues.

"It's the way he and Duncan looked at each other before they left. I know that look."

She hunted for a lid for the container she'd put the leftover taco meat in. Ben's cooking repertoire was limited, but he fixed great tacos and sizzling chili. "What kind of a look was it?"

"The kind they used to give each other when Charlie was about to pull some crazy-ass stunt. Duncan always seemed to know when Charlie was ready to cut loose. God knows how he could tell, but he could. That's usually how I knew Charlie was up to something. He and Duncan would look at each other that way." He rinsed the last plate. "The two of them have always been pretty tight."

None of them seemed to have been close to Ben. He'd been the oldest, the responsible one. The one who took care of the rest after their parents died.

He was still trying to take care of them. He made her ache. Gwen yanked off a paper towel and marched to the sink, where she wet it. "Did Charlie pull a lot of crazy stunts?"

"Oh, yeah." His grin was grudging, but there. "Nothing criminal, just stupid. He was pretty wild back in high school."

"He isn't in high school anymore," she said as reassuringly as she could.

"Some things don't change." Ben shut the dishwasher, then just stood there, scowling at it.

She busied herself wiping down the counter. Ben didn't move or change expression. Finally she said, "Listen, would you like to postpone our date? I wouldn't mind. If you need to talk to your brother tonight…well, family comes first."

The scowl lightened. "Are you sure?"

"Absolutely." She looked around. Everything was clean, dammit.

He came over and gave her a quick, one-armed hug. "Thanks. You're being good about this."

No, I'm not, she thought miserably. She was being a coward. A confused coward. "So should we cook or order in a pizza?"

They had pizza. Duncan and Charlie had picked up a couple of perfectly awful Japanese monster movies, planning to watch them with Zach while Ben and Gwen went out. Instead they all ate pizza in the den and watched the first movie together.

For once Duncan didn't leave right after supper. After Zach went to bed, the four adults played poker in the kitchen.

At eleven, they were playing dealer's choice with a dime limit on raises. Charlie had the deal. He'd set the game at five-card draw, jacks or better to open, nothing wild. The radio was playing a song about a cheating man whose woman had walked out on him.

Gwen was trying not to listen. Country music wasn't her favorite, but she hadn't wanted to complain when Ben selected it.

Charlie had, and loudly, but he'd argued for a different country station, not another type of music. In the end they'd compromised—an hour on Ben's station, then an hour on Charlie's.

Duncan had smiled and said nothing. What kind of music did he like? she wondered. Country, like his brothers?

It was her turn to open. She'd drawn three cards and had managed, for once, to match one of the cards she'd kept—a queen. Compared with most of her hands this evening, a pair of queens was exciting. At least she *could* open.

She was having a wonderful time. "This one's worth two cents, at least," she announced, and added two pennies from her dwindling hoard to the small pile in the center of the table.

Ben made a disgusted noise and tossed his cards on the table facedown. "I'm out. Someone needs to get the deal away from that cardsharp."

"I'll do my best." Duncan pushed in five pennies. "See you and raise you three."

"Oh-ho." Charlie surveyed his brother lazily over the top of his cards. "Think you have something, do you?"

Duncan met Charlie's gaze, lifting his eyebrows slightly. "Do I?"

Gwen felt free to study Duncan, too. He was leaning back in his chair, his cards in a neat pile on the table in front of him. One hand rested near them, utterly relaxed.

He had nice hands, she thought. The fingers were long and oddly graceful for so masculine a man.

He glanced at her, his rain-colored eyes curious. "Something wrong?"

"I don't know," she said darkly. "How can I? You look the same whether you've got an ace-high flush or a pair of deuces. She gestured at him, appealing to the others. "Look at that face. He's devious."

"That's our Duncan," Charlie agreed. "Calm, cool, collected. And sneaky. I'm betting he's bluffing this time. See you and raise you a nickel."

Gwen looked wistfully at her two queens and folded. The betting between Charlie and Duncan continued for another three rounds before Charlie ended it by calling. Duncan laid down his hand—an ace, a king, a seven, a five and a deuce. Different suits.

"Look at that," Gwen said, incensed. "My hand was better than that."

"He didn't win," Ben pointed out. "That sneaky cardsharp sitting beside you won."

"But he might have, and he didn't even have openers!"

Charlie chuckled and drew the pot to him. The pile of pennies in front of Charlie was twice the size of anyone else's. "That's called bluffing. He's good at it. Ante up," he added cheerfully, shuffling. "I need to build my retirement fund."

"Speaking of retirement funds," Ben said as he picked up his cards, "is yours in any trouble?"

"That was slick." Charlie grinned at him. "You're getting better at worming things out of suspects. You'll be happy to hear that my 401-K is fine. I sold my rig, though."

Very quietly, Ben repeated, "You sold your rig."

"'Fraid so. Pot's light. Who forgot to ante?''

"You've got contracts with Timberlane.''

"That's who I sold it to. Gave them a decent deal on it in exchange for releasing me from the contract.''

Ben scowled. "I can't believe you sold your rig. If Timberlane wasn't treating you right, you should have told me. Better to pay a penalty for defaulting on your contract than to lose your truck.''

But Charlie was shaking his head. "That's not the problem. I'm sick of driving.''

Ben tossed down his hand. "Where the hell did this come from? You always talk about how much you like seeing the country, keeping on the move.''

"I like that part. But…'' Charlie sighed and put down his cards, too. "I'm twenty-eight years old, Ben. I've been driving a truck since I turned nineteen. I don't want to do it the rest of my life.''

"So go out on your own,'' Ben said stubbornly. "You've been talking about having your own trucking firm.''

"If I'm sick of trucking, how would it be better to own a trucking firm? You like running things, Ben. I don't.''

Gwen could tell Ben was trying to keep a lid on his temper, but the effort not to raise his voice made it come out in a low growl. "So what the hell are you going to *do?*''

Charlie leaned back in his chair. "Damned if I know. Maybe I'll try dealing in Vegas. Maybe I'll see if I can find a freighter captain desperate enough to hire me and work my way to Singapore. Maybe I'll stick out my thumb and just drift awhile. Hell, I might end up in college—though I do have trouble picturing me in a classroom.'' He shrugged. ''I've got savings. I can take my time figuring things out.''

''You don't have anything lined up,'' Ben said, his voice rising. ''There's nothing you want to do, but you sold your rig, anyway. So you can hop a freighter or hitchhike.''

''That's about it.''

For a long moment, no one spoke. Gwen's hands were clasped tightly in her lap, her left hand holding her right, the thumb stroking firmly, as if she could push the tension out. Ben was going to yell at his brother or lecture him. Or both. Then they'd argue, and she didn't know what to say, how to help.

Duncan would know. She didn't question that sudden certainty, but glanced at him hopefully.

His eyes were filled with sympathy, but he was looking at Ben, not Charlie. As if it was Ben who was hurting or likely to be hurt.

Ben stared at the table, frowning mightily. ''You never told me you were unhappy. I thought you liked driving.''

''It snuck up on me. I kept blaming everything else—the paperwork, the tight schedules, the routes I'd been drawing lately. Then one night on I-20 I realized I just plain didn't want to do this anymore, much less for the rest of my life.''

Ben set his shoulders and scowled at his six-foot-five-inch little brother. ''You know you can bunk here if you need to. Or whatever. If you need money—''

''I know.'' Charlie's voice was oddly gentle. ''Thanks, but my bank account is healthy enough, and this is something I have to do for myself.''

Another silence fell. Ben wasn't yelling. No, he was looking miserable. And both his brothers had expected that. Gwen kept looking from one to the other of them, trying to understand what had just happened—and what hadn't happened.

"I'm sick of that station," Duncan said suddenly, pushing his chair back and standing. "I'm switching it."

Startled—disappointed—Gwen frowned at him. This was no time to start an argument over what radio station they listened to.

"Hey, I thought we'd agreed," Charlie said. "My pick first, then Ben's."

Duncan turned the dial and the music faded into static. "Gwen is tired of listening to songs about drinking and cheating, but she's too polite to say so." For some reason he winked at her. The way he was standing, she didn't think the others saw him do that.

Ben frowned at her. "Do you want to listen to something else?"

"Even if she does," Charlie announced, "that doesn't mean we have to put up with that screeching and yelling Duncan prefers to real music."

Gwen might as well have not been there for the next couple of minutes, in spite of the fact that the brothers kept referring to her musical preferences—without giving her a chance to tell them what those might be. After a moment she noticed a comfortable rhythm to their bickering, an ease that hadn't been there moments ago. Even as the brothers insulted each other, they relaxed.

This was safe, she realized. They knew how to argue about music—they'd probably been doing it all their lives. And it had never mattered one bit in the way they felt about each other.

Understanding, Gwen hid a smile. Duncan *had* known what to do, how to ease them past all those jagged edges.

Tentatively she offered her preference, breaking into the discussion to do so. "I like classical."

"Classical." Charlie's voice held exaggerated horror.

"It can't be any worse than that cross-over crap you made us listen to," Ben informed him, and picked up his cards. "Duncan, find something classical for Gwen."

"There isn't a classical station closer than Denver, and the mountains interfere with picking that one up." The static faded into the last few bars of a Metallica song. "Classic rock should keep us all lively enough for a few more hands."

"That's not rock, that's screeching. Try 101.3. They play the real thing."

The deejay plugged some diet aid that he swore worked without counting calories or doing exercise. The brothers argued about what constituted *real* rock. Gwen listened and smiled.

This was the kind of family she'd always dreamed of. They were loud, they were stubborn and they actually *liked* arguing—and that was okay. Each one of the brothers would do just about anything for the others. And each one of them knew it. If one of them robbed a bank and got thrown in jail, she thought, the others would give him hell for being such an idiot—and hire the best lawyer they could find.

If she married Ben, she'd be part of this family.

Oh, that was a happy thought. Foolish, maybe, but happy. Warmth and wishes sped through her as the brothers argued and the deejay started on the news. She glanced at Duncan, smiling. And the warmth shuddered to a stop.

He stood motionless, one hand in midair, as if some bizarre cold front had swept through the kitchen, missing the rest of them but freezing him in place. His face was blank, wiped clean…no, not that, she thought. Whatever struggled inside him, trapped behind the blind stare of his eyes, it wasn't clean.

It was the way his hand had stopped in midmotion over the radio that drew her attention to what the announcer was saying. *"…killed two and injured five others. The identity of the sniper has not been confirmed, but sources indicate he may have been a disgruntled worker. Police sharpshooters—"*

"Hey, Duncan, you going to turn that dial or do I have to get rough with you?" Charlie said with great good humor. He turned in his seat to look over his shoulder at his brother.

Gwen knocked her glass over.

Fizzy cola went everywhere, including Charlie's lap. She jumped up and exclaimed and apologized and ran for paper towels. By the time she turned back around, Duncan was entirely normal again. On the surface, at least. But she was beginning to wonder if the surface was all he let anyone see.

Gwen blotted the floor and apologized some more while Ben dug out another deck of cards—she'd soaked the best hand she'd held all night—and Duncan wiped down the table. Charlie pounced on the radio and found a station that played golden oldies. Ben started dealing, which naturally provoked an argument over whose deal it was. While they argued, she went to the sink to dampen some more paper towels so she could get the stickiness off the floor.

Why had she done that? She hadn't even thought—she'd just acted. She couldn't let Duncan's brothers see him like that.

It had been an impulse, and a stupid one. She had no right to make such judgments. Except that she was still stupidly, irrationally certain he would have hated being exposed that way, that it would somehow have made things worse for him.

When she turned around he was right there. In front of her. Gwen's heart jumped into her throat.

"Trade you," he said, handing her a full glass of cola.

"I'm glad you'll trust me with another glass after what I— Oh, no," she said when he tried to take the damp paper towels from her. "I made the mess. I'll clean it up."

He gave a small shake of his head and took her hand in both of his. Gently he opened her fingers. His eyes weren't rain-colored now, but darker. Like the sky before a storm, she thought. His voice was quiet. "No. You've done enough."

Chapter 10

Sleep was a successful fugitive that night. Gwen chased it for more than an hour after the house was dark and quiet, but couldn't even find the trail. She was too busy traveling in circles, tripping off down the paths of her own whirligig thoughts.

He'd known. Somehow Duncan had known she'd spilled the glass on purpose and probably why she'd done it. She could have sworn he hadn't seen her—that he hadn't seen anything except whatever demons had been conjured up by the news of the sniper.

She must have given herself away somehow.

Gwen rolled onto her side, careful not to wake Zach, and punched her pillow into a new shape. It didn't matter, she assured herself. He hadn't sounded angry.

But who could tell, from the way Duncan sounded, from the way he looked, what he was really feeling?

They'd played cards for another hour and he'd teased and joked and won a few hands. He'd probably bluffed on one of them—everyone else had dropped out and he'd refused to show his cards, which had irritated Gwen no end. Everyone had thought her reaction was funny.

Duncan was too good at bluffing. Too good at keeping everything to himself. And she'd helped him, dammit. Gwen flopped over on her back. She'd helped him hide.

But she knew what it felt like to have people, however caring, poke at places too raw for any touch. When her cancer was first diagnosed, she'd coped by tying a smile on her face, dreading pity even more than she'd feared the disease. She hadn't wanted to go to the support group her doctor recommended, but fears were like mushrooms. They grew like crazy in the dark. Hers had grown too big to balance on her own, so she'd given in and gone.

Thank God she had. It had been possible to say things in that group that she couldn't imagine saying anywhere else. No one there felt sorry for anyone else—they were all coping, that was all. They all knew, from the bones out, what it was like.

The group had originally met at the medical center, under the auspices of a therapist who served as a facilitator for their discussions. Gwen and five of the others had continued meeting after the official sessions ended, getting together every other week or so for lunch or dinner. She'd never been closer to anyone in her life than she was to these women, though on the surface they had little in common.

Gwen was the youngest of them. At seventy-one, Louise Bell was the oldest, a lively widow who'd been talking marriage with the widower she'd been seeing at the time her cancer was diagnosed. He hadn't been able to deal with her disease. She hadn't dated since.

Emma Fowler was fifty-nine, a former hippie who

worked as a highly paid lobbyist now. She was soft-spoken, tough-minded and recently divorced. Her husband had coped with her diagnosis by having an affair. She'd found out in the middle of chemo.

Not all men were bastards. Hillary Friedman was fifty-two, a surgical nurse who cursed like a dockworker and hugged like a grandma. She'd been married for more than thirty years to the same man, a blacksmith who sang tenor with the local choir and was devoted to his wife, from what Gwen could tell. Hillary had joined the group after losing her second breast to cancer.

Linda Blackman was forty-five, a minister's wife with four children, three still at home. Her husband Ed, fifty and pudgy, had taken a year's sabbatical to care for Linda and their children while she underwent surgery, radiation and chemo. When her hair fell out in clumps, he'd shaved her head—and his own. They'd been quite a sight for a while, the two of them walking around bald as eggs, holding hands and smiling.

Gwen didn't think she was the only one who envied Linda.

Then there was Kelly. Just thinking of her made Gwen smile. Opinionated, funny, with the hoarse voice of a former smoker, Kelly Morales was the closest to Gwen's age in their group. She'd been fast-tracking her way up the corporate ladder, having crashed through the glass ceiling by the time she was diagnosed with cancer at age forty. At some point between surgery and radiation, she'd decided the whole boardroom bit was a crock and quit. These days she called herself a born-again hedonist.

Kelly had been divorced twice. Last year she'd re-married her first husband. The two of them argued a lot, couldn't keep their hands off each other and desperately wanted a child. They were on a cruise now that Kelly had dubbed the fertility tour.

Which was just as well, because Gwen suddenly craved her friend's voice and good sense so much she might have picked up the phone and called her if she'd been home. Not a good idea, she thought, lying flat on her back and staring up at the darkness. It would be after two in the morning in Florida.

"So what should I do, Kels?" Gwen whispered.

Her mind furnished the reply in Kelly's dry tone: *About what? The man you want, the man you think you should want, or the fact that you're lying awake talking to someone who isn't there?*

That made her grin and toss back the covers. She might not have answers to the first two questions, but the third was a familiar problem—at least, the sleepless part was. No point in grimly trying to force sleep on herself. It wasn't happening. She might as well get up and work awhile.

Nothing woke Zach from a sound sleep except light. Daylight, moonlight, the light from a computer monitor—any increase in light would have his eyes snapping open. So she slipped on her robe and headed for the stairs, leaving the door open. Just in case.

At the foot of the stairs she paused, glancing at the front door and thinking of the times this past week she'd awoken to the sound of Duncan's door opening or closing in the middle of the night.

He hadn't gone running tonight. Maybe having Charlie home helped. She headed for the den.

It was a cozy little room that might have been intended for a study when the house was built, but was used now as a TV room. The end tables and shelves were solid, scarred oak; the big recliner that faced the television was new and cushy. One wall was floor-to-ceiling shelves crammed with books and old board games. Gwen studied the titles. A twenty-year-old encyclopedia, some recent thrillers, an assortment of westerns and a surprisingly extensive collection of nonfiction historical books.

Ben's? she wondered, crouching and letting her fingers slide from *Soldiers, Suttlers and Settlers* to *Paul Revere's Ride*. Or Charlie's? Or were they Duncan's?

Never mind, she told herself sternly. She could speculate about that tomorrow if she just had to. Right now she needed to think about something—anything—other than the McClain men.

Most of the books were on American history, but there were quite a few on European history, too, including three on the Napoleonic wars. In the end Gwen curled up in the big recliner with Henry VIII. The Tudor king did the job, providing just enough distraction for sleep to sneak up on her without being compelling enough to chase it away again. The second time her bobbing head jerked her awake, she yawned, stretched and headed back upstairs.

It was dark and silent and her feet were freezing. She was thinking sleepy, unhappy thoughts about having to buy a pair of slippers when she passed Duncan's closed door.

From inside came a muffled shout.

She stopped, instinctively reaching for the doorknob. A nightmare? Illness? Her better sense caught up with her before she turned the knob. Duncan wasn't her son. She couldn't just barge in.

On the other side of the door there was a long, low groan. Oh, God. She had to do *something*.

She rapped on his door. "Duncan? Are you all right?"

She heard him mutter, then movement, as if he were thrashing around without waking. She knocked again. More muttering. Dammit, he must sleep as soundly as Zach.

Gwen turned the knob.

Moonlight spilled through the slats of the blinds to stripe the sheet twisted at his feet, the taut, white sheet beneath him and his legs. The bands of light ended at midthigh.

He was naked.

Gwen stopped dead, trapped by the sight of him—shadowed, yes, but not enough. This was wrong, barging in on him this way. She was invading his privacy. Best if she went back in the hall, slamming the door behind her. Surely that would wake him. She reached behind her, finding the doorknob by feel.

His head thrashed on the pillow. "No," he said clearly. "No, no, no."

Gwen let go of the doorknob and took a single step forward—and nearly jumped out of her skin as two large hands gripped her shoulders from behind, stopping her.

"I'd better do it," a voice said from several inches above her ear.

The quick, frightened hammer of her heart didn't die down even when her brain identified the voice as Charlie's. He moved her aside and went to the bed. He wore a pair of jeans, and nothing else.

"Hey," he said, reaching down to shake his brother's shoulder. "Better wake—"

Duncan exploded in silence. Moving so fast it was a confusing blur to Gwen, he shot up, seizing his brother and twisting. Somehow he ended up on his knees with his forearm across Charlie's neck, one hand gripping the

other to lock that deadly hold in place. Charlie's back
was arched. He was utterly still.

Slowly Duncan's arm relaxed. His breath shuddered
out in what might have been a sob as he released his
brother and sank back on his heels.

Charlie leaned forward, rubbing his neck. He cleared
his throat. ''Okay, I know you don't like to be woken
up, but don't you think you're overreacting?''

Duncan made a hoarse sound caught between misery
and amusement. His chest heaved once, twice, but when
he spoke, his voice was steady. ''Sorry about that.
You're going to have to be quicker or learn to sleep
through my racket. I don't want to kill you, too.''

Too?

Shaken, Gwen fled before Duncan could spot her lurking in his doorway, seeing and hearing what he wouldn't
want her to see and hear. Back in her room she flung
her robe on the floor and climbed into bed with her
sleeping son. And shivered.

Duncan had killed. In the line of duty, yes, but that
didn't keep it from haunting him, wrecking his sleep and
freezing him in place when he heard news of a sniper.

He'd said he was a sharpshooter. Like the police
sharpshooters who had killed the sniper? She supposed
it must be similar. And wondered what it did to a man
to do that—to take slow, careful aim on another man
and wait for a chance to kill him.

Her mind replayed the scene in his bedroom again and
again, looking for hints, hoping for understanding. And
catching, lingering in spite of herself, on the dimly
glimpsed shadows and planes of his body. Then, she'd
only been conscious of the violation of her presence
when he was naked in every way. Now she couldn't
ignore another reaction.

She moved restlessly. Hunger twitched and itched beneath her skin. Her breasts felt full and achy, and she
rolled onto her stomach, turning her head to stare bleakly
at the darkened shapes of her borrowed room.

Charlie had shown up awfully fast. That first, muffled
shout must have woken him, but he hadn't had to stop
and figure out where the sound came from or what was
happening. He'd taken the time to pull on his jeans, but
that was all, before heading straight for Duncan's room.
Where Duncan had tried to choke him.

No, she amended quickly. That wasn't fair. Duncan
had reacted, that was all, reacted from training and instinct, from the depths of whatever nightmare had
wrenched those terrible groans from his chest. He'd
sobbed—maybe it had been a sob—when he released
Charlie.

Who hadn't been all that surprised. She lay still, absorbing that. Accepting that she'd been even stupider
than she'd realized. Covering up Duncan's earlier lapse
had been a mistake, all right, but not for the reason she'd
thought. Because it had been unnecessary. Charlie had
been all too ready to intervene in his brother's nightmare. He *knew*. And Ben…well, Ben nagged. He
showed his worry by fussing if Duncan didn't wear a
hat and trying to talk him into leaving the service. So
he had some idea of what demons were stalking Duncan.

A better idea than Gwen had, probably. Duncan's
brothers knew him. She'd been foolish to think she'd
seen something they hadn't. And doubly foolish, unfor-
givably so, to think he might need her. Or that, if he
did, she would be able to help.

Lying on her stomach wasn't improving her other
problem. Her pulse throbbed between her legs, making
her want more pressure there, more… *God*, she thought,

If offer card is missing write to: Silhouette Reader Service, 3010 Walden Ave., P.O. Box 1867, Buffalo NY 14240-1867

NO POSTAGE
NECESSARY
IF MAILED
IN THE
UNITED STATES

BUSINESS REPLY MAIL

FIRST-CLASS MAIL   PERMIT NO. 717-003   BUFFALO, NY

POSTAGE WILL BE PAID BY ADDRESSEE

SILHOUETTE READER SERVICE
3010 WALDEN AVE
PO BOX 1867
BUFFALO NY 14240-9952

Get FREE BOOKS and a FREE GIFT when you play the...

LAS VEGAS
GAME

Just scratch off the gold box with a coin. Then check below to see the gifts you get!

YES! I have scratched off the gold Box. Please send me my **2 FREE BOOKS** and **gift for which I qualify.** I understand that I am under no obligation to purchase any books as explained on the back of this card.

345 SDL DUYH   245 SDL DUYX

| |
FIRST NAME   LAST NAME

ADDRESS

APT.#   CITY

STATE / PROV.   ZIP/POSTAL CODE

(S-IM-03/03)

7	7	7	Worth TWO FREE BOOKS plus a BONUS Mystery Gift!
🍒	🍒	🍒	Worth TWO FREE BOOKS!
🔔	🔔	♣	TRY AGAIN!

Visit us online at
www.eHarlequin.com

Offer limited to one per household and not valid to current Silhouette Intimate Moments® subscribers. All orders subject to approval.

rolling onto her back again, throwing her forearm over her eyes. Had she wanted this? Had she actually prayed to feel like a woman again?

Her lips twitched wryly. *Be careful what you ask for…* Life had returned all too insistently.

Gwen had always had an active libido, an easy enjoyment of the thrill of desire. Maybe too easy, she'd thought after she found herself pregnant and alone. Pregnancy, childbirth, the exhaustion of trying to work and care for a baby—it was no surprise she'd had little interest in men after Zach was born, but she hadn't expected that to be permanent.

Then had come the diagnosis, the discovery that her body had betrayed her. Surgery had followed, then radiation, then the drug that suppressed her body's production of estrogen, which was a likely culprit in the form of cancer she had. The tamoxifen had finished destroying her sex drive even as it threw her into premature menopause.

That, thank God, had been temporary, but desire hadn't returned along with her periods. Until now.

No doubt if it had been Ben she'd seen naked instead of Duncan, she'd be obsessing over his body now. Maybe she should creep down the hall and try to sneak a peek and find out whose body kept her awake.

That thought brought amusement, but it died all too quickly. Maybe she should stop dragging her feet. Ben had asked her to marry him. If his motive wasn't romantic, he was still a good man, the kind of man she'd always hoped to find. A man she'd been attracted to once. One she was growing to care about now.

Maybe she did need to find out if Ben's body could stir her.

It was a long time before exhaustion finally claimed

her, dragging her down to sleep. When it did, she dreamed—confusing snatches, fragmented bits and pieces. Some of the bits were sexy. Some were frightening. And all of them were about the wrong brother.

Chapter 11

His family was falling apart, and he hadn't been able to get a handle on what was wrong, much less figure out how to fix things for his brothers.

Ben's brow furrowed as he slowed for the turn onto Oak. Duncan had always been the quiet one, slow to anger, steady as a rock. All of a sudden his temper was on a hair trigger. The change had something to do with Duncan's last mission, Ben was sure of that much. No point asking what, though. It had probably been covert work, hush-hush stuff he wasn't supposed to talk about.

Dammit. Ben turned down his street. When you added the military's passion for secrecy to a naturally deep reserve, you got a man who could give clams lessons.

If that wasn't enough, now Charlie was talking about hitchhiking around the country. Christ. Couldn't the idiot find himself while driving his truck?

Idiot was right, Ben thought, scowling. Charlie had obviously lost whatever sense he used to have. He'd proved that this morning when he dropped by the site and starting making those stupid hints.

"Dad, you know that big machine? The one that looks like a dinosaur getting ready to chomp on things?"

Ben's heart lifted. For all that was wrong right now, one thing was very right. "The trackhoe? The big Caterpillar that was digging today?"

"Yeah, the Pat-a-piller."

Ben glanced at the boy belted into the passenger seat of his truck. Zach had gotten such a kick out of going to the site with him the other day that he'd repeated it. The boy was crazy about the earth-moving equipment. "What about it?"

"I saw one like it at Roy's Toys, except it was little. But it looked like yours."

Ben grinned. "It's not mine, son, just leased. A toy trackhoe, huh? Where's this Roy's Toys?"

"Back home. It's a real cool place," Zach said with relish. "Is there a Roy's Toys here?"

The words *back home* pinched Ben's heart. He didn't want his son's home to be halfway across the country from him. But he couldn't say that to Zach, so he filled the last few blocks to *his* home with a description of local toy stores while arguing silently with his conscience. Would it violate his promise to Gwen if he bought Zach a toy bulldozer?

No, he decided as he pulled into the driveway. One toy wasn't an avalanche. But he'd tell her first, so she wouldn't think he was trying to go behind her back.

He felt another rush of gladness as he climbed out of his truck. Usually he didn't come home for lunch. What was the point in rushing away from the job to eat in an empty house, then rushing back again? But the house wasn't empty now. He wanted to believe this was the way things could be from now on. He wanted to come home for lunch often and find Gwen waiting for him.

Of course, he had some work to do there, he thought as Zach raced ahead to the door. She didn't *see* him. Oh, she saw her son's father and seemed to like what she saw that way, and that was a start. But she wasn't seeing him as a man.

That would change, he told himself as he stepped inside.

The house was quiet, and he hadn't seen Duncan's car out front. He wondered if Charlie was home, and if he'd have to apologize. Probably, he thought, heaving a sigh at the unpleasant duty. He'd been pretty mad earlier, said some things he shouldn't have.

Not that Charlie hadn't had it coming. What was wrong with the boy? Duncan might be going through a rough patch, but he hadn't turned into someone else entirely. Maybe Charlie had caught Duncan looking at Gwen a time or two. So what? Looking didn't hurt anything, and Duncan wasn't dead. Gwen was a pleasure to look at.

Delicious smells drifted through the house, grabbing Ben's attention before he had time to talk himself back into a good mad. He smiled as he reached the kitchen. This was just about perfect—coming home to family, to the homey smell of food he hadn't cooked. Fantasies stirred at the back of his mind.

"Something smells great," he said. The table was set, he noted with pleasure. Napkins, plates, glasses, even a pitcher of tea made and waiting. Two of the places already had steaming bowls of soup.

"Vegetable soup," Gwen announced. She stood at the stove filling a third bowl, her back to him. She was wearing jeans, and he gave their fit an appreciative glance.

"You'll probably want a sandwich with yours. There's some leftover roast in the refrigerator."

Ben knew a hint when he heard one. He sighed as the soap bubble of one fantasy burst, but the savory smell of homemade soup reconciled him to fixing his own sandwich. "Where's Zach?" he asked, opening the refrigerator.

"With luck, he's washing up." She turned, holding a brimming bowl.

There was a heaviness about her eyes, a hint of shadows underneath. Panic and guilt touched him—one lightly enough for him to ignore, the other more heavily. After all she'd been through, she didn't need a man who sat around expecting to be waited on. She needed someone to take care of her. "Sit down," he said gruffly. "You like mustard with roast beef, right?"

"Thanks, but I don't want a sandwich. The soup will be plenty." She did sit, though.

He considered pointing out the obvious—she was too thin and needed to build up her strength. Long experience told him that would be a mistake. People never liked being told the obvious. He'd make her a sandwich and maybe she'd eat some of it, he decided, slicing into the roast. "Have you seen Charlie?"

"I think he and Duncan went somewhere."

"Didn't they tell you?"

"They were gone when I got up." Her smile flickered. "I was lazy today. I went back to bed after you and Zach left."

Was she coming down with a bug? He studied her face as he brought their sandwiches to the table. She didn't look rested. The faint flutter of panic was stronger this time. "You feeling okay?"

"I'm fine. I didn't sleep well last night, that's all, so

I took advantage of the fact that you were taking Zach to the site to get caught up. Ben, I told you I didn't want a sandwich.''

Ben ignored that and set her plate beside the one that held her bowl of soup. He couldn't ignore the little nips fear was taking out of him. ''There's a lot I don't know, a lot I still need to learn about you, but you aren't lazy. If there's something I should be aware of, something about your condition, I mean—''

''I'm all washed! See?'' Zach sped into the room at warp speed, flashed his hands in the air, then launched himself into the chair beside Ben. ''You shoulda seen this Pat-a-piller, Mom. It dug up humongous piles of dirt and it growled real loud. Like this.'' He demonstrated.

Obviously he couldn't bring up Gwen's cancer in front of their son. Ben abandoned the subject, secretly relieved. *Later,* he promised himself. He'd bring it up later, make sure she was okay. Not now. Not when there was such pleasure in sharing a meal with her and Zach.

She was a good mother. A great mother. He watched her smile at Zach and encourage him to eat some soup in between growls. Funny how he'd forgotten how pretty she was, he thought as he nudged her sandwich closer to her while she wasn't looking. So maybe she was too skinny. What there was of her was shaped just fine.

This was the first time he'd seen her in jeans. They were dark blue and probably new, which made her look like one of the tourists that descended on Highpoint during skiing season, but they did great things for her trim little bottom. Her top was bright green, long-sleeved and ended at her waist. It was made from some kind of stretchy stuff that snuggled up to her breasts without being too tight. In fact, it fit so comfortably it seemed to breathe right along with her. Ben was enjoying watching her breathe when she said something about who was fixing supper.

Maybe it was the remembered echo of Charlie's words. Maybe it was his appreciation of the way those jeans fit her. Whatever the reason, he saw his chance and took it. "We missed out on our date last night," he said casually, reaching for the pitcher to refill his glass. "How about we let my lazy brothers fend for themselves tonight and go out? We can grab something to eat, go to a show."

She looked down at her lap, smoothing the napkin she'd put there. "Sure," she said after a second's pause. "That would be great."

It wasn't the kind of enthusiasm he'd like, but it was a start. "What would you like to eat? Chinese, maybe?" She seemed to enjoy that sort of thing.

"I want a cheeseburger," Zach announced.

"You'll have to ask your uncles about that," Gwen said. "If they agree, they'll be in charge of you and dinner."

Zach's face fell into a scowl. "I want to go, too."

"Not this time. Here, wipe some of that temper off your face along with the soup." She handed him his napkin.

The stormy look on Zach's face said he wasn't finished arguing. Ben frowned. It was only natural for the boy to resist sharing his mother, but he hadn't seemed jealous before.

Of course, he hadn't had much reason. They'd done everything together until now. "Not this time," he echoed Gwen firmly. "We'll be going to one of those places with cloth napkins where you'd have to sit still and mind your manners. Then we'll go to a grown-up movie."

"With kissing?" Zach looked disgusted.

"Probably."

He sighed heavily. "Gross. Can I rent a movie, Mom?"

She agreed, and they discussed what he wanted to watch. And sure enough, while she was talking to Zach, she picked up the sandwich he'd fixed her and absently took a bite. Satisfied, he reached for the pepper. The soup was good, but a little bland. No meat. He could be flexible, though. If she was crazy about vegetables, he'd eat them.

That made him think about her family being "in produce," and the soup lost its savor. He hadn't come up with a solution for that problem yet. Maybe he should talk to a lawyer about a prenuptial agreement—though that wasn't much of a solution. The money would still *be* there.

He'd work it out, he promised himself, one way or another. First things first. She wasn't noticing him yet, not the way he needed her to, but tonight should change that.

"It was a tie," Charlie insisted.

Duncan glanced at his brother. Charlie's sweatshirt was wet across the chest and under the arms. He was still breathing hard. "Tie? Where the hell do you get tie? I was ahead two games."

"The last game was a tie. Up till then I was taking it easy on you."

Duncan snorted. Sweat trickled between his shoulder blades. He felt good—loose, relaxed. More like himself than he had in a long time. Somewhere between the first and second game of one-on-one, a few things had fallen into place. "Tell me one I'll believe. You, little brother, are out of shape."

"Yeah," Charlie said sadly. "There was a time when you couldn't have snuck in that last basket on me."

"Hard to stay fit when you're behind a wheel all day, every day." He turned off on Oak. Almost home, he thought. Gwen would be there.

His heartbeat sped up. He ignored it. That was what he had to do for another four days, all he was going to do. Duncan had his share of flaws, but he was hell on wheels when it came to setting and meeting goals. He could ignore what he felt for that long. Then she'd be gone.

If that made him feel hollow, he could ignore that, too.

"How's the arm?" Charlie asked.

"Good." Duncan flexed it experimentally. It hardly ached at all. "Thanks for the game."

"Next time I won't hold myself back," Charlie said smugly, reaching for the door.

Duncan snorted. "If you want to be punched, try something I might believe." He ducked the lazy swing Charlie aimed his way and was grinning as he stepped inside.

Zach's voice, high and excited, came from the living room. "I bumped you! Look, Mom, your car has to go back to start 'cause I bumped you!"

Duncan's grin widened. Sounded like another McClain male was enjoying the thrill of competition.

He heard Gwen murmur something, then as he reached the doorway, Zach again, highly indignant. "Hey! You bumped me!"

Gwen and her son sat on the floor with an old board game between them. Her back was to Duncan. Sunlight washed it, making her short, pale hair glow almost molten. "That's right. Now *you* go back to start."

Zach's face puckered up in a scowl so familiar, however condensed on that smaller, rounder face, that Duncan's throat closed up.

"Sounds like a cutthroat game," Charlie said from behind him. "Just my kind."

"Hi, Unca Duncan! Hi, Unca Charlie! I'm winning!"

Gwen looked over her shoulder, smiling. "Want to join us?" Her gaze snagged on Duncan's for a second—and quickly skipped past him to Charlie.

His heart hitched in his chest. Four more days…

"Mom, they'll never catch up. You guys can play with me after supper," Zach told them generously. "You're gonna be in charge of me then. I want a cheeseburger."

"If that's okay," Gwen said quickly, picking up the dice. "Ben was supposed to ask, but he had an errand to run."

"Sure," Charlie said easily. "You and Ben going out?"

She nodded, her attention on the dice in her hand.

If she left without getting herself committed to his brother, he could go after her. He'd given Ben his chance, hadn't he? He'd held back, let Ben do his best to win her—hell, he was going to watch their kid tonight so they could be together. Surely that was enough nobility for any man.

"Mom, it's my turn."

"Oh—yes, so it is." She handed Zach the dice. She didn't look up.

He couldn't go in there. His feet wouldn't move.

"I'm going to wash off some of the sweat Michael Jordan, here, forced me to work up." Charlie slapped him on the arm and headed for the stairs.

On his *injured* arm. It hurt. It also jarred him into

speech. Had Charlie done it on purpose? "Cheeseburgers for supper sounds good. I'd better go wash up, too."

That had come out okay, he thought. He started for the stairs. His foot was on the first step and Charlie was halfway up when he heard Zach's voice again.

"Mom, are you gonna marry my dad?"

Duncan froze.

"What in the…where did you get that idea?"

"From my dad. He told Mr. Hampton at the site maybe you would."

"Your dad has been jumping to some big conclusions," she said grimly.

"I like it here. I want to stay. If you an' my dad gets married, we'd stay here all the time."

Duncan forced himself to start moving. His heart was beating harder than it had in the middle of the fast and furious third game of two-man basketball.

God. Had he been patting himself on the back for deciding to wait four whole days? What an ass he was. What a selfish ass. If there was a chance that boy could have his parents together, Duncan had no business messing with it. Even if it meant waiting four months or four goddamned years. Even if it meant never.

Highpoint had more restaurants than Gwen had expected in such a small town. Skiing meant tourists, and tourists meant shops, cafés and restaurants, bed-and-breakfast inns, two nice hotels and a posh resort just outside town.

The movie theater was old but had been recently renovated, with comfortable seats. She and Ben went to an early showing of a new Kevin Costner film, then to a little Italian place with red tablecloths and a pesto that rivaled any she'd had anywhere.

He'd held her hand at the movie. His hands were what she remembered best about him—big and gentle. She'd felt cared for, protected…and a little restless. She kept having to shut out the memory of another man's hands.

Gwen hadn't wanted Ben to put his hands anywhere else. And he hadn't.

But then, Ben wasn't a grabber. Gwen wasn't normally a fan of the "good old days," but Ben possessed an old-fashioned courtliness she couldn't help but be charmed by. It was more than just holding doors or consulting her on where they would eat. When Ben took a woman out, he gave her comfort and enjoyment his complete attention.

And that, she found, was both appealing and distressing. What woman wouldn't enjoy being the focus of such solicitous masculine attention? Yet it felt impersonal, a tribute to her gender rather than herself. He would have devoted himself to the comfort of whatever woman he was with because he considered that the right thing to do.

Between the salad and the pasta courses a thought flew into her head: living with someone who always did what was right might just drive her crazy.

She escaped to the ladies' room. It was, happily, empty.

Idiot, she told herself as she fluffed her hair with her fingers. Would she rather have a man who *didn't* do what was right?

None of this had bothered her five years ago. Had his courtesy been just as generic then as it was tonight? She sought the memories she'd repressed for so long and couldn't be sure, but something else did become clear. Five years ago she wouldn't have cared if his attention was truly personal or not. She'd needed exactly what he offered—the care, the sense of safety, the certainty that nothing would happen she didn't want.

Five years ago that had made her want him. Tonight it didn't.

Was sex so important?

She bit her lip. She was afraid that, for her, it probably was. But it was juvenile to think that passion had to strike like a bolt out of the blue. Surely it could grow out of friendship.

She and Ben could be friends, she thought, digging through her slim black evening bag for her lipstick. Couldn't a marriage be based on liking, and couldn't liking grow into love over time?

The memory of another man's touch drifted over her…Duncan's hands, closing around hers when he took the paper towel from her and told her she'd done enough. She shivered.

Dammit, she was with Ben tonight, and he deserved better. She ran the lipstick over her mouth quickly and shoved it back in her purse.

Maybe he deserved better than she could give him.

Earlier they'd talked about his parents. His father had been a wanderer, just as Mrs. Bradshaw had said, an archaeologist who was out of the country more than he was home. Ben's mother had gone with her husband whenever possible. His parents' passion for other places had eventually robbed their children of them permanently. They'd been killed on a dig in Egypt when their car rolled over.

Ben had taken over their roles. At an age when most young men were kicking up their heels, dabbling in adulthood without really committing to it, he'd assumed responsibility for three younger siblings. And she wondered if he'd been doing that all along in some ways, if all his life he'd been the one others depended on.

And that, she thought sadly, was what had drawn her to him five years ago. In the wake of her father's death she'd wanted—needed—a man she could depend on. Those lean-on-me vibes he gave off like a stove radiates heat had been irresistible.

Now they felt smothering.

Gwen gave the skirt of her little black dress an impatient twitch, making sure it was settled properly over her hips. She was overreacting. Ben was protective and a bit bossy, but he was no tyrant. After a last check in the mirror, she marched out of the ladies' room.

Ben stood and held her chair for her when she rejoined him. She wanted to tell him she was capable of seating herself without assistance. *Still overreacting,* she thought, and smiled and thanked him.

"I ordered coffee and tiramisu," he said. "It should be here soon."

"But I said I didn't want dessert."

He smiled. "Wait till you taste it. They do great tiramisu here."

The waiter arrived before she could snap at him. The dessert was delicious, but she was full. She put her fork down after a single bite and picked up her coffee cup. "It must have been difficult to put your own life on hold to take care of your brothers and sister." He'd intended to be an architect, he'd said. He'd been working summers at a construction firm while he went to college.

He shrugged. "It was hard on all of us. Hit Annie the hardest in some ways—she did go on to be a teacher, which was what she'd always wanted, but she sort of tethered herself to Highpoint. Wouldn't go far from it."

"But she's in Sri Lanka now."

"Jack persuaded her to look at things differently."

Jack was her husband. They'd married a little over a year ago. "What about Charlie?" And Duncan. Only she couldn't bring herself to ask about him.

He grinned. "Charlie did stop talking about being a country-and-western star, but I kind of think he would have given up on that, anyway. He can't carry a tune with a shovel." His grin faded. "He stopped talking about college, too. Just like Duncan. Neither of them would even consider it, no matter how much I tried to talk some sense into them. I've wondered…"

"What?"

"Maybe it was because of me." Ben had that heavy, brooding look again. "I didn't think about it at the time, but maybe they were worried about being a burden. They both jumped from high school straight into jobs—Charlie took a course in truck driving and Duncan went into basic. And look how well that worked out. Charlie wants to take off and find himself, and Duncan got shot up."

"You can't blame yourself for that," she exclaimed, laying her hand over his. "They made their own choices."

"I should have seen what they were doing, found some way to make it clear they weren't any kind of burden." He turned his hand over to clasp hers. "I didn't take you out so we could talk about family history, Gwen."

Her heart beat a little harder. "I know. But if…" It was ridiculously hard to come out and say it. She made herself press on. "If I did agree to marry you, they'd be my family, too. And I like that idea. I like them."

His grip tightened. "I'd like to think there's more to like about me than my brothers."

She felt an urge to yank her hand back. He was holding it too tightly. Not hurting her—Ben would always be careful of his strength with a woman. Just…holding on when she didn't want him to. "There is, of course, but I'm going to be blunt. We aren't in love. If we were to marry, it would be for other reasons, and your family is one of the reasons I'm considering it. Zach needs family."

"I care about you."

"I'm glad. But, Ben…" Gently she tugged until he released her hand. She used it to smooth the napkin in her lap and tried a teasing smile. "Admit it. You would have asked me to marry you if I'd been…oh, Cruella DeVille or Lucretia Borgia. Because of Zach."

His face relaxed into a slight smile. "Maybe. But if you were Lucretia Borgia, I'd be having some second thoughts."

She laughed. "Well, then. Honesty is a good starting point, isn't it?"

"If honesty is what you want, I'm in luck." He was still smiling, but his eyes were very direct, very dark. "I'm better at saying things straight out than I am at tact. I want you, Gwen."

She believed him. For the first time, she felt that he wanted *her,* not just her son. It stirred her, made her feel uncertain, flattered—and restless. She uncrossed her legs and recrossed them the other way. "But what do you want or expect from marriage? Other than Zach, that is."

"Family. I want a family. I want kids running around on the lawn, getting in trouble and needing bedtime stories read to them. I want to *be* there the next time a child of mine is born."

Quietly she said, "I'm not sure I want to have more children. It's a health issue for me."

That bothered him. She saw it in the way his eyes left hers, in the slight twitch of his shoulders, as if he'd tried to shrug it off. And couldn't. She waited for him to ask what was wrong, to ask *why*.

He didn't. "There's adoption, if we decide we want more children."

Duncan would have asked. As quickly as the thought arose, she shoved it away. "I don't know. It might not be easy for me—for us—to adopt. I'm not sure an adoption agency would consider a woman who's had breast cancer a good candidate."

His face took on a stubborn look she recognized from having seen it on her son's face at times. "Kids aren't all I want. I want someone in my bed at night and across the breakfast table from me in the morning."

"Don't we all," she said wistfully. She thought of the dream-fuzzy images that came to her at 2 a.m. when Zach was running a fever, images of a faceless man who shared the work and the worry. A man she could bitch to when things went wrong at work. One who would lie down with her at night and be there in the morning.

How many times had she longed for someone to hold her? Just hold her. Someone who loved her, who would let her talk about the cancer and how it had changed her life. Her mother hadn't been able to do that.

Ben wasn't, either, she thought sadly. He slid off the topic as if it were greased every time she brought it up. "It makes a difference, though, who that someone is. I'm not sure we have enough in common to make a marriage work."

"Sure we do. There's Zach, of course. We both want what's best for him, and it's best for a kid to have his parents together if at all possible. And we're both stubborn. That might lead to arguments sometimes, but if we get stubborn about making our marriage work, what's to stop us?''

''If all it took to make a marriage was stubbornness, there wouldn't be so many divorces.'' She took a deep breath, let it out. ''What about my money?''

He claimed her hand again. ''I'm not saying we won't have a lot to work out. Just deciding where we're going to live will probably take some high-powered negotiating.''

This time she did yank her hand away. ''You're going too fast. I'm not ready to start negotiating yet. I'm not ready.''

''You're leaving in four days. That doesn't give me much time.''

''And is that the last you'll ever see of me? You can't come to Florida?''

He shook his head impatiently. ''You know what I mean.''

Actually, she didn't. She felt pressured, defeated by his lack of understanding. She picked up her fork and fiddled with the dessert she didn't want.

''We have other things in common,'' Ben said. ''Remember what we talked about the night we met?''

That made her smile. ''As I recall, we argued about politics.''

''That wasn't all we talked about. I complained about the bureaucratic hoops a builder has to jump through.''

''And I said you needed a good real-estate attorney.'' She smiled. This was the first time either of them had referred to that night. That was progress, wasn't it?

''We started something then, something that could have been good for both of us. I screwed it up, I know that. I want another chance.''

''That's what this is about, isn't it? Tonight, I mean.''

Nervous, she picked up her coffee and took a sip. It had grown cold. "Ben...did you have any regrets? Did you..." *Think about me at all?* She put the coffee cup down. It was too cold to drink. "Be honest, now. You said you were good at honesty."

He grimaced. "Blunt is what I'm usually called. Yeah, I had regrets. I'd like to say I was sorry I broke off with you, but I didn't think of it that way. I thought I'd done what I had to do, so mostly I regretted the necessity."

"You were sorry I had money." She fiddled with the handle of her cup. "You still are. So what's changed?"

"I'll be forty next December. And I think you need me now in a way you didn't then."

What did that mean—that he was desperate enough to take her, money and all? Well, she'd asked for honesty. "Because of Zach, you mean."

He shifted uncomfortably. "Partly."

Maybe he meant that he wasn't the same person he had been. Lord knew that was true of her. "I guess I could stay a little longer. Another few days, anyway."

"Yeah?" He brightened. "That would be great, Gwen."

He seemed so cheered by her concession that she felt guilty. She turned the conversation to more impersonal matters, and they talked about Highpoint, the construction business and their opposing views on the current president until the waiter brought the check.

She'd forgotten how much fun she'd had arguing politics with him. She was laughing at a crack he made about lawyers when they got in his pickup, and she stayed relaxed until they neared his house. Then it occurred to her what came next.

He wouldn't try to pressure her into bed. That wasn't

his style, especially when his brothers were there, and Zach. But he'd expect a good-night kiss.

Her ease and pleasure slipped away, much to her irritation. Good grief. This was one of the reasons she'd gone out with him—to find out if there was a spark waiting to be rekindled. She didn't exactly owe him a kiss, but…

"Dammit," he muttered. "I thought those idiots had a few grains of tact. Looks like I was wrong."

"What?" she said, dragged out of the confusion of her thoughts. "Who?"

"My brothers," he growled, turning into the driveway.

She realized the lights were on downstairs—every light except the porch light. "You're mad because they forgot to turn on the porch light?"

He shut off the engine and turned to her, draping one arm over the back of the seat. It was hard to tell in the uncertain light, but she thought he looked sheepish. "I probably shouldn't admit this, but we have this understanding. If one of us goes out with a woman, anyone who's home stays back in the den and turns out the rest of the lights."

"Oh." She was amused. "Just in case you, ah, get lucky?"

"Something like that." Definitely sheepish.

She chuckled. "Relax, Ben. I haven't been picturing you living like a monk the last five years."

"Thank God for that. You're a rare woman, Gwen." He touched her hair lightly. "Sensible and rare and lovely."

She didn't let herself stiffen.

His hand slid down to her shoulder. "You never said what you want from marriage."

Someone to love who loves me. She shook her head, trying to be sensible. "The same things as you, I suppose. Fidelity. That's important to me."

His mouth crooked up. "Something else we have in common." He pulled gently, bringing her closer. "Here's another."

He kissed her. His mouth was firm and gentle, clever in its courting of hers. One big hand cupped her head while the other stroked her arm. After a moment she put her hand on his shoulder and kissed him back, and her body stirred, drifting toward pleasure in a way that was easy, familiar—and distant.

Only her body was involved. The rest of her was sitting back, watching to see what happened, how she reacted. Wondering if Duncan knew she was out here kissing his brother.

Gwen pulled her head back, distressed.

He smiled and smoothed her hair away from her face. "Don't worry. I won't push for more than you're ready for."

Ben sounded satisfied. She turned away the moment he released her, too agitated to wait for him to open her door as he undoubtedly intended to do. She climbed out and took in a deep lungful of air.

Ben's kiss had been pleasant. It had proved she could respond to him. It had upset her badly, and she didn't know why. She didn't *want* to know why. It was all she could do to keep from scurrying ahead of him into the brightly lit house.

He took her hand again when he joined her. She let him, mostly because she was too lost in confusion to care. They walked in silence to the door. He stopped.

When he tugged on her hand as if he would turn her

to him, kiss her again, her breath caught sharply. She pulled away, summoning an apologetic smile.

He studied her face for a moment, but whatever he thought of her refusal he kept to himself, getting out his key and opening the door.

Moving from the shadowy porch to the brightness inside made her feel exposed. Even the hall light was on. She ran her hand up and down the strap of her purse. ''I should check on Zach.''

''He's bound to be asleep by now. It's after eleven. How about a drink to relax with before you go to bed?''

''I don't think so. I—''

''Gwen.'' Duncan stood in the arched doorway to the living room. His face and body were utterly still. For no reason at all her heart began to pound in alarm. ''Your mother called.''

Chapter 12

The soprano's clear voice soared into the refrain of "Amazing Grace." Other voices, less perfectly pitched, joined hers in the muggy air that carried the scent of carnations and lilies. Overhead the sky was a strong, bright blue.

Gwen couldn't sing. Every time she tried, her throat closed up on her, so she swallowed and waited. Her eyes were hot and dry.

She hadn't cried when Duncan gave her the news two nights ago. She'd been too shocked, disbelieving. Her first tears had come on the plane, with her head turned toward the window for whatever privacy she could find. Last night, home in the empty house where she'd lived the past four years, she'd all but cried her eyes shut. She'd wanted Zach. She'd wanted Natasha, but her cat was with her mother.

She'd wanted to be held. By Duncan.

This morning her insides felt like her eyes did—tender, puffy and tired, but all cried out.

The singing ended and the minister suggested a moment of silent prayer or contemplation according to their faiths. She bowed her head and prayed for her friend, and for the man standing in the front row with what was left of his family.

Someone sniffed. She glanced to her left and saw tears running down Kelly's face. Silently she slipped an arm around her waist. It was a lopsided hug; Kelly was a full seven inches taller than Gwen.

Ed finished the simple service with a reading from the Torah followed by a Zen *koan* and a quotation from Joan Rivers that brought watery laughter from most of the mourners. It was so very Hillary. When she'd known she was dying, she'd written her own funeral service reflecting her eclectic beliefs and had asked Linda's minister husband to lead it.

"I am so mad at her," Kelly said as they walked away from the gravesite. "I can't believe she didn't tell us the cancer had metastasized."

It had spread fast. Only four months had passed from the day Hillary had realized something was wrong to the day she died. The first two months she'd been able to keep coming to their meetings; after that she'd claimed that the hospital had switched her shift. "It's just like her, though. Hardheaded. She didn't want us dripping tears all over her."

"I had a right to drip tears if I wanted to," Kelly said furiously, and sniffed.

It felt strange to be the one doing the comforting. Kelly was usually the one to offer counsel, often with a quip. "You okay?"

"Of course not. I hate it when people die on me. I'm

angry, I'm sad, I'm scared. If Hillary's cancer could come back like that, it could happen to any of us."

Gwen nodded. Most of her tears last night had been for Hillary and her family. Not all of them, though. It was one thing to know intellectually that the cancer might return. It was another to see it happen to one of them, and especially frightening, in a way, for that one to be Hillary Friedman.

As a nurse, Hillary had known what her odds were and how to better them. Of all of them, she'd been the most knowledgeable about both traditional medical treatments and the untraditional, ranging from herbal remedies to meditation. She'd done every thing right, dammit. She'd fought her cancer with everything she had.

And still she'd lost.

Gwen and Kelly walked on in silence, trailing some of those who had attended the graveside service while others followed behind. The grounds of the cemetery were lush, fragrant with flowers. Birds called. The quiet voices of others, now seen, now hidden as the path curved among the trees, blended with the birdsong. Somewhere a child exclaimed in excitement.

Life seemed to burst from every bush, blade and petal, vibrant and beautiful, as the path they walked wandered among the graves of the dead. Gwen thought of the words from the thirteenth century poem with which Ed had opened the service: "In the waves and underneath, there is no volition, no hypocrisy. Just love forming and unfolding."

The juxtaposition of life and death wasn't incongruous. It was natural. Hillary was underneath, part of all that was or had been. Part of the mystery. Something that had been clenched inside Gwen relaxed. She felt sad, yet fiercely glad to be alive.

Stepping from the graveled path to the hard, sun-warmed asphalt felt like another goodbye. She turned to Kelly. "Doughnuts?"

"We'll take your car."

They went to the Krispy Kreme shop near Gwen's house. Somehow it had become their "deal with it" spot, the place they went when one or both of them needed a burst of pure indulgence. At this hour—eleven in the morning—it wasn't crowded.

Gwen ordered two chocolate-cake doughnuts with chocolate frosting. Kelly had her usual cinnamon roll. The coffee was hot and reviving.

Kelly sat across from her, a small frown making a V between the straight slashes of her eyebrows. Those eyebrows were the only straight thing about her. Everything else was curves. Gwen had told her once she looked like a redheaded Sophia Loren.

"Sophia plus fifty, maybe," Kelly had grumbled, referring to her weight—and, as usual, exaggerating how many extra pounds she carried. She'd been on one of her diets at the time, obsessing over calories. Gwen had been delighted when Kelly remarried Freddie. He agreed with her that Kelly's weight suited her. She looked voluptuous, robust.

"I'm really glad you're here," Gwen told her.

"Me, too." She pulled off a strip of cinnamon roll.

For a moment they concentrated on the calories they were splurging on.

Kelly spoke first. "I miss Freddie. I wish I hadn't talked him out of coming with me."

"You wouldn't want him getting sick all over again."

She and Kels, Linda and Louise and Emma had met before the funeral to hold their own version of a wake for Hillary, sharing memories. That was when Gwen learned that Kelly and Freddie's cruise had come to a screeching halt two days before when Freddie had come down with stomach bug. They'd left the ship and were staying in a hotel in Bermuda when Linda tracked them down with the news of Hillary's death. Kelly had flown back to the States alone, not wanting Freddie to get on a plane when he was still nauseous.

"Well, no. But funerals make me horny."

Gwen choked on a laugh that insisted on coming out while a bite of doughnut was trying to go down.

"What?" Kelly demanded. "There's nothing wrong with that. It's the old reaffirm-life-in-the-face-of-death bit."

A sip of coffee helped get the bite of doughnut down. "It's just the way you come out with whatever's in your mind—do not pass Go, do not collect any inhibitions. Anyway, if Freddie's sick, he wouldn't be able to, ah, help you out."

"The man would have to be dying before he lost interest in helping me out that way." She sounded smug. And happy. "So why are you here by yourself? Did things not work out with Zach's dad?"

Kelly was the only one she'd confided in about that. Now she wished she hadn't. Gwen grimaced. "You know that old saying, Be careful what you wish for?"

"You mean you've got him, only now you don't want him?"

"Something like that." She sighed. "I've been doing it again."

"What?" Kelly grinned. "Having sex?"

"I wish." Her answering grin faded. "No, I've been trying to do everything right again—be sensible, be responsible, follow the rules. If I'm a good little girl, Mom and Dad will love me.''

''Your mother wasn't exactly thrilled with you taking Zach to Colorado to meet his dad.''

''No, and my father's dead, so I can't please him anymore. But that's not what I mean, exactly.'' She crumbled a bit of doughnut. ''I've been trying to be safe. To do the right thing, color inside the lines, so bad things wouldn't happen anymore. But there's no way to keep bad things from happening. There are big risks and little risks, but there's no such thing as safety.''

''No. There isn't.'' Shared pain and understanding glowed in Kelly's dark eyes. Gwen knew she was thinking of Hillary, too. Hillary, who had done everything right.

Gwen broke off a piece of doughnut. ''I'm not saying rules aren't important—''

''Thank God. You scared me for a minute—thought you might be going crazy on me, really cutting loose. Start jaywalking or something.''

Gwen threw the piece of doughnut at her.

Kelly's eyes lit up. ''Food fight!''

Gwen laughed. ''No, no—peace. I don't want to get kicked out of here.''

''Then don't start something you aren't ready to see through.'' Kelly stuffed a piece of cinnamon roll in her mouth.

''I think I already have.''

''Can we take this discussion out of the abstract and down to the nitty-gritty? What have you started, and does it have something to do with Zach's father? And *why* aren't you having sex?''

''Because the man I want to have sex with is Zach's uncle, not his father.''

Kelly's eyes widened. "Well. This *is* juicy." She made a come-along motion with her hand. "Out with it. I want the rest of the story."

So, in between bites of doughnut, Gwen told her. About Ben and how wonderful he was with Zach. About their date, and how stable and good he was, everything she ought to want. Only she didn't, not in the way she needed to. She'd wanted so much to do the right thing...but she'd also wanted to make things tidy again. Falling in love with Ben would have given her the kind of life she understood—sane, sensible. Safe.

But safety was an illusion. Big risks and little risks, that was reality, and you couldn't always tell which was which.

Kelly pointed her last piece of cinnamon roll at Gwen. "Of course you wanted to be in love with Ben. That would have justified what you did the last time you cut loose. It would have made it all right to have had sex with him way back when. You wouldn't have made—" she shuddered dramatically "—a *mistake*."

"You really are obnoxious, you know that?"

"It's part of my charm. You obviously think a lot of Ben, since you left Zach with him when you came here. Not that I think you're overprotective or anything."

"Wait until you have one of your own. You'll want to wrap him or her up in cotton."

Sadness flickered in Kelly's eyes. "Maybe so. I don't know if I'll ever find out."

"Kels, I'm sorry." She put her hand on her friend's. "It will happen, sooner or later."

Kelly shrugged. "We're talking about your problems now. You haven't said much about the man you *do* want."

"Duncan." Gwen rubbed the side of her cup with her

thumb. "He's in the army—Special Forces. About my age, I think. Tall—"

"Everyone seems tall to you."

She stuck her tongue out, then went on, "He's quiet, doesn't say much. But what he does say…matters." She found it hard to put words to what she thought—what she felt—about Duncan.

Kelly looked surprised. "I always thought that when you fell, it would be for someone outgoing, uninhibited. The opposites-attract thing."

"I haven't fallen for him! I mean…I don't know what I mean," Gwen admitted. "But whatever this thing is I have for Duncan, it's obvious I can't marry Ben."

"I knew you had some sense. So, are you going to have a flaming affair with Duncan?"

"You don't understand. He's all wrong for me, or I'm all wrong for him. Or both. He's…" She paused unhappily. Spilling Duncan's secrets—what little she knew of them—didn't feel right. "He's got…issues. You know how I am, Kels. Shoot, one of the things I like best about you is that I don't have to guess. Everything's out there for me to see, and if it isn't, you blurt it out."

"That's me—all surface, no substance."

"That's not what I mean and you know it. You let everything out in a way I wish I could. Even I can tell what you're feeling. Duncan…he's so private. Nothing shows. He bluffs at poker," she said, and sighed. "I ask you, is that the kind of man I need? I'd never be able to figure him out."

"Yet you can't get him out of your head." Her friend hummed a few bars of the old song with that line, then shook her head, smiling. "If it doesn't make sense, it must be love."

"Oh, God." Gwen dropped her head into her hands. "I think I'm hyperventilating."

"A perfectly reasonable reaction to falling in love."

"Stop saying that."

"Okay. So what are you going to do?"

Gwen lifted her head. This much she knew the answer to. "Fly back to Highpoint and tell Ben I can't marry him. But before that—" she took a deep breath "I have to get some boxes, start packing. And talk to my mother."

"Ye gods. Are you going to move there? Just like that?"

"I don't know. I don't know what I'll do in the long run. But Zach and Ben—they need each other. And I need to find out what I want. I…damn, I'm doing it again. Hedging my bets." She swallowed. "The bottom line is, I'm pretty sure what I want. It scares me to death. I don't know if it's possible, I don't know if it's right. But I'm going to find out."

Colorado, three days later

Sleet hissed against the windshield. It had been raining in Denver when Duncan picked Gwen up at the airport, but there was snow and ice in the mountains. The Mustang's headlights showed a road black with rain, but rapidly turning white on the shoulders. The air was a dingy gray edging toward darkness. It was four-thirty, and visibility was lousy.

This morning, the forecast had been for clear skies and chilly temperatures. Ben and Charlie had taken Zach to "Pony Day" in Egerton, a town on the other side of Ray's Pass. It was an annual event that combined a horse auction with other western-themed events, including pony rides for the kids. Zach had been desperately eager to go. Ben had put in a lot of extra hours to free up enough time to take him.

Charlie had decided to tag along. Duncan hadn't. Though he'd privately cursed himself for an idiot, he hadn't wanted to leave the house. Today, Gwen would be back. Well after Ben, Zach and Charlie returned, or so they'd thought. But Duncan hadn't wanted to leave.

He was glad now that he hadn't. When the weatherman started talking about a freak spring storm with ice and snow, Duncan had called Ben's cell phone and left a message on his voice mail. Gwen had no business driving in this. She wasn't used to snow, ice and mountains.

He'd driven to the Denver airport and waited.

Gwen's face had lit up when she'd seen him. Then she'd decided she was insulted by the idea that she couldn't handle a little bad weather. She hadn't argued for long, though. Duncan couldn't help hoping that meant she'd been glad to be with him.

And indeed, for the first part of the drive she'd been animated, as if some private excitement simmered inside. She'd asked about Zach. He'd asked about the friend whose death had pulled her back to Florida. They'd talked about Florida weather and Colorado weather, and he'd teased her about buying the new, heavyweight jacket she'd tossed in the back seat.

It hadn't seemed to matter what they talked about. He didn't know if she took as much pleasure in the sound of his voice as he did in hers, and he didn't let himself think about it. But for the past twenty minutes she hadn't said much. Not since the rain turned to sleet.

The radio was tuned to a classic-rock station. The windshield wipers were working hard, as was the car's heater. Duncan hummed along with the music. He didn't look at the woman beside him. He needed all his attention for the road, and he didn't need to add to the physical ache she brought him. But he felt her presence the way he felt the air from the vents.

He was happy.

Ben would be waiting when they got home. Even if Duncan lost every gram of honor and common sense between Denver and Highpoint, there wasn't a damned thing he could do about it. He had her all to himself, yet it was safe.

"You can talk if you want, you know," he said at last. "I'm capable of driving and listening at the same time."

"I'm trying to figure out how to admit you were right about me driving in this."

He grinned. "You don't have to. I already knew it."

"Pig." She hesitated. "The road looks icy."

"Not yet." It would be soon, but they only had another twenty miles to cover and on a road he knew well.

"I didn't realize how much worse the weather would be up here. I'm not used to driving teensy little winding roads up a mountain in a blizzard."

"Hardly a blizzard," he said dryly. When she didn't respond, he risked a quick glance. She was looking down at her lap, fiddling with her ring. It was the one she'd worn the first time he'd seen her, the silver one with the pearl. "It's okay, Gwen. I'm not in any difficulty here. I'm used to this."

"Oh, that's not… I trust your driving. You said Ben has snow tires?"

Now he understood. "He does, and his truck is heavy enough to hug the road. Ben won't take any risks when he has Zach with him."

She sighed and relaxed. "I'm being ridiculous, but I can't help worrying. Mother guilt, I suppose. I've never been away from Zach this long before."

Since she'd called Zach every day, he didn't think she needed to hear again that her son had handled her absence just fine. But she did need some kind of reassurance. "He missed you. He nearly drove us crazy every day, asking if it was time for you to call."

"Oh…" She gave a little laugh. "You do know the right thing to say. I couldn't stand it if he'd cried himself to sleep, but I'm not ready for him to be too independent yet, either. Maybe I'm a little jealous of Ben, too. The two of them became close so quickly, which is just what I hoped for, but…I'm not used to sharing Zach."

"It took guts to decide to do that. Any regrets?"

"No…no, not about that. But—oh, never mind. How's your arm?"

That was abrupt. "It's fine."

"I wonder," she said thoughtfully, "if you said the same thing when you were shot. I can see it now. Your captain comes up to you and you're bleeding all over the place—but you still salute, of course. Only your arm flops around in a most unmilitary way, not being attached properly anymore. So your captain says, 'My God, Sergeant, your arm!' And you say, 'It's fine, sir.'"

He laughed. "You must have hung around soldiers before. Or nurses—from what I've seen, they enjoy the same kind of black humor."

"It's a survival skill." She was twisting that ring again. "Duncan…I know you don't like to talk about what happened, but…was there a point when you thought you were going to die?"

His mind blanked. After a moment he realized he was holding his breath and let it out. "Yes," he said, speak-

ing carefully. She'd just come back from burying her
friend, who had died of the same disease she'd been
treated for. Death was on her mind. He'd give her what
he could, but he didn't know how much good it would
do her. "For a while it seemed real likely."

She didn't respond right away. When she spoke, the
words came slowly at first, as if she had to gather them
one by one. "When I realized I could die, it changed
me. Not as much as it should have, maybe." Wry humor
touched her voice briefly. "But I'm not the same person
I was, and I can't go back. That's the part I struggle with
sometimes—I can't go back to the way things were. Forward is all I've got, only I can't always tell where forward is. I don't know who I'm becoming well enough,
so sometimes I flail around in all directions."

"Yes. Yes, that's what it's like. You can't go back."
His hands tightened on the steering wheel. "Life doesn't
come with a reverse gear, so you have to go on. But I
don't know where forward is. I don't have a clue. I'm
frozen between what I used to be and whatever I am
now."

Silence fell. His words echoed in his mind. Where had
that come from? And how had she known? He swallowed. "What, no advice?"

"I'm terrible at advice," she assured him. "I can't
spot my own forward. I'm not about to guess at yours."

He was smiling. He wasn't sure why. "Right now
forward seems to involve Highway 191." They were
passing the resort, visible only as a few dim lights shin-
ing through the murky air. Snow was mingled with the
sleet now, wet, white flakes drifting down in leisurely
swirls.

Highpoint lay just around the next brawny shoulder

of mountain. His time alone with her was nearly over. "We'll be there soon."

"Good. I'm ready to stretch." She leaned forward, hunting on the floorboard for the smart little purse she'd carried. "Will this storm interfere with Fed Ex deliveries?"

"It shouldn't. This wouldn't qualify as a storm if it weren't so late in the season. You ought to see the real thing sometime—we've been known to get three feet of snow in twenty-four hours."

"Ugh. I can hardly wait." She took out a lipstick and began smoothing it over her lips.

His heart skipped a beat. She meant that she'd be back with Zach in the winter. Surely that was what she meant. "You expect to be here next winter?" he asked carefully.

"Ah…that just slipped out. I hadn't planned to say anything until I talked to Ben."

She was going to marry his brother. Sick disbelief rose in his throat like bile. He wanted to stomp on the brakes, stop the car and shake her, make her deny it. He couldn't speak.

The little click as she snapped her purse closed sounded very loud. He didn't turn, didn't look at her, but he was as aware of her stillness as his own. Finally she cleared her throat. "I'm going to stay in Highpoint awhile. I don't know how long. That will depend on— on how things go. Zach needs… Damn," she muttered. "I'm doing it again."

"You're going to marry Ben." The words sounded no more real when he said them than when he thought them, but the sickness increased.

"No."

The breath he drew was shaky. The relief was huge.

"You're staying in Highpoint so you can get to know him better, then."

"No. I want Zach to be near his father, but I can't marry Ben. Getting to know him better won't change that. I thought…but that's what I meant about flying around in all directions. I shouldn't be telling you this," she finished miserably. "He deserves to hear it first."

Duncan couldn't hear the music from the radio anymore. Or the rhythmic slap of the windshield wipers. All he heard was the sudden rush of his blood echoing surf-like in his ears, driven by the pounding of his heart. Hunger, so long denied, burst over him in a flood.

He was going to have her.

Soon, he told himself in a desperate grab at sanity. Soon, but not yet. She had to tell Ben, make it clear he had no claim on her. "You probably shouldn't have said that. I'm having a helluva time paying enough attention to my driving to keep this car on the road."

She made a choked sound—a laugh maybe, strangled by the same tangle of honor and restraint that kept him from reaching for her.

"And I shouldn't have said what I just did." He forced himself to relax, easing off on the accelerator. They were passing the army-navy store on the outskirts of town. Soon they'd be home—home to Ben's house. His mouth tightened.

They'd reached the first traffic light. He slowed to a stop. There were other cars around them now, their headlights cutting through the drifting white. The sense of being surrounded by other people helped Duncan get a firmer grip on his control.

Technically the house was his, too, and Charlie's. The tiny efficiency apartment where Duncan bunked when he was in the country was only the most recent of a series of places to sleep. Home was Highpoint and that big old house.

But the house was more Ben's than his. Far more.

It was just as well he was taking her there, though. The sooner she told Ben, the better. And then…then, or very soon after that, the fat would hit the fire, when Ben realized Duncan meant to have the woman he wanted for his own.

"I wasn't sure," she said softly. "Until you said that, I didn't know if you…but even if you didn't, I couldn't marry Ben."

He didn't have to ask what she meant. He knew. He wanted badly to reach for her hand, to touch her. "My leave is up soon. I have to be back at the base by the first of May."

"So soon! I mean…I knew you'd be leaving, of course." She looked down and picked some invisible spot of lint from her creamy wool slacks. "Where are you stationed?"

"Georgia." A helluva long way from Colorado.

"Well." She swallowed. "I'll need to find a place to stay. Obviously I can't stay with Ben once I've told him. That's why I asked about Fed Ex. I packed up a few boxes while I was home—books, toys, some kitchen things. A friend of mine will ship them to me when I have an address to give her. Maybe you have some ideas?"

"What kind of place?"

"An apartment, I guess. I don't want to sign a long lease. If…I suppose I may end up buying or building a house if I move there permanently."

If. Such a small, sensible word. "You aren't sure you're going to stay, then."

She shook her head. He caught it out of the corner of his eye. Her voice was very soft. ''It depends.''

Did it depend on him? On what he decided to with his own life? He wanted to grab her and shake her, tell her not to make plans based on him. Then he called himself an idiot. Naturally she would want to see how well she liked living in a small town high in the Rockies, so vastly different from what she'd known all her life, before making the move permanent. And Zach, too— she was moving there for him. She'd want to see how he adjusted.

For some reason that line of thought didn't make him feel any better.

They'd reached the turnoff for Sentinel. Oak Street lay only three blocks away—Oak Street, home...and Ben.

Duncan slowed, signaled and found the first patch of ice as he made the turn. The rear end skidded slightly. Gwen didn't seem to notice, lost in her thoughts. He stole a quick glance. She was looking at her lap, twisting that ring again. Her expression made it clear those thoughts weren't happy ones.

He should warn her. He was too big a risk. He should at least make it clear he wasn't in any shape for commitments—hell, he couldn't even commit to what he would do for a living two months from now. Nightmares dragged him from sleep half the time, and a few of the local cops had started keeping an eye on him when he went running. Sane, respectable people didn't haunt the streets at night.

The last turn was upon them, onto Oak. ''What about Zach? What will you tell him?''

He didn't add ''about me.'' They'd both been careful not to quite put that into words, as if by leaving it unspoken they weren't really betraying Ben. *We aren't,* he told himself. *If she says Ben has no claim on her, then he doesn't.*

The acid in his stomach called him a liar.

"He said he wants to stay here. Not that he really understands what that means, of course, but I know he…" Her voice faltered.

"He wants his mother to marry his father."

"You heard that? Well, yes, that's what he thinks he wants. Naturally. He's too young to understand what it means, any more than he realizes what it will be like to live in Highpoint."

Suddenly he'd had enough of pretending. His voice came out harsh. "I'm a mess, Gwen."

"So am I." She sounded surprised.

"As messes go, we aren't even on the same scale. You'd be better off with Ben."

"You're probably right."

Startled, he stole another quick glance. She was sitting very erect, her hands resting loosely in her lap, smiling at him rather shyly.

In spite of everything, an answering smile tugged up one corner of his mouth. "Not going to argue with me, huh?"

"If you're going to say stupid things, I can, too."

His smile lingered until he pulled into the driveway. It died before the car came to a complete stop.

The lights were off. All of them.

Ben wasn't back yet. No one was. He and Gwen would be alone in the big old house.

Chapter 13

"We can handle this," Gwen said firmly.

Outside, the sleet had stopped entirely. There was only snow, soft with silence, falling now.

Inside it was pretty quiet, too.

They were standing in the kitchen. Duncan had just played back the message Ben had left on the answering machine an hour ago. A tractor-trailer had tipped over, spilling its cargo all over the only highway through the pass. By the time the road was clear it would be too icy to be safe, so he and Zach and Charlie were putting up at a motel in Egerton.

She and Duncan were alone. They would be alone all night.

Duncan ran a hand over his hair. The lines of his face looked taut, as if he were clenching his jaw. "We'll handle it. But I think we'd better go back to pretending there's nothing to handle."

* * *

They played Monopoly.

"Come on, dice, be good to Momma." She rolled a seven and chortled. She'd hopped over Boardwalk again—which Duncan owned, the rat.

"What a competitive monster you are," he said. He was sprawled on the other side of the board, propped up on his elbow. His eyes looked darker than usual, but that might have been the lighting. They were on the floor in the living room with only one lamp and the fire for light.

His body looked relaxed. Long and lean and deliciously fit...

She jerked her eyes away from his body and collected her money from the bank for having passed Go. "I'm not the one who piled up hotels on Boardwalk and Park Place."

"No, you put them everywhere else." He picked up the dice. "Vicious."

"Me?" She was indignant. "You're the one with a monopoly on the railroads!"

"Yeah." He grinned and rolled. "So I am. I'm going to put you out of business, lady."

Outside, the light had faded from dim to black. The last time Gwen had checked, snow had still been sifting down and the window felt icy. Gwen did not approve of snow after Easter. She wasn't sure she approved of it at any time. The darned stuff was cold.

But there were compensations. It was cold out there, but inside, she was snug and warm. No more cold feet. Though she hadn't broken down and bought slippers, she had picked up several pairs of thick socks before returning to Highpoint. She was wearing a pair now, along with new wool slacks and a cherry-red sweater. A fire crackled merrily in the fireplace...and Duncan was with her.

She hadn't been sure he would be. Oh, even Duncan wouldn't go running in this weather, but she'd been afraid he might vanish into his room. She'd asked him to build a fire in the fireplace. He'd given her a long, level look, then nodded and headed for the living room. She'd dug up the game and made sandwiches, which they'd eaten off paper plates, sitting on the floor by the fire while they made every effort to destroy each other at Monopoly.

It was like other nights she'd spent here. It was completely different. They were alone in the house. And now she knew beyond any doubt that he wanted her.

What else he felt, she had no idea.

Firelight loved him, she thought, watching the subtle dance of shadows over his face. He had beautiful cheekbones. Not sharp like some starving male model, but high and clearly drawn. There was strain around his eyes, but his mouth was relaxed. Not quite smiling, but easy.

"Hey, you going to hang on to those dice all night?"

She flushed. "It's my new strategy. Not letting you roll." She put the dice on the board near him. They were both being careful. No touching.

"Ha!" she cried when he landed on Marvin Gardens. "Pay up."

They were dealing with this just fine. Maybe another kind of excitement simmered beneath the thrill of seeing her opponent land on the hotel she'd just bought for that space, but she was a big girl. She knew right from wrong. She wouldn't *do* anything, and neither would he.

He put the play money into her outstretched hand. Their fingers didn't touch. "I should have let you stay with your strategy. If I don't roll, I don't land on any of your hotels.''

"You're right. I need a new strategy.'' She rolled. "Where did you get that scar?''

"Which one?''

"Here.'' She touched her own cheekbone, not his. "It's shaped like a little sickle.''

"That's where Annie clobbered me with a golf club.''

"She *what?*''

He told her about the time he and Charlie and their sister had decided to create their own golf course out back, and how he'd ended up needing stitches because he'd been standing too close to her backswing. She listened and chuckled and watched his hands. And ached.

It was getting harder to ignore the restless energy skimming along just under the surface of her skin. *We don't have to wait forever,* she reminded herself. Tomorrow she'd start looking for a place to stay.

Fortunately he was doing a better job of suppressing all that teeming lust than she was. She had to smile ruefully at the thought. It *was* fortunate. Not flattering, but fortunate.

He raised his brows. "When you smile like that, I think I should count my money just to be sure.''

"Nonsense. I don't have to resort to theft to win.'' She moved her marker—the shoe—missed his railroad and smirked. "See?''

"You do like winning, don't you.''

"Yes,'' she admitted. "I'm disgustingly competitive. I don't know how much of that is nurture, how much is nature, but the plain fact is, I hate to lose. To fail. When I found out I had cancer, I felt like I'd failed in some way. Oh, good grief.'' She shook her head and reached for the dice. "Listen to me. Sometimes I drag every subject back to cancer, as if everything revolved around it, and that is not a healthy way to live. It's a bore for everyone else, too. I'm sorry. I shouldn't—''

''Gwen.'' His hand closed over hers, preventing her from rolling the dice. ''Shut up.''

His touch startled her as much as his words. Her eyes flew to his.

He pulled his hand back. ''Don't censor what you say to me. For God's sake, do you honestly think you *bore* me when you talk about your cancer?''

Nervously she licked her lips. ''Some people feel that the cancer is in the past, that I should leave it there. And probably I should. I don't want it to define me.''

''But you're still finding your forward, aren't you? You don't have yourself figured out yet.'' He paused. ''You just came back from burying a friend.''

''Yes.'' She ducked her head. The little metal shoe was still in her hand. She turned it over, studying the tiny marker as if it held answers. ''I've tried to do everything right. I researched the disease, participated in the decisions made for my treatment, changed my diet. I even learned to meditate. Well, sort of. I'm not very good at it yet, but meditation is something I can do to help myself, so I'm working on it. Only...''

''Yes?''

She swallowed. ''Hillary did everything she was supposed to do, too.''

''The friend who died.''

She nodded.

''Did you and she have the same kind of cancer?''

''No.'' She exhaled heavily. ''That's what makes it so stupid for me to feel this way. Hillary had been fighting cancer for over twenty years. She'd already had it come back once, when she had her second mastectomy.'' Blindly she turned the little metal shoe over and over in her hand, unable to look at him. ''We all like to think we're brave, or could be if we had to be. I haven't much liked learning that I'm not.''

''Gwen.'' His voice was gently chiding. ''What makes you think that?''

''I'm scared. Scared of dying. It's been nearly a year since the treatments ended, and I'm still scared.''

She felt his fingers first, drifting across the side of her head, sifting through her hair. Chills whispered up her spine. Then his hand cupped her chin, tilting her face so that she looked into his calm gray eyes. ''I'm told that bravery consists of doing what we have to do, even if we're scared.''

She tried to smile back. ''You don't sound as if you believe that.''

''Sometimes I do. Sometimes, when I wake up in a cold sweat, I think it's a crock. When do you not feel brave?''

''Almost any morning at 3 a.m., if I'm awake then. And sometimes I wake up a lot.''

His hand moved, but he didn't pull it away. Instead, he turned it, skimming her cheek with his knuckles. ''Now, there's a cowardly act—waking up in the middle of the night.''

Each light stroke of his fingers drew another pulse of that restless energy closer to the surface. Her fingertips tingled. ''Then we're a pair of cowards, I guess. You wake up a lot, too.''

His eyes were shadowed, the glow of the fire not reaching them. ''Have you heard me?''

''Duncan...why do you run?''

His hand stopped moving. She held her breath, waiting for him to reject the question, to pull away.

He didn't. "I feel better when I'm running. Even when it hurts, I feel better. Maybe it's like your meditation. Running is something I can do for myself."

Or maybe he wants it to hurt. Maybe he's punishing himself. The flash of intuition so startled Gwen that she acted without thinking, reaching up to take the hand still resting against her cheek.

He never gave her a chance. His fingers tightened on hers so hard, so fast, she didn't have time to respond rationally. His eyes went from smoke to darkness so quickly she couldn't doubt that he needed her—right this moment, truly *needed* her. How could she protest when he leaned across the game board?

How could she fail to lean toward him, too?

And when his mouth settled on hers, it felt so right she could do nothing but part her lips on a shuddery sigh.

There was no storm outside, no board game between them, no merry fire in the fireplace. There was only the taste of him painted across her lips with the sweep of his tongue. The firm pressure of his fingers on the nape of her neck, tilting her head. The sigh of her breath as she fell into the moment and his kiss.

The little shoe fell, forgotten, to the floor as she reached for him.

He murmured something against her mouth. The words were lost in the liquid rush of pleasure as their bodies touched. She gloried in it. He was firm and warm, known and unknown—a man's body, hard where she was soft, the wall of his chest delicious against her breasts. He was Duncan.

They were both on their knees—when had that happened? His arm tightened around her waist, pulling her tight against him. His hand skimmed along her side, thigh to hip to waist, ribs, breast. Her breath caught, and his kiss turned fierce.

Quick as the snick of a key in a lock, pleasure turned to need. She moaned that need into his mouth, her hands seeking him, finding shoulders tense with muscle, the strong line of his back, his buttocks.

He kneaded her breast. Delight shivered through her.

"You son of a bitch."

Ben. Oh, God. Those growled words had come in Ben's voice.

She jerked away. She had one glimpse of Duncan's face as she turned, still on her knees and awkward with haste and horror.

Ben stood in the doorway arch. Charlie was behind him. And Zach.

"Come on, buddy," Charlie said, scooping Zach up and striding out on his long legs for the back of the house. "There's an argument about to happen, and grown-ups need privacy for that. Let's get something to collect some snow."

"But my mom—"

"Last snow of the season—we should save some. It's a tradition," Charlie said, his voice fading as they vanished toward the back of the house.

Gwen pushed to her feet. Ben's face was stone-hard and colder than the weather outside.

"I'm sorry," she stammered. "I'm so sorry, Ben. I meant to tell you before—"

"Before you started rolling on the floor with my brother? Hell, if I'd known you were so hard up I'd have taken care of you before you left town. Looks like you need it pretty regular, and if you don't care who you—"

Duncan launched himself at Ben, connecting in a low tackle. They went down in a tangle of fists and blows.

Gwen froze. The sudden violence was so alien to her that she just stood there, stunned. There was a sickening smack of fist on flesh, then the men rolled together, bumping a table. The lamp tottered.

She leaped for it, righting it—and someone's leg crashed into her, nearly sending her to the floor. She lurched back.

They rolled the other direction. Ben ended up on top. He reared back. His fist landed heavily in Duncan's midsection. Duncan's hand shot up, clipping Ben on the chin. Then he did something with his legs that tumbled Ben off him, and seconds later he was on his feet again.

This time Ben was the one who launched himself at Duncan. Duncan danced away, but Ben's fist caught his shoulder.

"Stop it!" she cried. "Both of you, stop it!"

They didn't hear. Or maybe they couldn't stop, as caught by this frenzy as she and Duncan had been caught in passion moments before. Ben swung and Duncan ducked.

Ben was forty pounds heavier and ten times angrier than Duncan—who was recovering from being shot, dammit! Frantic, she looked around, as if an answer might float by in the air or be sitting on the mantel, waiting for her to pick it up.

Should she get Charlie? Could he stop them?

Then she remembered the only other violence she'd ever witnessed. Dog fights.

She ran for the front door, flung it open. There should be a hose, a water hose, on the porch—Ben had gotten it out to give the bushes a drink before she'd left. She remembered because he'd drained it afterward so the water wouldn't freeze in it and damage the hose—it was something that would never have occurred to her. But was it still there?

A loud, horrible crash from inside made her jump.

Yes. There it was, coiled neatly beneath the spigot. Her breath sobbed in her throat as she fumbled to screw it onto the faucet. Then she turned it on. Water spurted. She squeezed a kink into the hose, stopping most of the flow, and raced back into the house, water dripping and spurting on her and the floor.

Broken crockery announced that the lamp hadn't fared well in her absence. Neither had the table it had been on. Next to the remains, Duncan crouched, his arms loose and ready, facing Ben. Half his face was covered in blood. "Enough, Ben. I don't want to hurt you."

Hurt *Ben?* Was he crazy?

Ben rushed Duncan again. Gwen unkinked the hose with her finger over the end to make the spray come out hard right where she wanted it. Icy water streamed over Ben, Duncan—and the couch, the floor, the wall.

The men jumped apart.

"What the *hell?*" Ben sputtered.

"No more." Gwen's hands shook as she bent the hose, kinking it so the spray dwindled to a freezing drizzle that soaked her sock-clad feet. Only then did she notice that she was crying. Her face was wet with tears, and she hadn't even noticed. "No more, both of you."

Chapter 14

"But how come we have to stay *here?*" Zach's voice held that particular whiny note four-year-olds use to drive their mothers crazy. He kicked one of the chairs tucked up to the small round table. "This is a dumb place. I hate it."

Gwen sprinkled cleanser in the stained sink and prayed for patience. Guilt alone ought to grant that to her. But after most of an afternoon of listening to that whine, it took her a moment to get her voice to cooperate with her intentions. "There weren't many two-bedroom furnished places available. This was the best of the lot."

"I'm bored. There's nothin' to do here."

The snow had melted, but it was too muddy for him to play outside. And she couldn't go down and watch him yet. "How about coloring in your new coloring book?"

"Coloring is dumb. I want my Legos."

"Your Legos are in Florida, honey. It will take a while to get all your things shipped here."

His lower lip was sticking out so far she could have used it as a shelf. "I want 'em now."

Gwen scrubbed harder on the sink and held her tongue. Zach wasn't upset because of the lack of a particular toy. She didn't think he was upset about the apartment, either.

She'd been lucky. After last night she'd been determined to move into her own place right away, but if the ski season hadn't been over, she wouldn't have been able to find anything this fast. Gwen glanced around the tiny kitchen.

Her new landlady—a friend of Mrs. Bradshaw's—was an eighty-year-old widow who lived on the bottom floor of her old family home and rented out the converted second floor. The sink was stained, but the window over it looked down on a big backyard with a tire swing and an old picnic table. At one end of the galley-style kitchen, two more windows made a sunny nook for the dinette set. If the curtains were faded, they were clean and cheerful. She'd set a pot of pansies on the table, and that brightened things, too.

More practically, the apartment came with linens, a few pots and pans and cheap tableware. She'd still had to do some fast and frantic shopping, but they had what they needed for now.

All in all, it wasn't the sort of place she was used to, but it would do for now. Besides, it had a certain shabby charm. More than the only other real prospect she'd looked at, a furnished condo with all the personality of a hotel room.

Her mother would have a fit if she saw where Gwen

and Zach were living. A very dignified fit. That image brought the first hint of humor to her day.

"I liked it at my dad's house."

The whine was gone, leaving a wistfulness that made her drop the scrubber in the sink. Two steps took her to him in that little kitchen. She knelt and smoothed his hair back from his sad, stubborn little face. "I know you did. But we couldn't stay there forever."

"We could if you an' my dad gots married."

"But I don't want to marry him, honey." His scowl as he struggled with that idea was so much like his father's. "I love you very much, but when a man and a woman get married, they need to have very special feelings for each other. Your dad and I don't have those. But you and I will be staying here in Highpoint a long time, so you'll get to see your dad a lot."

His lower lip stuck out. "How long is long?"

"I don't know yet." Would she stay here if Duncan didn't? He wanted her, but if all he wanted was a flaming affair... She shut that thought away. "Certainly long enough for you and him to go on that camping trip you told me about."

That brightened his face some. "We can stay out all night?"

"If he says that's okay. Tell you what. Why don't I order a pizza, and we'll watch *Aladdin* together while we wait for it." She'd picked up the movie, one of Zach's favorites, in hopes that watching it would make him feel more at home here. She'd intended to save it for after supper, maybe use it to occupy him while she made some concrete plans for her future.

But Zach didn't need to be told to go play, or to watch a movie by himself. He didn't need more words, more explanations. He needed *her*.

Gwen didn't have local phone service yet, but she had her cell phone. A few minutes later she and Zach were cuddled up on the worn blue sofa. In lieu of an afghan, she'd spread her long robe over the two of them. On the TV—another of her hasty purchases—a young thief and his pet monkey outraced the people wanting to cut off his head. Zach was a warm and welcome weight against her side.

Gwen's muscles ached as if she was coming down with something. It had been a rough day.

She hadn't seen or heard from Duncan. When she'd gone downstairs to Ben's kitchen this morning, Duncan had been gone. He'd left last night, Charlie had said, to stay with a friend. He'd also left her his car keys.

The irony hadn't been lost on her. She'd stuck to her guns when she first arrived in Highpoint, making sure she had her own transportation. And hadn't really needed it. Now, when she did, she'd had to borrow a car.

"Mom?" Zach said.

"Yes, honey?"

"Are you still mad at my dad?"

"A little bit. We didn't move out because I was mad, though. We'd never planned to stay there more than two weeks, remember?"

"We weren't going to stay here at all. But now we are."

She stroked his hair and wondered how to answer. Though Zach might not realize it, moving to Highpoint was going to be harder on him than not having a live-in dad. That, for him, was a temporary disappointment. When parents divorced and the father moved out, the children's sense of stability was shattered. But Zach had only met his father two weeks ago. He was used to Florida—to oceans, not mountains. "Do you miss your grandmother, sweetie? And your old room?"

He nodded.

"We'll be heading back to Florida to pack up the rest of our things and get Natasha soon. You'll see your grandmother then."

He thought about that, his face screwed up. "It isn't the same."

"No, it isn't." She thought that, in the long run, living near his father would make up for the homesickness that was sure to hit at some point. And for seeing so much less of his grandmother.

She hoped it would. One thing she'd figured out about being a mother, though, was that half the time her decisions were little more than best guesses. And the other half she was winging it.

On the TV an enormous blue genie was singing that Aladdin had never had a friend like him before. Zach didn't sing along, though he knew most of the words. After a moment he said, "Dad was mad, too, last night. He didn't like Unca Duncan kissing you."

Her heart cramped. "No, he didn't."

"Do you like Unca Duncan better than my dad?"

"I like him in a different way than I like your father."

"Do you got special feelings for Unca Duncan?"

"Very special." Her heart was beating hard.

"Are you gonna get married with him?"

"I don't know, honey. Grown-ups usually take a long time to decide things like that."

His face took on that familiar, determined frown as he tilted it up to her. "I like Unca Duncan, but I got special feelings for my dad."

"Well, that's good." She smiled and touched his nose. "Though those aren't exactly the kind of feelings

I was talking about. Your dad will always be your dad, Zach, no matter what. Just like I'll always be your mom.''

He thought about that for a minute, then nodded and snuggled closer. Just when she thought he was caught up in the movie he said, ''Mom?''

''Yes?''

''That lady said we could have pets here.''

''Yes, I wanted a place I could bring Natasha.''

''Dogs are pets, too, you know.''

She laughed and rumpled his hair. ''Point taken. Now, let's watch the show, okay?''

Gwen tried to pay attention to the movie. She wanted to shut off her mind for a while. It didn't work. She was too busy listening for a phone that never rang.

After dousing the men last night, she'd tossed the hose outside, wiped the tears from her face and hurried to the kitchen—and panicked. No one was there. After a moment her overloaded brain had taken in the fact that the back door was open, and she'd gone outside to find Charlie and Zach filling a pan with snow.

Bless Charlie, she thought, stroking Zach's hair. She'd expected him to hate her for causing trouble between his brothers, but he'd done everything he could to help. Today he'd taken her to rent a car and promised to give Duncan and Ben her new address. He'd managed, with utmost tact, to let her know why he and Ben and Zach had shown up with such disastrous timing last night. The storm had been much milder on the other side of the pass, so when a trucker had told Ben that the road was clear, he'd decided to head home, after all.

And last night—oh, for what he'd done then, she could have kissed him. No, cancel that. Gwen grimaced. She'd been kissing too many of the McClain men. But

Charlie deserved a medal for getting Zach away so fast and then distracting him.

Since Zach had never seen snow before, Charlie's distraction had worked—to a degree. But Zach had known something was wrong. With the adults in his world behaving like raving idiots, of course he'd known.

Being Zach, anxiety had turned him hyper. And stubborn. He'd wanted to build a snowman and have a snowball fight. He for sure hadn't wanted to go upstairs and take a bath, though it was past his usual bedtime, and had thrown one of his rare screaming fits.

Zach's temper fits were, thank God, as brief as they were wholehearted. He'd fallen asleep quickly.

She hadn't.

The doorbell rang before she fell back into the same pit she'd spent the night in. "Bet that's the pizza-delivery guy."

Zach scrambled from her lap and bulleted for the door. Gwen paused the movie, grabbed her purse and followed more slowly. "Hold on, tiger. Don't open that door until I see who it is."

"I know who it is," he said with great certainty, and managed to get the lock turned. He pulled the door open.

It wasn't the pizza-delivery guy.

"Hello, Ben," Gwen said quietly.

He shifted uneasily from foot to foot, a big man in a flannel shirt, a lightweight jacket and a grim expression. His left eye was swollen nearly shut. "May I come in?"

"Hi, Dad!" Zach tilted a sunny face up to his father. "You gonna have pizza with us?"

"Pizza, huh? Sounds good, but I don't think so this time." His gaze lifted and met Gwen's. "I need to talk to your mom for a few minutes."

Zach tugged on Ben's hand. "Your eye is hurt. What hurted it?"

Ben touched the skin beneath his eye gingerly. It was green and yellow with some purple mixed in. "Quite a shiner, isn't it?"

"A shiner." Zach repeated the word, committing it to memory. His forehead creased. "Did you—"

"Come in," Gwen said quickly. So far, she didn't think Zach realized his uncle and his father had argued physically. She wanted to keep it that way if she could.

Ben looked around as he stepped inside, frowning.

"Are you mad at my mom?"

Ben looked startled. "No."

"She's not mad, either, 'cept a little bit. We're watching *Aladdin*," Zach announced. "C'mon and watch with us. The genie's gonna make Aladdin a prince."

"I don't think—"

The doorbell chimed again.

This time it was the pizza.

They left Zach in the living room with the pizza, *Aladdin,* and a promise to plan the camping trip when Ben finished talking to his mom.

Ben supposed he must have lived through worse days in his life. Sometime. Even if he couldn't remember when at the moment. Lord, he'd been dreading this moment.

"This place isn't what I expected." He'd known she was leaving his house. She'd told him so this morning, very stiff and polite. He didn't blame her for that, though he regretted it. Along with a lot of other things.

"Oh?" She sat at the little dinette. "Have a seat, Ben."

He paced the narrow length of the kitchen, turned. "I

figured you'd rent one of those pricey condos on Wilshire, not a made-over place like this." He frowned, looking down. "The sink is stained."

"I know. I liked this better than the condos. It has personality—and a backyard. Ben—"

"Would you have liked it better five years ago?"

Puzzlement broke through her chilly formality. "I don't know. Maybe not. I didn't think in terms of what a little boy needs back then."

He nodded and looked down. She'd tried to tell him more than once that she'd changed, that she wasn't the same woman he'd met on that soft Florida night. He hadn't understood. "I came to apologize."

"Well." She clasped her hands together on the table. "That's generous of you, under the circumstances." She bit her lip. "Is…is Duncan's arm all right?"

"What do you think I am? I didn't hit his wounded arm, for God's sake! Not that it seemed to be giving him much trouble," Ben grumbled. "I was lucky to get in a decent blow anywhere. Probably couldn't have if he hadn't been holding back."

"He was holding back? Dear God, he let you beat him bloody—"

"He didn't *let* me do anything," Ben snapped. "He wasn't going at it all out, that's all. If he had been, I'd have some broken bones now." Or worse. Ben didn't underestimate his own abilities, but Special Forces personnel didn't accomplish their missions by blacking an opponent's eye. They were trained to kill or disable.

And Duncan was damned good. Quick. Absently Ben touched his eye again.

"It looked like the two of you were trying to kill each other."

"Never seen a fistfight, have you?"

She shook her head. "It was…upsetting. I appreciate your apology."

"I wasn't apologizing for that. We should have taken it outside, but Duncan swung first and I was damned if I—" He shook his head. This wasn't what he'd come here to say. "Never mind. I'm ashamed of the way I spoke to you. It wasn't true, any of it."

She stared. "I will never understand men. Never. Ben, for heaven's sake, sit down."

Reluctantly he pulled out a chair and sat across from her. There was a pot of bright purple pansies in the center of the scuffed old table. "Pretty flowers," he said, touching one bloom. He was still having trouble fitting his idea of who and what she was into this setting.

"I found them at the grocery store. I'll accept your apology, Ben, if you'll accept mine." She grimaced. "Not that the blame is even. I am so sorry, so very sorry for the way… I realized while I was gone, you see, that I couldn't marry you. I intended to tell you before…" Her voice trailed off.

"You have feelings for Duncan."

She nodded, her face sad and solemn.

He sighed heavily. Charlie had tried to warn him.

"I guess your living room is a mess."

He waved that aside. "Does Duncan share your feelings?"

"I…we didn't talk about it. It didn't seem right, when I hadn't spoken to you. Are you and he going to be okay? I mean—oh, shoot. To put it in Zach's terms, are you still a whole bunch mad at him or only a little bit?"

He scowled. He hadn't seen his brother today. He hadn't wanted to. He still didn't. "That's not your problem."

"If I've caused trouble between you two, it certainly is my problem."

"You didn't cause anything. If he'd kept his hands to himself—"

"Ben, he didn't seduce me or anything like that."

"You're not responsible for what he did. So, are you staying here awhile? Here in Highpoint?"

She eyed him as if she wanted to argue some more, but answered his question. "For six months, anyway. Maybe for good. You were right about one thing—Zach needs you in his life, and a weekend now and then isn't enough."

Relief crashed over him, so big he had to close his eyes for a second. Big enough that it almost drowned out the question of whether she was staying so she could carry on with his backstabbing brother. "That's good. That's really great. I hope you'll make it permanent. Well." He cleared his throat and shoved his chair back. "I'd better go make plans for a camping trip."

"He's excited about it," she said, standing, a tentative smile on her face. "It's very early in the year for camping, though, isn't it?"

"It'll be another month before we can go, but we can start getting him ready for it. A short hike, maybe. There's an easy trail to a picnic spot west of town."

Her smile warmed and steadied. "On the plane on the way here, he asked if he could climb one of your mountains."

They were standing close. He looked down at her smooth skin and hopeful eyes, at the mouth he'd tasted again after five years.

Why couldn't it have been him? Why did she have to choose his brother? "I didn't have a chance, did I?" he asked abruptly. "Not this time around. But the first time—we might have made something good then, if I hadn't blown it.''

"Who knows?" Her voice was soft. "Might-have-beens can eat us alive if we let them. But, Ben, you still have most of what you wanted. Zach won't be living with you all the time, but you'll be able to have him a lot. We'll work that out, put it in writing.''

She didn't have a clue. The realization hit Ben hard. She thought it had been all about Zach, not about her.

Maybe it had been at first. And maybe it was best she go on thinking that way. He turned away. "Yeah," he said. "That'll be good. I'd appreciate that, Gwen.''

He walked back into the living room, shoulders squared, ready to smile for his son. Half a dream was better than none.

Chapter 15

Duncan drove around the block four times. The first time he didn't stop because Ben's truck was out front, parked between an old Chevy and a Jeep. The next three times he didn't stop because he was an idiot. A scared, witless idiot.

He'd told himself he wouldn't go to her. Ben wouldn't forgive easily, but forgiveness would come in time if Duncan stayed away from Gwen. And she would be better off with someone else. He didn't doubt that.

Yet at eight o'clock he'd climbed in his car and driven to the address she'd given Charlie, just as if that had been his plan all day long. So then he told himself it was only right to see her, that he was going to break off with her. It would be easier on her if he did that before they became lovers.

That was a lie, too. He wasn't thinking of what would be easier on her, better for her. Some remnant of honesty finally forced him to admit the truth: he was afraid she'd realized the truth herself last night, that she would be the one to end things.

He was just as afraid that she wouldn't. Truth doesn't always make sense, he supposed, but he'd never been this ripped up by his own contradictions before.

It was no wonder he kept driving around the block. More surprising, maybe, that he finally pulled into the only open spot in front of the house—the same place Ben had parked.

Following in his big brother's footsteps, wasn't he? In more ways than one. The twist to his mouth was bitter when he climbed out of his Mustang.

The night was crisp and cool, the sky as clear as if twenty-four hours ago it hadn't dumped rain, sleet and snow on them. He tipped his head back. Were there really more stars over Highpoint, and could they really shine brighter here than anywhere else? Or was it just that this was home?

Funny. He'd almost forgotten what it felt like to truly come home. Yet he'd been coming here for years on holidays or to touch base with his family. He shook his head and headed for the house.

Canned laughter drifted through the walls of the old frame house as he followed a narrow sidewalk to the outside stairs. The sound was coming from downstairs. At the top of the stairs, a porch light glowed.

Gwen had probably turned it on for Ben when he left. Had she forgotten to turn it off? Or was she waiting— hoping—Duncan would come? His heart pounded as he climbed the stairs.

He knocked on the door. A moment later it opened.

Her skin was pale, almost translucent. There were faint mauve shadows under her eyes, two pale freckles on that slightly crooked nose and questions, instead of a smile, in the green eyes raised to his. She wore a pale yellow sweater, neatly pressed jeans. And no shoes.

Hunger rose in him, and longing. He stuffed his hands in his pockets to keep from reaching for her. Once he touched her, there would be no talking, no turning back. Not for him, anyway. "The first time I saw you," he said quietly, "you blindsided me. I opened my door and stared at you like an idiot. Now I'm at your door. May I come in?"

Color washed over her cheeks and set her smile free. She nodded and stepped aside.

Her new living room was small, seriously tidy and splashed with color. The walls were pale lemon; lime green throw pillows enlivened a dark green couch a few years past its prime. An area rug banded in green and turquoise covered most of the wooden floor. The huge old étagère that held the television, some books and a few toys had been painted turquoise, too, at some point. The blinds weren't in the best shape, but the windows were tall and would let in plenty of light. She'd put ivy on one of the deep windowsills, some kind of flowering plant on the other.

He smiled. "I can't believe how much this place looks like you already."

Her eyes lit up. "I got lucky, didn't I? Um…do you want something to drink? I don't have much, I'm afraid—I just picked up the essentials. But I can offer you some orange juice. Or I could make coffee."

"I don't need anything to drink." Her. He needed her. He could feel his pulse pounding in his throat, and lower down. "I'm afraid to touch you."

"Oh. Well, then, I have an idea." Her smile flickered as she moved toward him. "I could touch you, instead." She stopped in front of him and slowly unzipped his jacket, then rested her hands on his chest. "If I do anything you don't like or that frightens you, just tell me. I'll stop. Probably."

Laughter rolled up from his middle, surprising him. He put his arms around her and held her, just held her, his face pressed to her hair.

The laughter died as suddenly as it had come. "Gwen," he said, and couldn't remember what to say next. They needed to talk…but her hair smelled like apples, and her body was warm and soft and willing in his arms. And his was hard and ready and hungry. So hungry.

He stroked her back, trying to soothe himself. "Are you okay?"

She frowned at him. "That should be my line. Your arm…Ben said he didn't hit it, but the way you two were rolling around—"

"No new damage."

She touched the butterfly bandage Jeff had put on the cut on his forehead, her fingertips gentle. "What about your head? Did all that blood last night come from this?"

"Head wounds bleed a lot," he said absently. "Besides, Jeff patched me up when I got to his place." It was a very pretty sweater she was wearing, but he wanted it off. He wanted to feel skin when he stroked her. He shook his head, trying to be civilized. "What about Zach?"

Tiny diamond studs in her ears winked at him when she tilted her head. "He's asleep."

"No, I meant…" One of his hands had drifted down to cherish the soft, round curve of her bottom. He lost what he was going to say. "Damn. I can't think when I touch you. I meant that he might not be okay with me being here. Especially after last night.''

''If I thought it would hurt him for you to be with me, you'd be on the other side of the door right now.''

He knew that. He knew it, yet… ''He wanted you to marry his father.''

''Duncan.'' She was patient. ''Of course he wanted that. He's four and a half years old. He wants a dog desperately, too, but the lack of one hasn't warped him or made him hate my cat.''

So he was like her cat, was he? Not Zach's first choice, but with luck her son wouldn't hate him. He managed a half smile. ''I didn't know you had a cat.''

''Natasha. She's a crotchety old thing. I'll have to go back home to get her and my car, among other things.'' She touched his cheek. ''You haven't shaved in a while.''

''I should have, but I was pretending I wouldn't come here tonight.''

''Well.'' Her hand fell away. ''That's honest. I guess it explains why you didn't call, too. It was just a kiss, after all. I suppose I read too much into it.''

''No.'' He closed his hands around her arms. ''No, there's more than just a kiss between us. I couldn't stay away from you.''

''But you wanted to.''

''I don't know what I want these days, remember? Except you.'' He ran his hands down her arms to capture *her* hands. ''I know I want you.''

''Something tells me you spent the day trying to talk yourself out of it, though.'' She hesitated. ''Ben was here earlier.''

''I know.'' He touched one of the little studs, then traced the curve of her ear. ''I saw his truck.''

"He apologized. Not for the fight." She rolled her eyes. "He seemed to think that was perfectly acceptable. For what he said to me. I thought that was generous of him, under the circumstances."

"Ben always does what he thinks is right."

"You sound bitter."

"Maybe I am." He tested the word in his mind, seeing how it fit. "I love Ben, but he's not an easy act to follow."

She was silent a moment. "Is that a problem? With me, I mean. With us."

"I'm not sure." The first, raw hunger had eased, but it wasn't gone. He had trouble balancing his need against hers. Right now, she needed reassurance, but all he could offer was honesty. "Yes. It's a problem. But it isn't something we have to fix tonight."

Her eyes were very large, very serious, as they searched his. "Is there going to be an 'us,' then?"

"I thought there already was." Even though they weren't lovers yet. Even though he'd never taken her on a date, never done with her any of the things couples do. Even though, until last night, he'd thought of her as his brother's woman... Duncan took a deep breath. "You know my leave is nearly up."

"I know. You haven't promised me anything, Duncan. I understand that."

Did she? Could she protect herself against all that he wasn't promising? "You must have noticed that Ben's the dependable one. For some reason you've decided you want me, instead. I don't know why—maybe because he let you down once. But if you're thinking I won't ever let you down... Gwen. Don't count on me for too much."

"I'm not in love with Ben. That's why I don't want him."

Staggered, he could only stare, his hands tightening on her arms. She hadn't said she was in love with *him*, just that she didn't love Ben. But the distinction didn't seem to matter to his whirling thoughts or his pounding heart.

Now, his body screamed, every muscle tight with need.

Now, he agreed, instinctively widening his stance as he pulled her to him. Hunger roughened his voice. "For someone who talks like a sensible woman, you sure like to gamble."

"I guess I do," Gwen said, and she cupped the back of his head with her hand and pulled his mouth down to hers.

Their first kiss had been discovery, sweet and drugging. This time, heat hit fast and hard.

Gwen felt the quick shudder that went through him. Then his arms tightened so hard she couldn't breathe. But she didn't need breath. She needed this—his arms, his urgency, the press of his body against hers. His mouth, hard and demanding. The heady male scent of him and the dense muscles of his back beneath her hands…the flexing of those muscles as he swept her into his arms.

"Duncan! Your arm—"

"It's fine," he said, and a smile touched his mouth.

She smiled back at him, smiled through the dizziness of being carried and kissed on her chin, her shoulder— whatever part of her body he could reach, he kissed. He carried her into the bedroom she'd never slept in, and she rejoiced that for this first night here, he would be with her.

The light was on. And the bed was occupied—by her suitcase. She'd forgotten to put it away. "I forgot," she said, her face flaming as if she'd committed some terrible social sin.

Show-and-tell time was here. And she wasn't sure she was ready.

"No problem." He put her down—slowly, so that their bodies ended up touching. He kissed her again, his mouth testing, retreating, returning.

Shaky, she pulled away. "You'd better close the door."

She hurriedly removed the suitcase and folded back the covers. "I bought the comforter today. Down-filled. I wanted something warm for your cold Colorado nights."

"It's very pretty." But he wasn't looking at her bed. His eyes remained steady on her. "Beautiful, in fact."

Her smile wobbled.

He came to her, rubbed his knuckles along her cheek. "You're nervous. Second thoughts?"

"No, only…it's been a long time." She forced humor into her voice. "Maybe I've forgotten how. Or something might have rusted."

"You've seen *my* scar."

How did he know? How could he pluck her fears right out of her head that way? "It's not the same. Your scar is on your arm."

He nodded seriously. "I see. If the bullet had taken a chunk out of my nuts instead of my arm, it would change how you feel about me. Seeing me naked would be a turnoff. You'd be kind, I imagine, try to hide your revulsion or disappointment, but—"

She put her hands on his shoulders, leaned in close—

and nipped his chin. "I'm having a crisis here, and you make me sound ridiculous."

"Because you're being ridiculous." That slow smile eased across his face, but his eyes were hot, the lids heavy. "You can't really believe it will matter to me, can you?"

All sorts of feelings fluttered in her stomach trying to break free. "Show me," she whispered.

The smile lingered on his mouth. Deliberately he bent and pulled off his shoes. Then he straightened, put his hands on her waist—and tumbled with her onto the bed.

They landed with Gwen on her back, laughing in surprise. He was stretched out half on top of her, their legs tangled. His eyes shone. Her skin tingled. She drew a foot along his calf and enjoyed the little hitch in his breath.

He slid a hand up under her sweater, pausing at her waist. "I've dreamed of touching you here." He stroked the tender skin just above her jeans. His fingers were warm. "God knows I tried not to, but I wanted so much to be free to touch you."

That wasn't all he wanted. It wasn't all Gwen wanted, either. But there was a delicious languor in lying quietly while his hand made light, careful magic on her skin.

Then he slid the hem of her sweater up to her waist and met her eyes. "Let me show you how you make me feel, Gwen."

She stiffened—she couldn't help it. She wasn't wearing a bra. But it was time, past time, to stop feeling sorry for herself because of a little inconsistency between her breasts. "I'll do it."

He shifted to one side so she could take the hem of her sweater in her hands and lift up enough to tug it off over her head. She tossed it away, paying no attention to where it landed, and lay back down. Her heart was pounding, and it wasn't all from desire.

She was very aware that when she lay on her back, her breasts practically disappeared. Gwen had never much minded being small there, perhaps because of the example of her mother, who had always seemed the height of grace and elegance. But when a bite has been taken out of a peach-size breast, the lumpy plum left behind just isn't very pretty.

She couldn't tell it by Duncan's reaction, though.

He was propped on one elbow, gazing down at her. No way could he have faked that look of arousal—the pleasure-dilated eyes, the slight, excited flush on his cheeks.

Her hands, which had been tensed into fists at her side, went limp. "Maybe I should have asked if you were a breast man."

"Oh, yeah," he said, shifting so he could run both his hands up her midriff to her breasts. He cupped them, lifting. "Definitely. Also a lip man." He licked the hardened tip of her left breast—the lumpy plum. She shivered. "A hip man, a leg man—I've never seen the point in specializing."

He settled in to enjoy himself then, and that destroyed the last of her doubts. He wasn't trying to convince her of anything. He didn't pull her nipple into his mouth because he wanted to prove she was desirable. Plainly, obviously, he was pleasing himself…and her.

She forgot which breast was lumpy, which one whole. Both received attention. Both sent the most incredible sensations shimmering through her. She reveled in those feelings, let go and sank into them, rolling up her mind and tucking it away for later. Feeling was enough.

Feeling sent her hands over his shoulders, his chest,

but there was too little of him she could reach. And too much cloth in the way. So she tugged on his sweatshirt and he let her pull it off. Then she had his chest to enjoy—the hard muscles, the arrowhead of hair right in the center. And there was his scar to be kissed, too, and the hard curve of his shoulder to lick, and somewhere along the line he decided she didn't need her jeans anymore. Or her panties.

She agreed. The hard knot of need was tightening in her belly, the pulse between her legs growing stronger, more insistent. She wanted his jeans off, too, but he told her, "Not yet," and her hands forgot how to deal with a zipper as he cupped her between her legs. She arched into his touch, her breath lost in a gasp. For a few minutes she was helpless, her hands clutching him, the covers, kneading whatever they landed on as he licked and sucked while his hand worked her.

The quick buck of climax surprised her, slapping her into a white-hot burst of pleasure that left her limp and panting. She lay in a damp, naked sprawl, her mind hazed, while he took care of the zipper that had defeated her, pulled something from his pocket and shoved his jeans down.

Finally he was as bare as she was. The sight of him did nothing to clear her mind, but a great deal to chase away the drowsy fog.

He sheathed himself and knelt between her legs. She raised her knees, cradling him, and he kissed her. Then he was at her entrance, rubbing against her as their mouths clung.

She pushed up, he pushed in and she held him inside her.

He was thick, filling her so snugly she could feel him

pulsing against her inner walls. Her muscles contracted in a spasm of pleasure. He groaned.

"Oh, good," she gasped, shifting her hips to seat him more fully. "Looks like my parts are still in working order. Nothing rusted."

Delight lit his face. He bent and kissed her ear and withdrew very slowly, murmuring that yes, her parts seemed to be working very well. Then he thrust home, hard. And his control broke.

That closed, unrevealing face lost all its guards. He drove into her as if he couldn't stop himself, as if she held the answer to every secret yearning he'd never dared speak. He was naked now, truly naked to her for the first time, and the power of that stripped her of speech and thought even as her body answered his in the wild ride toward glory.

Chapter 16

The new comforter was on the floor. Duncan was lying on his back, his chest heaving. Gwen was puddled across that chest, boneless, as words drifted back into her keeping. She was smiling. "I think I'm still breathing. Would you check, please?"

"I don't know if I can. Someone is panting on my chest, though. I thought it was you."

She moved one hand enough to pat the firm surface beneath her cheek. "It's a magnificent chest."

"No—" his hand moved lazily to cup her breast "—*this* is magnificent."

No one had ever called her chest that, even before one breast was turned into a lumpy plum. But he meant it. Suddenly she needed to see his face. "We may have to agree to disagree on that." She rested her forearms on his chest, propping herself up.

He looked so relaxed. Happy. She wondered if her

smile was goofy with love for him. Her heart certainly was. "You're so beautiful."

Was that a faint rose flush beneath the tan on his cheeks? "Afterglow is having an odd effect on your vision."

Her smile widened. She'd embarrassed him. "The beard stubble is very sexy, in a rough-around-the-edges way. Beneath it you have the loveliest cheekbones. Elegant." She drew her fingertips across them. Definitely a flush, she decided, tickled.

He shifted, obviously uncomfortable. "Are you one of those women who wants to chat after sex?"

"Certainly. You aren't one of those men who fall asleep afterward, are you?"

His smile took on another cast—wicked, that was what it was. Definitely wicked. "I'm not sleepy."

He took his time proving that.

It was very late when they left the bedroom. Reluctantly they'd decided it would be best if he didn't stay the night. At least, Gwen was reluctant. She couldn't tell what he felt. Duncan had stopped being naked before he pulled his clothes back on.

"Zach is too young to understand the implications of a man staying the night with me," she said, handing him his jacket. They were in the living room.

"He's also too young to understand the need for discretion," Duncan said.

"I don't understand the need for it, either. I'm not ashamed of what I've done."

"I'm glad." He took the time to drop a kiss on her mouth, then shrugged into his jacket. "But Zach is likely to mention it to Ben if I wake up in your bed in the morning."

"Ben is going to know about us. Sooner or later he has to know."

"Later would be better. I'd rather not rub his face in our relationship. We've already done that once." He looked grim.

"Duncan, Ben asked me to marry him because of Zach, not because there's anything between us. We shared one kiss, that's all—no intimacy, no promises."

"You share Zach—that's an ongoing commitment. The two of you *made* Zach. That's a pretty major intimacy."

She bit her lip. "You did say you had a problem with my history with your brother."

"It's Ben's feelings I'm worried about now, not mine." He put his hands on her shoulders gently. "You don't have a clue, do you."

"But his feelings weren't deeply involved! Surely he won't be angry with you for long. If you just talk to him—"

He snorted. "You don't know my brother. He changes his mind about as easily as rivers change their courses. It can happen, but it helps if there's an earthquake to move things along. Whatever his reasons for asking you to marry him, the fact remains that he'd settled on you for his wife. He won't forgive or forget what I've done anytime soon."

"That's exactly right," she said quietly. "I don't know Ben, not really."

That startled him enough that she got a glimpse inside. Sadness mixed with warmth in his rainy-day eyes. "Okay." He dropped a kiss on her nose. "Point taken. I'll come by around noon, if that's okay."

Of course it was.

The moon was high when he left. Gwen's feet were

freezing. Still she stood in the doorway and watched him go, watched until the dome light in his car shut off as the door slammed shut.

Back in her bed with the lights turned off and a warm pair of pajamas pulled on, snuggled into the sheets that smelled of him—and of sex—she hugged her pillow. Was she wrong to have held back the words she wanted to give him? He hadn't spoken of love. No, he'd warned her not to depend on him. But his eyes…

For a while, when he'd been truly naked, his eyes had sung all the poets' words to her. Hadn't they?

Maybe she was fooling herself. Lord knows she wasn't great at reading people. Gwen punched her pillow into a different shape, plopped her head down on it and closed her eyes, determined to sleep.

Duncan wondered why she'd chosen him, instead of Ben. It was hard to put into words. There were so many reasons. Passion, of course—the sheer physical splendor they shared did matter. But great sex by itself wasn't reason enough to gamble everything on a man she'd known for less than a month.

She admired him—his courage, the clear-eyed compassion he offered everyone but himself. Then there was the loyalty he felt for his family. Even if that loyalty had taken him away from her tonight, she admired it. And his silence, that deep, calm well of silence…oh, she loved him for that. His was the kind of quiet that listened, an involved, accepting sort of quiet. With him, she felt free to be the woman she was becoming.

But what could she give him in return? So far, it seemed she'd brought mostly grief. The older brother he loved wasn't speaking to him. He'd moved out of his home because of her.

Another woman, she thought, flopping over onto her

back, might be able to mend the breach. She didn't have the foggiest idea how to do that.

But she wasn't giving up. She wasn't going to back away from the choice she'd made, no matter how risky the road ahead looked.

But May first was only nine days away. She didn't have much time.

Her eyes snapped open. This wasn't working. Maybe she should see if meditation helped with lovesickness as well as it did with other anxieties.

I breathe in, my body is calmed. Breathe out…

Every breath brought the scent of him into her lungs. Gwen sighed and promised herself a nap tomorrow. She was going to need it.

The basketball looped the edge of the rim once, twice—and fell through.

"I think it's coming back to me," Charlie said. He was bent over, his hands on his knees, dragging in air.

"Your aim, maybe. Your wind is still lousy." Duncan was breathing hard, too. He used the hem of his sweatshirt to wipe his face and caught a glimpse of his watch. Their time was up. The girl at the front desk had said one of the YMCA teams would need the court at six.

"Speaking of coming back, when are you? Coming home, I mean. Jeff must be sick of you by now."

"I'm not coming back to Ben's house." Duncan walked over to retrieve the ball. "Want a Coke?"

"If you're buying, sure. Make it a Dr. Pepper." Charlie headed with him to the hall, where half-a-dozen preteens were giggling and dripping on the floor. Swim class was over, obviously. "Ben wants you to come home."

"Try again." Duncan fed quarters into the machine.

"Maybe he...thanks," Charlie said, taking the can Duncan held out. "Anyway, it's your house, too. And I want you there. Unless you've got a better deal? Are you and Gwen—"

"I haven't moved in with her." Duncan started walking, unable to handle the conversation standing still. God knew, leaving her got harder every time. Not that there had been that many times, he reminded himself. They'd only been lovers for four days...and nights.

He was leaving in six days. He'd made the reservations yesterday.

"I think Ben does want you to move back into the house. You know him—he won't come out and say it."

"Oh, he's said a few things," Duncan replied dryly, popping the top on his can.

"I, ah, gathered you'd spoken to him. That's progress."

"You could call it that, I guess." When Ben came looking for Duncan yesterday, he'd had plenty to say, all right—but even the most confirmed optimist couldn't have found much to encourage him in any of it. Duncan shoved the big glass door open and stepped out into the slanting sunshine of late afternoon. "He doesn't want me anywhere around him right now, Charlie. He's hurting."

"A grizzly with a sore paw," Charlie agreed. "But he's not nursing a broken heart."

"That's what Gwen believes." He would see her soon. For the first time he was taking her out for an adult evening—dinner and dancing. Zach was staying with Ben tonight because they were going hiking in the morning.

"But you don't?" Charlie shook his head. "Usually you're so sharp about this sort of thing, too. Ben isn't in love with her. He's in love with the idea of being married. Sooner or later it will occur to him that he could marry someone other than Gwen.''

Maybe Charlie was right. And maybe, when that did occur to Ben, he'd forgive Duncan.

"He does seem to have some screwed-up ideas," Charlie went on. "Seems to think you're using Gwen. I told him that was bullshit. You wouldn't have started something with her, not under these circumstances, if you weren't serious.''

Duncan didn't know what to say to that. He stopped and took a deep drink of his cola, then stood frowning at the can. "He told me I'd damned well better be planning on marrying her.''

"Hell, Duncan, you know Ben. He couldn't just ask if you've set the date yet.''

"I told him I wasn't going to marry her.''

Charlie grimaced. "And you're supposed to be the smart one—the one who's good at handling our pig-headed brother. I know Ben can make a saint curse sometimes, but you usually keep your temper when he starts throwing orders around. Why didn't you just tell him it was too soon to talk about marriage?''

"Because it isn't true." Duncan was tired. Not the healthy tired that comes from a good workout. Bone-deep, used-up tired. "I won't marry her.''

"You want to tell me what's going on in that head of yours? Because I don't buy that. I've seen how you look at her.''

"I'm heading back to the base next week." Duncan started walking again, heading into the parking lot for his car. Tired or not, he couldn't stand still. "I've only got six more days with her.''

Charlie's long legs kept pace with him easily. "I

know it would be hard, working on a relationship when she's here and you're in Georgia. But I don't think that was what's bugging you.''

Oh, it was bugging him, all right. Maybe that was why he was so tired. It took a lot of energy to keep from thinking about how little time he would have with her. ''You're assuming I re-up. That I'm staying in the service.''

''If you don't, where's the problem?''

He spun and slapped the hood of the nearest car. ''*I'm* the problem, Charlie! Don't you remember what happened when you woke me up? I was freaking over a nightmare and damned near choked the life out of you for your trouble!''

Charlie just looked at him, his long face grave. ''Tense,'' he pronounced at last. ''Real tense. I would have thought a man getting sex as regular as you are would be more relaxed. What happened when I woke you up that night...'' He paused, scratching his chin. ''I have to think you can tell the difference between me and Gwen. Even when you're mostly asleep, that should be obvious. She's a lot shorter.''

Duncan's laugh was short and harsh, but it did ease him slightly. ''Yeah,'' he said. ''She's got better legs, too.''

''There you go.''

In unspoken agreement, they started walking again. After a moment Charlie asked, ''You heading over to see her tonight?''

As if he could stay away. He nodded.

''Tell her hello for me, then. And, Duncan...'' They'd reached his car. Charlie's old Ford was parked on another row. ''Gwen strikes me as a patient woman. Hell, she must be to put up with you, right? Besides, seems she's willing to wait, give you time to work things out for yourself. The least you can do in return is be patient, too. With yourself, I mean.''

An hour later, showered, shaved and wearing dress slacks and a dress shirt, Duncan was in his car again. Gwen's place wasn't far from Jeff's apartment, where Duncan had been staying the past four nights—whatever portion of the nights he didn't spend with Gwen, that is. In fact, on the way he passed the 7-11 where he'd run into Jeff all those weeks ago. Sure enough, Jeff's car was there this evening.

That was one good thing, anyway. He'd managed to leave before Jeff got home. Much as he appreciated Jeff letting him bunk on his couch and use the facilities, he didn't need another sales pitch for the Highpoint PD.

Gwen's street was two blocks past the 7-11, in a mixed neighborhood. Some of the old houses were on the seedy side, while others had been renovated or converted to offices. The sidewalks here were canted, the street steep. The trees were old, their branches spreading over the narrow street. There were a few kids still out— he passed a pair on in-line skates, and a teenager was washing his car on the lawn with the bass on his stereo turned up to earthquake level.

He hadn't been able to stop thinking about what Charlie had said. And the more he thought about it, the madder he got.

Gwen hadn't said one word to him about what he planned to do when he went back to the base. Not one word. And it wasn't because she didn't care, he thought, pulling up to the curb. Maybe she hadn't put her feelings in words, but she was in love with him. It fairly shone from her.

And what did the damned woman do when the man she loved planned to leave her and hadn't had the basic decency to explain himself? Not one blasted thing. She left it all up to him.

She deserved better, dammit. She should insist on being treated better. And if she didn't see that, he'd make it clear to her.

He took the stairs two at a time and pounded on the door.

Seconds later, she opened it. She took one look at him and frowned. "Are we going to fight? You know I'm not good at it."

Just like that, she punctured his anger. It drained out, hissing like a wet cat as it went. He sighed and wrapped his arms around her. "What am I going to do with you?"

She snuggled close and kissed his chin. "You've come up with some pretty good ideas so far. I hope you'll delay any new notions until after dinner, though. I spent a ridiculous amount of time shopping and then primping for our first date."

Holding her was having a predictable effect on him. He eased back slightly and looked down at her. She'd smudged dark, sultry stuff on her eyes. Her dress was short and sleek and shiny red, like her mouth. There wasn't much of it. "I'm not sure I should take you out in public in that dress. You might incite a riot."

That turned her smile pleased, a little cocky. "You think so? Wait until you see the back." She pulled out of his arms and did a slow twirl.

"Gwen, I hate to mention this, but you've been gypped. There is no back to that dress."

She craned her head, looking over her shoulder. "Why, I believe you're right! Imagine that." She looped her arms loosely around his neck. "Too late for a refund now. I'll just have to wear it, anyway."

He couldn't ignore that shiny red mouth a second longer, so he kissed it. And showed his approval for the backless dress in other ways.

Several minutes later she handed him a tissue. "Now that we've settled that," she said, slightly breathless, "do you want to tell me what was really bothering you?"

He wiped his mouth carefully. "Nothing reasonable."

"I don't insist on reasonable."

"You don't insist on anything!" He paced away, picked up a book she'd left on one end table, then put it down again. He wanted to hurl it against the wall. "You haven't asked me a single question, Gwen. Not one. You know I'm leaving in six days, and you haven't asked me anything about what happens after that."

She didn't say anything until he turned to face her, then she spoke quietly. "I haven't asked because there was no point in it. You don't know what you're going to do. If you did, you would have told me. You don't need me badgering you for decisions you can't make yet, or throwing out ultimatums. Especially since I wouldn't mean them. I'm not going to toss away the best thing that's ever happened to me just because it might not last."

His eyes squeezed closed. When he opened them, she was still standing there, looking beautiful and sexy and sad. He crossed to her and took her hands in his. "I don't deserve you."

"Usually you only speak when you have something worth saying. Not always, apparently." She tipped her head to one side, smiling. "Come on—you promised me dancing."

Chapter 17

One of the slats in the blinds was stuck and hadn't closed completely. Moonlight slipped through the opening, striping the sheets and the naked back of the man lying beside her, one arm curled over her waist. He was asleep.

He must be very tired to have dozed off so quickly. She knew he didn't intend to stay the night with her. She'd have to wake him soon. But not yet. Not quite yet.

How very strange men are, Gwen thought, her fingers lightly stroking the nape of Duncan's neck. She'd given him exactly what he asked for—*Don't expect too much of me*, he'd said. And that had made him angry.

But for once the reason was obvious, even to her. Or maybe she was getting better at reading him. Duncan hadn't really been mad at her. He'd been furious with himself. He still was, she thought, watching him sleep. And maybe that was at the heart of his problems. He hadn't forgiven himself for whatever had happened when he was shot.

He hadn't forgiven himself for wanting a woman he thought belonged to his brother, either. At least, she thought that was how he saw it. Men were quite irrational about some things.

Gwen sighed and let her mind drift back over the evening. Duncan was a marvelous dancer. She'd thought he might be from the way he moved, the way he made love. Dancing had taken them away for a while into a world with only the two of them.

Unfortunately that world didn't really exist. They'd gone to the ski resort just outside town. It was one of those expensively rustic places, and did a booming business during the ski season, Duncan had said, when they had a live band every night at the supper club. Tonight, being off-season, there had been a deejay.

Before the dancing, though, they'd run into a couple Duncan knew. The man had gone to school with Ben. They'd known who Gwen was. And whose son Zach was.

The woman's eyes had held the gleam of gossip. Her prying questions hadn't bothered Gwen all that much, though Duncan had been terse to the point of rude. It was the man who'd upset Gwen. His eyes had been cold with disapproval, and it had been aimed at Duncan.

Why did people who knew nothing about a situation feel compelled to judge, to take sides?

Of course, Gwen reflected ruefully, the woman *had* done her best to find out everything she could.

Gwen hummed a few bars of one of the songs they'd danced to, dreaming a little on the memory. Duncan didn't stir. He was sleeping so soundly she was reminded of Zach, and smiled. How lovely it would be if this were their usual life—both of them working in the days, staying home with Zach most evenings but going out once in a while, just the two of them. Then coming home to make love. Or even coming home just to sleep together. It was so lovely, lying here with him this way…

Her eyelids were heavy. *I'll just close them for a minute,* she thought. She still had to wake him up, after all. In just a few more minutes…

Something jabbed her in the side. Hard. Gwen's eyes flew open.

"No," Duncan muttered. His head thrashed back and forth. "No, no, no." He flung out one arm.

This time she saw it coming and rolled away, ending up kneeling at the foot of the bed. Her heart pounded. Her mouth was dry. She didn't know what to do. She remembered very clearly what had happened when Charlie shook Duncan awake from a nightmare.

So she wouldn't shake him. "Duncan," she said firmly. "Duncan, wake up."

His lips moved, inaudibly this time. His face was shiny with sweat and twisted with pain.

Sooner or later he would wake up on his own even if she did nothing—but he was suffering. She couldn't stand it. But what…oh, he wasn't Duncan in his nightmare, was he? She made her voice as deep as she could and barked, "Sergeant McClain! On your feet right now, Sergeant!"

His eyes flew open. His chest heaved once, twice. "Oh, God," he said, and sat up, holding his head in his hands.

She licked her lips. What was she supposed to say? "You were having that nightmare."

He made a harsh noise that was closer to a groan than

a laugh. "No kidding. Now you know why I don't want to sleep over."

"Is this a male-ego thing? You don't want me to see you when you're…upset?"

He lifted his head. "I don't want to belt you one in my sleep."

"Oh. Well, you didn't. I mean, you did poke me in the ribs, but any restless sleeper might do that." She tried a smile. "I'm fine."

"You're perched on the edge of the bed as far away from me as you can get." His mouth twisted. "Good thinking."

So far she was failing dismally at reassuring him. She tried another tack. "It's not easy to talk about this sort of thing, but it helps. What's your nightmare about?"

"Death."

She sat back on her heels, her breath huffing out. "Okay, that's a start, but you might help me out a little here. Add a few details."

"It's a good thing you decided to be a lawyer, not a head doctor. Cross-examining the witness isn't the accepted style for therapists."

"I'm not a courtroom attorney." Worry wrinkled her forehead. "Duncan, can't you talk about it at all?"

"I killed Pat."

She jumped.

His mouth twisted bitterly. "Oh, not personally. But I'm responsible for the bullet that pulped his brains." He twisted, sitting on the edge of the bed, his clenched fists between his knees.

She swallowed, sorted through myriad questions clamoring for answers and picked one. "Who was Pat?"

"A corporal in my squad. My friend. The best damned poker player I've ever crossed aces with." He shoved to his feet. "I dream of him. Night after night, I dream of him with his face blown off, trying to talk to me."

Gwen bit her lip and thought frantically. The therapist who had led her cancer-survivor group used to say that everyone who appeared in a dream represented some part of the dreamer.

What part of Duncan was faceless and bloody? She shivered. "Maybe you should ask him what he's trying to say?"

"Great idea. Yeah, Pat, what do you want to tell me? That I got you killed? Sorry about that." He stalked over to the window. The stripe of moonlight fell across his chest now.

"It happened during the mission when you were shot."

"It happened because of me." He spun, his body all lean, deadly grace, his face savage. "We had one chance, just one. We were screwed six ways from sideways, but we could complete our mission, at least. *I* was that chance—our sharpshooter. And I screwed up. I missed the shot. I missed my goddamned shot."

The hot demand of tears pressed at the backs of her eyes. She refused it. He didn't need her to weep for him. "It was all your fault?" she demanded. "Nothing else went wrong?"

"Hell, yes, things went wrong." He started pacing. "Everything went wrong. We were dropped eighty miles from where we were supposed to be, practically in the lap of government forces. We'd been sent to hunt terrorists—one man in particular—not supposedly neutral troops. We couldn't afford to be caught. We hid out, made it to the pickup point." He stopped, scrubbing the hair back from his face. "We damned near made it."

"They caught up with you?"

"The wrong bunch stumbled across us. Or the right bunch—the ones we'd been sent to find. Only not quite the way it worked out. The odds were long, but the lieutenant thought we had a chance of finishing part of the mission, taking out the man we'd been sent there for. He thought that because I told him I could make the shot. I was to take my target out, then we could get the hell out of there. The rest of them laid down covering fire. I made it to the ridge, had the drop on the target. If I'd made the shot…" He stopped and grabbed his pants from the floor.

Gwen pushed to her feet. "Was it a hard shot?"

He stepped into his pants, not bothering with underwear. Ignoring her.

She grabbed his arm. "Was it a hard shot?"

"The bastard moved. The stupid bastard moved just as I squeezed off the shot. Then some other bastard shot me. The bloody SOB I was supposed to take out walked away, but Pat didn't. He and Crowley came to get me off the ridge and Pat got his face shot off." He jerked his arm away. "Don't talk to me now. You mean well, but don't talk to me. I'm going running. It's the only thing that works."

In silence she watched as he pulled on socks and shoved his feet into his shoes. She didn't talk to him. He pulled on a sweatshirt and left. Just like that, he left.

When the door slammed behind him, she sat back down on the bed, cold and naked. "Okay," she said to the empty room, her voice shaking, "that went well, didn't it?"

At least now she knew. Duncan wasn't haunted because he'd had to kill in the line of duty. He was haunted because he'd *failed* to kill. And in trying to save him, his friend had died.

She was hopelessly out of her depth.

What had Duncan said? Courage was doing what you had to, even when you were scared. Well, she was scared spitless. But she had to do something. Duncan hadn't told anyone else what he'd just told her—she was sure of that. It had come spilling out like pus from an infected wound, but she didn't think he'd drained off enough to do him much good. He'd still needed to run.

So he needed help, but she was all the help he was going to get. What a terrifying thought.

Or was she?

For long minutes Gwen sat still and thought. Finally she noticed the chill bumps. She got up and pulled on a robe, then went looking for her address book.

When Ben brought Zach home late the next afternoon, her four-foot jack-in-the-box was bouncing off the walls. Zach adored hiking. He was crazy about the mountains, couldn't wait for the promised camping trip and needed urgently to tell her all about it. Gwen had her hands full, but she managed to keep Ben from leaving and, eventually, to distract her wired son with a blatant bribe—a radio-controlled car she'd been saving for his birthday.

Zach and the car were crashing around in the backyard when Gwen motioned to Ben to join her several feet away.

This time his frown looked more like impatience than anger to her. "If this is about the camping trip," he began, "we can—"

"It's about Duncan."

"I'm not going to discuss my brother with you."

"Yes," she said firmly, "you are. Because he *is* your

brother, and you may be mad at him, but you love him.
And he needs help.''

That changed the texture of his frown without erasing
it. ''I can't help him. Hell, I'm not even talking to him
right now.''

''Then you'd better get over it. Listen, Ben.'' She put
a hand on his arm. ''Last night he—he told me some
things. About how he got shot and everything that went
wrong. It was bad,'' she said quietly. ''From what he
said, things went badly wrong. And he's blaming himself.''

Now Ben's frown was frankly worried. ''I'd guessed
as much, but he won't talk about it. You know how he
is. I can't help him if he won't talk to me.''

''He doesn't need to talk to you. Or to me, for that
matter. He needs to talk to people who have been where
he is. They're the only ones he could open up to.''

''That leaves me out,'' Ben said curtly.

''No, dammit, it doesn't. He won't listen if I tell him
he should join some kind of talk-therapy group.'' Not
that she knew if she'd have a chance to tell him anything. He hadn't come back last night. She didn't know
if he planned to come back at all. She took a deep,
steadying breath. This wasn't about her. ''A man like
him doesn't deal with problems that way. Besides, I'm
a woman. He'll think I don't understand. But he'll listen
to you.''

''He hasn't listened to me since he was eight years
old, and he didn't listen too well then. Get Charlie to
talk to him. The two of them have always been tight.''

''He needs to hear it from you,'' she insisted. ''You're
his big brother. He respects you, looks up to you,
and…he needs your forgiveness.''

Ben took his time thinking it over. He rubbed his face,

looked down, looked away, then sighed heavily. "All right. If I can do something…what is it I'm supposed to tell him?"

She let go of the breath she'd been holding. Her smile broke through. "I called my therapist in Florida today and got some information. There are groups that can help him, some within the military and some outside it. Groups of soldiers and former soldiers who have dealt with PTSD—post-traumatic stress disorder."

Binton's was packed, even though it was a week-night. Duncan had turned down two offers from women he didn't know and brushed off a friend of Jeff's from the police force.

He didn't want company. He just wanted to get drunk—stinking, roaring drunk. He frowned at the beer, wondering why he'd ordered it. Beer was going to take too long.

He raised a hand to signal to the waitress.

"You buying?" a deep, gravelly voice said from behind him.

Duncan turned around, his face expressionless. "You just scared a year off my life. Didn't know you could creep up on me that way."

Ben grabbed the other chair at Duncan's table, turned it around and straddled it. "Creeping up on people is more your style. The place is noisy, that's all." He studied Duncan intently. "Or maybe you were sunk too deep in that pit you've been digging yourself into to hear much of anything."

Duncan looked away, picking up his glass. "I'm not in the mood for a lecture."

"Tough. You're getting one. Not about what you should do with your life. Stay in the service, join the

police force, take up knitting—that's up to you. And—''
he looked away briefly, his mouth thinning ''—not about
Gwen, either. Though you're being a damn fool there,
too. If you can't see she's the best thing that ever happened to you…never mind. Hell. I'm not going to talk
about that.''

Voice carefully neutral, Duncan asked, ''What,
then?''

''Why the hell didn't you tell me what was going on
with you? You think I'm so dumb I've never heard of
this PTSD stuff?''

''PTSD,'' Duncan repeated blankly.

''Yeah, you know—'' Ben waved vaguely. ''Post-
traumatic stress disorder. The nightmares, insomnia,
mood changes—all those are part of it. You don't want
to talk about your problems, fine. But it seems you're
too thickheaded to get some help, and that's just plain
stupid. So you get the lecture whether you like it or
not.''

''You think I'm, oh—disordered. That I should talk
to a shrink or something.''

''I think,'' Ben said flatly, ''you've been through hell,
and part of you got stuck there. You ought to know you
aren't the only one. Men have been going to war and
coming home shot up and shook up for a helluva long
time. I think you need to talk with other soldiers who
are trying to get those last few pieces of themselves back
from hell.''

Ben's words hollowed Duncan out, leaving him
shaky—and glad. Profoundly glad. Ben had forgiven
him. He swallowed and looked away, grabbing for control. After a moment he found his voice. ''And I think
you've been talking to Gwen.''

"Like I said, she's the best thing that ever happened to you."

Duncan met his eyes. "Yes. She is." Their gazes held for a moment, then Duncan's shifted.

"What is it?"

"I don't know." Jeff was threading his way toward them, and the expression on his friend's face made Duncan's gut knot. He knew that look.

"How many of those have you had?" Jeff asked the second he reached them, nodding at Duncan's still-full glass.

"This is my first. Why?"

"We've got a situation we need your help with."

He didn't even have to think. "No."

Ben spoke. "What's going on?"

Jeff flicked a glance at him. "The police department needs a sharpshooter."

Ben scowled. "You've got men with badges who can handle a gun."

"No one like Duncan." Jeff switched back to Duncan. "The perp who's been robbing convenience stores hit the 7-11. Only he wasn't so careful this time. This time the store wasn't empty. A uniform saw it going down, but the perp made him. And instead of taking off, the stupid bastard ran back into the store. We've got a hostage situation, highly unstable. One officer has already been shot."

Oh, God. Duncan's stomach churned. He thought of the young mother he'd met that night, Lorna, her name was, the one who was taking night classes. His right hand opened and closed. "I'm not a cop. I can't go around shooting people."

"The chief has okayed it—there's an old law on the books that will let him deputize you."

Duncan shook his head. He couldn't do this. He didn't want lives depending on him ever again. His hand clenched tight. He couldn't be counted on. "Anyone down?"

"Not yet. Duncan—" his gaze flicked to Ben again and back "—your lady is in the store with her boy. They're with the hostages."

Chapter 18

"**M**om." Zach's voice wobbled. "I don't like that man."

"Shh, honey." Gwen was sitting on the floor with Zach in her lap. They were all sitting on the floor, with rows of candy on the right and twelve-packs of soft drinks on the left—her, the clerk, an elderly man, everyone in the store except the man with the gun. He crouched at the end of the aisle, his attention split between them and the window at the front of the store. Her cell phone was stuck in his jacket pocket.

Gwen couldn't see what was happening out there. Her world was limited to chocolate bars and advertising slogans on the twelve-packs of soda. And to the others trapped here with her.

The poor clerk sat across from her, hunched over and hugging her knees, her young face streaked with the dried tracks of her tears. The old man sat beside her, leaning against the shelves. He worried her. He was tall and looked as if he'd once been heavy, but his skin hung loosely on him now and had a grayish cast. She thought he'd been ill, sick enough to lose a lot of weight.

Earlier—before the police had reached him through Gwen's cell phone—when the sirens had first swarmed close and stopped, the gunman had been very agitated. He'd dragged the old man to the front of the store, using him as a shield. He'd pushed open the door, holding a gun to the old man's head, and threatened to kill him if the police didn't pull back across the street.

Ill or not, the old man was sitting up straight now, glaring at their captor.

Gwen had no idea how long they'd been here. Forever, it seemed. The robbery itself had happened so fast—she'd been pulling a gallon of milk from the cooler when the sound of a gunshot had smacked against her eardrums. She'd whirled, seen a grubby young man with a gun, grabbed Zach and hit the floor. They'd stayed down until the gunman ran out of the store.

Time hadn't slowed to a crawl until he'd come running back in.

"I wanna go home," Zach whimpered.

"I know, sweetie." She stroked his hair, keeping her voice soft, soothing. Inside she was shaking. "We can't go yet."

"What you talkin' about?" The gun swung toward them. The young man holding it had acne, bad breath and the deadest eyes she'd ever seen. He was short, no more than a couple of inches taller than Gwen. She suspected he had a drug habit he hadn't fed lately. "I told you to keep the brat quiet!"

The young woman in the clerk's smock spoke. Her voice quivered. "He's just a little boy. He doesn't understand."

"What's to understand? Whup him if he won't hush up. That's what my daddy did, and none of us backtalked him."

And what a sterling example of the benefits of corporal punishment he was. Gwen bit her lip to keep from saying that out loud. "If I spank him, he'll cry."

"Aww." He made an exaggerated face of concern. "Pore little boy might cry. Maybe I oughtta give him something to cry about." He straightened partway, keeping his head below the level of the top shelf.

"No! Y-you might not be able to hear the phone when they call back about your demands." *I have to distract him, keep him from seeing whatever they're doing out front. The police are out there...* With a shudder, she remembered the shot that had shattered the glass earlier, and the gunman's glee. He'd shot at a cop who'd been getting too close.

I have to keep him calm. "Why did you ask for a helicopter instead of a plane?"

"What d'you care, bitch? I know your type—prissy bitch like you wouldn't spit on a guy like me if I was on fire."

"I want everything to go smoothly so no one gets hurt."

"You better hope it goes smooth. You better hope they do like I said." He jiggled his weight from one foot to the other, casting quick glances out the window at the front of the store. "I need to get out of here. I need to go. What's taking those motherf—"

"Young man!" the old man barked. "You won't use language like that around these ladies."

"Oh, won't I? I'll say whatever I damn well please. *This* gives me the ticket." He waved his gun. "I got the gun, I got the ticket. I say what I want, do what I want."

"Let the women go." The old man spoke sternly. "And the child. At least let the child go."

"That boy, he's my ticket, too." He smirked. "They'll be real careful with me if I got that boy with me. Maybe I'll take her along, too." He turned his gaze on Gwen, looking her over slowly. He smacked his lips, but his eyes never changed. "Yeah, maybe I will do that. You wanna see Mexico, bitch? Might be worth it. Ask me real nice, maybe I'll let you come along with your boy."

Zach started crying.

"In Christ's name—" the old man cried.

"Don't you be talking Christ to me." His face contorted. "I don't need you, old man. Maybe I want to shoot someone." He moved closer. "Maybe I want to shoot *you.*"

He put the gun right up to the old man's temple. Gwen hid Zach's face against her, muffling his sobs. "Don't! You might…you might need him. H-he's another ticket. They did what you told them to do when you threatened him, right? And the clerk and me, we're too small to…to use the way you did him. You might need him again."

He slid his gaze at her again. His face contorted in anger, but his eyes…it was like locking gazes with an insect. There was no one home.

"Bang!" the gunman shouted, and jerked the gun back. "Bang, bang, you're dead." He giggled.

A bead of sweat trickled down the old man's face. His eyes closed.

"Are you okay?" she whispered.

"Shut up, bitch." The gunman giggled again. "Bang, bang, you're dead," he repeated, enjoying his little joke.

So far her plan to keep him calm wasn't working so well.

* * *

"He's been staying back, keeping cover between him and us," Jeff said crisply as he slammed his car door. "The only time he exposed himself was when he used the old man to force us back. No chance of a head shot then—not for those of us who were here, anyway."

Duncan nodded, standing still so he could take in the situation. They'd parked catercorner from the 7-11. Police cars blocked off the intersection; more police cars were parked directly across from the store, forming a metal wall for the officers to shelter behind. An older man in civilian clothes had a bullhorn. He glanced their way and gestured for them to approach. The rest kept their weapons trained on the cheerfully bright interior of the convenience store.

Gwen. Dear God, Gwen and Zach were in there. Not that Duncan could see them or anyone else inside the store from here. His forehead was cold and clammy.

He glanced at Ben. His brother's mouth was a tight, thin line, his eyes hard and desperate. He'd scarcely said a word since Jeff found them. "Cross to the first patrol car tucked down," Duncan told him, "like you were running for the goal line with a dozen mean-as-hell fullbacks on your tail. He'll have a clear shot at us part of the way, if he wants to take it."

"Civilians stay back." Jeff's tone allowed no discussion.

Ben didn't discuss, just said flatly, "I won't get in your way."

And there was no way, short of knocking Ben out, they were going to keep him back. Duncan didn't waste breath trying. He bent and started running.

No one shot at them. The older man in civilian clothes

was waiting. "This is the sharpshooter." He looked Duncan over with quick, cold cop's eyes.

"Yes, sir. Duncan, this is Chief Hendricks."

"Parker's told me about you. I watched you at the range one day. You're damned good when your target is a paper outline. How are you when it's a man?"

This was his last chance. If the chief knew how badly he was shaking inside, he'd send him away—leaving Gwen and Zach at the mercy of a head case who'd already shot one man. Duncan heard himself say flatly, "I'm good. Whether I'm good enough remains to be seen."

"All right, then. For the record, you've just been deputized. You'll need a rifle."

Jeff spoke. "I sent someone to Duncan's house to get his rifle. He should be here any minute."

"I can give you a Colt AR15."

Duncan shook his head. "My Remington's a bolt action. More accurate, and I'm used to it." His eyes were busy, searching out possible positions. "He's on the west end of the store?" he asked the chief.

"Yes. He's staying down, maintaining cover. We get a glimpse of him now and then—he's keeping track of us—but not enough for one of us to target him."

"He's a nutcase," Jeff added, "but he's a helluva shooter. He's got a feel for line-of-sight."

They'd need a head shot. It was the only way to be sure the gunman didn't kill any of the hostages. "You're in communication with him?"

"One of the hostages has her cell phone with her. Detective Parker knows her slightly, so we were able to get the number and call him on it."

Gwen's phone. Duncan felt sick, dizzy. He didn't glance at Jeff—who apparently hadn't told his chief that

Duncan's nephew and the woman he was involved with were in there.

So far, Duncan's take-charge brother hadn't said a word. The chief turned to him. "Who are you and what are you doing here?"

"Benjamin McClain," Ben snapped. "That's my—"

"He's my brother," Duncan said quickly. "He has some medical training." First aid, anyway. "He won't interfere." If the chief knew Ben's son was in there, he'd figure out Duncan's connection to two of the hostages soon enough. Chances were, he'd *un*deputize him immediately. "How did your patrolman get hit? Where was he?"

Ben must have realized what Duncan was doing, because he didn't say a word and stayed behind when Duncan moved away with the two cops. Duncan paced along the barricade, absorbing the details Jeff and the chief gave him, looking for his spot. A radio crackled inside one car. The officers were mostly silent, now and then making the kind of stupid jokes men did to ease the tension.

The officer who'd been shot had had the right idea. The best angle on the aisle where the gunman was holed up was blocked by Gwen's rental car, parked in front of the store. The officer had tried to get behind it, but there was no cover between it and them.

There was one other possibility. Duncan stopped when he found it.

One of the patrol cars occupied the spot. He glanced at Jeff, who had the officers move out of his way, then climbed into the car.

Yes. He saw movement—a sleeve. An elbow, covered in dark material. The gunman had to stay on one end of the aisle to keep an eye on them, and from here Duncan had a narrow slice of that space. Inches only—the check-out counter blocked most of it. He'd have to wait for the man to move into exactly the right spot.

Duncan climbed back out of the car. "The best chance will be when he comes out. Even if he uses a hostage as a shield…" His voice flattened as his mind threw that image up at him: Gwen, pallid with fear, held tightly in front of a killer with a gun to her head. Or Zach, crying, terrified… He made himself go on. "He can't shield himself from all sides. With a clean head shot, there's a good chance he'd never be able to squeeze the trigger."

The chief and Jeff exchanged glances. "We're working on drawing him out," the older man said. "But in my judgment he's unstable. He wants a helicopter set down in the parking lot. I'm making arrangements, but the bastards at—" His lips closed tightly on whatever he'd been about to say. "It will take some time to get a chopper here. He's growing impatient. He's threatened to shoot one of the hostages to prove he means business. If you have a chance at taking him out before the helicopter arrives, I want you to take it."

There was a dry roaring in Duncan's ears. Six months ago he would have been confident he could make the shot—*if* the gunman moved into position. Now he didn't know. His palms were damp. His heart was pounding. He didn't understand how the others could miss seeing that he was in a terrified funk. "I need my rifle."

His name was Frank. He'd feared the father who had "whupped him good" for talking back and was delighted the man was dead now. He had two brothers, whom he hated, and a dog he was going to miss when he made it to Mexico.

He seemed to believe that was possible—that the cops

would really let him leave in the helicopter he'd demanded, and that it could take him to Mexico. If he was aware of the limitations imposed by fuel and distance, it didn't show.

He was twenty-two and not very smart.

Not entirely stupid, though—about ten minutes ago he'd made Gwen bring him a small mirror from another aisle. He used it to keep an eye on the front of the store without exposing himself as often.

Gwen had fallen back on the oldest rule on the books. When in doubt about how to handle a man, get him to talk about himself. Frank liked talking about himself. Sometimes he even liked it better than hurting or terrorizing people.

Zach was pressed tight against Gwen's side. He'd been silent ever since Frank made her leave him to get the mirror. Such stillness wasn't like Zach, and it worried her. So did the old man. He was unconscious. A dried trickle of blood on his forehead marked where the gunman had pistol-whipped him for speaking without permission, and his complexion was chalky. The clerk was moaning softly and hugging herself. Gwen didn't think she was aware of anything except her fear anymore.

Gwen was keeping Frank talking. It was all she could think of to do. "You like hot weather?" she asked brightly. "Mexico has plenty of sunshine."

"I like things hot." He leered at her, but it was perfunctory. He was antsy, shifting on his haunches, tilting the mirror this way and that. "You won't have to worry about cold toes in Mexico—me and the sunshine'll keep you plenty warm. If they ever get here…" His mood switched abruptly. He stuck his head around the corner of the shelves and pulled it back quickly. "Stupid sons of bitches. My copter should've been here by now. They're tryin' to mess with me. Won't let them get away with that, no sir.''

He pushed to his feet. "C'mere, bitch.''

It was chilly in the car, but a drop of sweat trickled down Duncan's temple. He ignored it. As long as it didn't get in his eyes, it wasn't a problem. His rifle was propped on the partially unrolled window. Lying prone would have been better, steadier, but the angle from the ground was wrong.

He hadn't spoken, moved or shifted his gaze for twenty-three minutes.

Twice he'd had the target's back in his sights. More often, it was his arm or his shoulder. The bastard had put his head out three times, but he was clever enough to use different spots. And he was quick, too quick. Duncan hadn't been able to site on him in time.

Or maybe Duncan was too slow. Too unsure. So many lives depended on him. Gwen's life. Zach's. Duncan inhaled slowly, careful not to let it disturb his aim.

Pat was back. Not the Pat with the ruined face who appeared in his dreams, but Pat the way Duncan remembered him.

Not really, of course. Maybe because this felt like old times, though, it was easy to imagine his friend sitting in the front seat giving him a hard time. Maybe saying something like, *Tensing up across the shoulders, ace.*

Duncan relaxed his muscles. Tense muscles made for jerky reactions. Sooner or later, the bastard inside that store would give him something to react to.

At least he knew Gwen was alive. He'd seen her. About ten minutes ago she'd come to the front of the store and grabbed what looked like a mirror. She'd cast one quick, frightened look outside and hurried back to the aisle where the gunman waited.

She hadn't looked hurt. For a few seconds his hands had trembled in the rush of relief.

They were steady when a head, dark-haired, popped around the corner of the aisle. Duncan shifted his aim a fraction—and the head was gone.

"Son of a bitch." Despair tasted like rusty iron.

Give it a rest. You can't win every hand.

If Pat had really been there, he would have said something like that. He was always comparing life to poker. *You play the hand you're dealt,* he used to say, *and if it's a bust, fold if you can afford to, bluff if you can't.*

They'd damned near all gone bust that last time out, hadn't they? No bluff possible, and folding meant death. Pat had drawn the big losing hand that time. Pain rode Duncan, familiar yet still fresh.

Give it a rest, will you? If I'd been the one down, you would've come for me. Hell, you'd done it before. You got lucky, didn't get your face blown off playing hero that time. I drew a bad hand. Duncan imagined Pat's shrug. *So?*

It wasn't really Pat saying that, of course. But it felt so much like what he might say—he used to drive them all crazy singing that Kenny Rogers song over and over, the one about the gambler who broke even. It wouldn't have been so bad if he'd been able to carry a tune. Duncan's lips twitched up ever so slightly.

Movement. A hand, this time, a flash of light. The mirror Gwen had retrieved—the bastard was using it to keep an eye on them. Duncan's whole being focused on the inches of space in his sites.

"I said, git over here!"

"No, Mom!" Zach clung to her, his breath hitching. "No, Mom, don't!"

"Ditch the rugrat or I'll do it for you."

His expression was ugly, and his eyes, those crawling, insect eyes... "We're going to be all right, honey. We have to do what the man says right now, but we'll be fine." She pressed a kiss to his forehead and passed him to the clerk. The young woman roused from her daze enough to take him, looking bewildered, but she held him, rocked him. "There, there, honey. There, there..."

Zach was sniffling, but no longer sobbing. Gwen stood. Her knees were shaky.

As soon as she was close enough, he grabbed her, making her crouch like he was. He smelled bad. The barrel of the gun touched her temple as his hand released her. She was faint with fear.

"You tell them I mean business." She heard the beep-beep-beep of the auto-dial. He thrust her cell phone into her hand. "I already called 'em. Now get out there." He shoved her, hard.

She half-staggered, half-fell into the center aisle near the checkout. The gun was trained on her. The eyes of the man holding it looked wild now, not dead at all.

Movement. An arm, down low—he was crouched down. Duncan lowered the tip of the barrel slightly. A flashing glimpse of part of the man's back—

And Gwen tumbled across his line of sight.

Duncan's head went light. The barrel of his rifle didn't move.

All he could see was her leg. The rest of her was blocked by the counter. Then, slowly, she stood and he saw her shoulders, her face. He didn't, couldn't let himself focus on her. His attention stayed fixed on the arm, covered in a dark sleeve—part of the body now, too. A shoulder.

He sited carefully a little less than a foot above that shoulder.

Gwen was holding something to her face. A phone. Her cell phone.

"H-he says he means business," Gwen stammered. She stared at the shattered glass at the front of the store, where a bullet had passed. The edges of things had turned unnaturally sharp and clear. Her mouth felt fuzzy and her head seemed slightly distant from her body, the way it did when she had the flu.

There were lights, so many flashing lights, across the street. So many officers there to help her and Zach get out of this. And none of them could do a thing.

"Are you all right, Ms. Van Allen?" a man's voice asked urgently from the phone.

"I—he hasn't hurt me. The old man—he knocked the old man out. But…" *He's going to kill me. He's going to shoot me to prove he means business.*

"Ask him if he can see you, bitch!"

"H-he wants to know if you can see me." *Not in front of Zach. Please, God, please. If I have to die, don't let it happen in front of Zach.*

"We can see you. Ms. Van Allen, try to draw him out. We have a sharpshooter out here. If you can get the gunman to move even slightly, we can take it from there."

"What did he say? Where's my damned copter?"

Duncan. Duncan was out there. Numbly she looked at the gunman. "He says he sees me. I'll ask about the copter." As she did, hope hit—a huge tidal wave that almost took her down as her knees went soft.

Duncan was out there. All she had to do was make the gunman move, just a little. Draw him out. Duncan would do the rest.

"Tell him the copter's on its way."

"Yes. Okay. Frank, it's on its way. I..." She looked right at the gunman and let her knees fold under her.

Gwen sank out of sight. Duncan's gun never wavered. His mouth was dust-dry and his heart pounded as if he'd been running for an hour. He didn't blink.

This is it, Sarge.

"What you doing, bitch?" the gunman screamed. "Stand up where they can see you!"

"I—I can't. So dizzy..." She leaned on one arm, holding the phone loosely in her other hand. Blinking, she let all the dazed terror she'd been repressing wash over her until she thought she really might faint. "Here. You...you better talk to him. I can't..."

She tossed the phone at him—a weak toss. It landed just out of his reach.

"Stupid bitch!" He leaned out, his arm extended.

Now!

A dark head, moving fast. Duncan tracked it. And squeezed the trigger.

Chapter 19

Duncan reached Gwen almost as quickly as she reached Zach. She was crouched on the floor, holding Zach and rocking him, keeping his head turned away from the body she'd had to step over to get to him. Gently Duncan pulled her to her feet, put an arm around her and led her with Zach in her arms away from the bloody mess that was all that was left of the man named Frank.

Then his arms went around them both—tight, crushing tightly. And what seemed like the entire Highpoint Police Department came racing through the doors—and Ben was with them.

Charlie showed up fifteen minutes later. The three McClain brothers stayed with her and Zach, shielding them when reporters shouted questions, helping her navigate the official maze—the police, the paramedics who wanted to transport them to the hospital. God knew why, since they had no injuries. But it helped, it helped enormously, to have Duncan's arm around her, his quiet presence steadying her.

He'd saved her life. Probably Zach's, too. At the time, she didn't think of what kind of a toll it must have taken on him.

Zach, thank God, hadn't seen the man killed. The clerk—her name was Lorna, Gwen learned later that night—had kept his head pressed to her shoulder, fearing that his mother was about to be shot.

In the end, Ben took them all home. Home to his house, that is. Gwen didn't protest. Ben had been through a terrible ordeal, too, with his son held hostage. He didn't need to be shut out. But she'd been surprised and so glad when Duncan looked at Ben and said, ''I'll be staying with Gwen tonight.''

Ben just nodded.

So all night she had the warm comfort of Duncan's body curled protectively around her, with Zach cuddled close on the other side. She kept jerking awake, so it helped to have him there.

She and Zach both slept late. When she woke up at nine, Duncan was gone. Not just gone from her bed, she discovered when she followed Zach downstairs. He'd left the house.

At ten-thirty she pulled up in the unpaved parking area next to the cemetery at the west side of town.

The sun was bright and, for once, truly warm. There were a few trees, all either in bud or with tiny new leaves unfurling. The cemetery boasted one ornate mausoleum, but most of the gravesites were marked by tombstones. Some of the older ones, near the blunt rise of a cliff that bordered the grounds to the west, had simple crosses.

The landscaping was sparse, almost barren, compared to the last place like this she'd seen at Hillary's funeral.

But the Rockies rose all around them, grand and enormous, and the sky rolled white puffs of cloud overhead. There was beauty here, too, she thought. And power.

Duncan was on the north side, sitting on the ground. The grass was a mingling of winter brown and fresh green as spring forced itself on the land. Gravel crunched beneath her feet as she took the path that led north. He saw her long before she reached him.

His eyes were very pale in the sunlight. "I suppose Ben or Charlie told you where I'd gone."

She nodded and stopped a few steps away from him. "I'm sorry if I'm intruding, but I've quit trying to do the right thing. Where people are concerned, anyway."

His eyebrows lifted slightly. "You have?"

"I had one of those lightbulb moments. If all the problems we make for ourselves and each other were put into a multiple-choice test, every one of the answers would be both 'none of the above' and 'all of the above.' There *isn't* one right answer, so I'm not going to waste time trying to find it anymore. All I can do is keep trying things and hope something works. That's why I'm here."

"You're welcome here," he said quietly.

She sat beside him on the ground beside a grave with a double headstone. The first line read, "Kelly McClain, beloved husband and father." Inscribed beneath that line was the next: "Mary Elizabeth Bright McClain, cherished wife and mother."

Gwen licked her lips. Resolutions and revelations aside, it was hard to know where to start. "I called my mother this morning and told her about…about what happened. She'll be here tonight."

"That's good. At least, I guess it is?"

"It's good. Zach has been missing her. I have, too,"

she admitted. That had surprised her more than it should have. "She'll butt heads with Ben, I expect. They both like being in charge. But she'll be very polite about it."

"That should be something to see."

He sounded amused, but she couldn't tell what was going on behind those calm, pale eyes of his. "Duncan, are you all right? And be warned," she added, "if you say you're fine, I'll hit you."

His mouth quirked up. "Then I'll just say I'm better. I found out I hadn't lost myself, after all. I can still do what I have to." The smile faded and his eyes turned somber. "How's Zach?"

"When I left, he was telling his father about the bad man with the gun." She remembered the way he'd grabbed Ben's cheeks, making his father look directly at him, just as he often did with her: *He was a bad man, Dad. He was very bad. He wanted me to shut up. He had a real gun, an' he was mean. So the please-man shot him.*

"I'd give damned near anything to have spared him that."

She threw him a suspicious look. "You haven't talked yourself into believing this was all your fault somehow, have you?"

"No." This time she could see the amusement dancing in his eyes. "I can occasionally tell the difference between myself and God."

She exhaled in relief. "That's good. At least you were able to spare him…" *Seeing me shot.* Gwen swallowed. Her son was better than her at putting the hard stuff into words. "That he's talking about it is a good sign, I think. When my little chatterbox can't talk about something, then I worry. Not that everything's okay. It'll take time for the memory to fade.'' She sighed and pulled idly at a tuft of grass.

''We want to shield them from everything,'' Duncan said. ''At least from the really hard things like death, pain, fear. But we can't.''

We. That had a good sound to it. She reached for his hand. For several minutes they sat in silence in the warm spring sunshine, holding hands and listening to a few lazy-sounding birds announce themselves.

Eventually he shifted, releasing her hand. ''I'd forgotten how angry I was after my folks died. Not at first, but for several months whenever I dreamed about them, I was furious. I'd yell at them for trying to trick me, pretending they were alive when they were really dead.''

''I did that, too,'' she said, surprised, ''after my father died. I would dream he was alive again, and I'd be so happy—then I'd realize he couldn't be, and I'd be angry.''

He nodded. ''I've been doing that with Pat. You were right, you know.''

''Was I?'' She smiled, pleased. ''About what?''

''I needed to know what he was trying to tell me in my nightmares. The message was pretty simple.'' His face eased into one of those slow smiles that melted her. '''Get over it.' That's what he wanted me to hear.''

''That's certainly simple.'' And not very helpful, she thought.

''It's what I needed to hear. I'd been so busy dragging Pat's death around with me I couldn't remember his life. What he was really like.'' The muscles under his eyes tightened, and his voice turned rough. ''He was one helluva good man, Gwen.''

She didn't answer with words, just scooted closer to him. He put an arm around her, and she leaned her head on his shoulder. "You were right about something, too," she told him.

"Oh?" He brushed her forehead with a kiss. "What's that?"

"I need to start asking you questions. No," she said, straightening so she could look him in the eye. "I need to make some things clear."

"Gwen—"

"I know you've got a lot still to settle," she said quickly. "Some of it you'll need to work out on your own. But you don't have to be *alone* while you're working things out. You don't know if you want to stay in the service or not. So what? Unless there's some other reason you don't want me around, I don't see any reason for you to...to end things between us when you go back to the base." There. She'd said it. Her heart was thudding against her ribs. She was terrified. "Unless you have a problem with my money, the way Ben did."

"I think I've got a handle on that. Seems to me that if you can deal with the fact that I shoot people for a living, I can adjust to you being rich."

The laugh that bubbled up was a trifle unsteady. "I'm not too crazy about you getting shot at, either. But I guess that's fair."

"Good. Gwen." He brushed a strand of hair back from her forehead. He was smiling. "I love you."

"Oh." Her body went light, as if all the sunshine in the world had just poured into her. "Oh," she said again, and touched his cheek. "I love you. I love you so much. I didn't think...Duncan?"

He understood what she was asking before she knew herself and answered with his arms, his lips and his body. All that sunshine bubbled up and poured from her to him, from him to her.

Very warm sunshine, it was. She was breathless when she settled her head on his shoulder, breathless and smiling. "That's lovely," she said, meaning all of it—the kiss, his words, his love.

He sifted his fingers through her hair. "I have a confession to make."

"Okay."

"You don't sound too worried."

"Because I know you don't have anything terrible to confess. You love me. I love you. The rest is details. I'm *good* at details."

"This is...a rather important detail. It's about your cancer."

That did send a tremble of alarm through her. She straightened so she could look at him. "Yes?"

He licked his lips and looked away. "It scares me."

She waited. "That's it? That's your confession?"

"You don't understand. I..." He scrubbed a hand over his face. "I know it's important for you to be able to talk about it. I've listened. I want to listen whenever you need to talk about it, but I don't know if...I'm scared of letting you down. Of saying the wrong thing, letting my own fear make yours worse. You need someone whose head is screwed on better, someone who doesn't break out in a cold sweat when he thinks about...about how it could come back."

"Duncan." She gripped his arms with her hands. "Are you going to deal with your fear by having an affair?"

"No! Good God. Of course not."

"Will you leave me because you can't deal with it?"

He shook his head impatiently. "That's not what I mean."

"Well, that's what *I* mean when I talk about real problems. What matters is that you'll stand by me and I'll stand by you. Maybe neither one of us will know what we're doing half the time. We'll muddle through.'' He didn't look convinced. ''Say the wrong thing to me,'' she demanded. ''Go ahead. Say the wrong thing and see if I fall apart.''

He looked away. ''This is stupid.''

''No, it isn't. There's something more bothering you. I can tell.''

''Can you?'' He met her eyes again. ''All right. I wish like hell you could have my baby someday. And I'm terrified you might try to.''

Her eyes filled. ''Me, too,'' she whispered. ''Oh, Duncan, me, too—both the longing and the fear.''

He caught her to him and held her close. A few tears leaked out of her closed eyes and she let them. He stroked her hair.

''See how well that works?'' she said after a moment. ''Talking about the details, I mean.''

She felt the muscles of his cheek bunch and knew he was smiling. ''While we're talking, there's another detail we need to discuss. Ah…whether you could be happy as the wife of a cop.''

''Duncan!'' She sat up straight. ''You've decided what you want to do? And you're asking me to marry you?''

''What did you think I meant when I said I wished you could have my baby?''

''It's not the same. You didn't ask.'' She waited, but he didn't get the hint. ''You still haven't asked,'' she pointed out.

He took her hand. His eyes searched hers, and they were as nakedly open to her as they had been the first time they'd made love. ''Will you marry me, Gwen?''

"Yes." She threw her arms around his neck. "Oh, yes."

He rocked her. "You don't have the foggiest idea how selfish I'm being, do you? You just went through hell. If I were a little less selfish, I'd give you a chance to get your feet under you again before tying you to me, but I'm not."

"Now, that's just dumb." She was getting distracted by the smell of him, a man-and-soap scent, mixed with something that was pure Duncan. She kissed his throat. "We need to work on this habit you've fallen into of thinking you don't deserve to be happy."

"Know what I think?"

"What?"

He cupped her face in his hands and kissed her lightly. "I think you're getting damned good at people stuff. And I...I've found my forward, and it's with you."

* * * * *

Don't miss Eileen's next exciting story!
Look for A MATTER OF DUTY
in the 3-in-1 anthology

BROKEN SILENCE,

available in May 2003
wherever books are sold.

Toward the end of 2003,
Eileen will have WITH PRIVATE EYES
in Desire in November and perhaps
Ben's story in Desire in early 2004!

The secret is out!

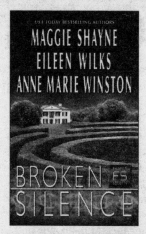

Coming in May 2003 to SILHOUETTE BOOKS

Evidence has finally surfaced that a covert team
of scientists successfully completed experiments
in genetic manipulation.

The extraordinary individuals created by these
experiments could be anyone, living anywhere,
even right next door....

Enjoy these three brand-new FAMILY SECRETS
stories and watch as dark pasts are exposed
and passion burns through the night!

The Invisible Virgin by Maggie Shayne
A Matter of Duty by Eileen Wilks
Inviting Trouble by Anne Marie Winston

Five extraordinary siblings. One dangerous past.

Where love comes alive™

In April 2003
Silhouette Books and bestselling author

MAGGIE SHAYNE

invite you to return to the world of
Wings in the Night
with

TWO BY TWILIGHT

Enjoy this brand-new story!
Run from Twilight

Savor this classic tale!
Twilight Vows

Find these seductive stories, as well as all the other tales of dark
desire in this haunting series, at your favorite retail outlet.

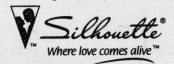

Silhouette®
Where love comes alive™

If you enjoyed what you just read,
then we've got an offer you can't resist!

Take 2 bestselling
love stories FREE!
Plus get a FREE surprise gift!

Coming in March 2003 to

I N T I M A T E   M O M E N T S™

The search for missing ARIES agent Dr. Alex Morrow
continues, and more FAMILY SECRETS are revealed in...

The Phoenix Encounter
IM #1208
by LINDA CASTILLO

Separated by a sudden explosion, badly wounded agent
Robert Davidson was carried away, unable to reach
Lillian Scott, the love of his life, where she was trapped
in a prison of flames.

Devastated, he never knew she survived—
nor the secret she survived with—until now....

FAMILY
SECRETS

No one is who they seem.

Join the search for Dr. Morrow in THE CINDERELLA MISSION
by Catherine Mann, IM #1202. And watch for the exciting
conclusion in THE IMPOSSIBLE ALLIANCE by Candace Irvin,
IM #1214, coming in April 2003.

COMING NEXT MONTH